Dark Whispers

Dark Whispers
Joanne Macgregor

Protea Book House
Pretoria
2014

For Stuart – my husband, my lover and my best friend, who puts bread on the table so that I can write.

Dark Whispers – Joanne Macgregor

First edition, first impression 2014 by Protea Book House
PO Box 35110, Menlo Park, 0102
1067 Burnett Street, Hatfield, Pretoria
8 Minni Street, Clydesdale, Pretoria
protea@intekom.co.za
www.proteaboekhuis.com

Editor: Danél Hanekom
Proofreader: Caren van Houwelingen
Cover design: Hanli Deysel
Cover images: Thinkstockphotos
Typography: 10.5 on 13 pt Arrus by Ada Radford
Printed and bound by Interpak Books, Pietermaritzburg

© 2014 Protea Book House

ISBN 978-1-4853-0015-1 (printed book)
ISBN 978-1-4853-0016-8 (e-book)

All rights reserved. No part of this book may be reproduced or transmitted in any form or by any electronic or mechanical means, be it photocopying, disk or tape recording, or any other system for information storage or retrieval, without the prior written permission of the publisher.

This is a work of fiction. All the characters, institutions and events described in it are fictional and the products of the author's imagination.

Website: www.joannemacgregor.com

nowhere in the corridors of pale green and grey
nowhere in the suburbs
in the cold light of day

there in the midst of it so alive and alone
words support like bone

dreaming of Mercy…

"Mercy Street"
Peter Gabriel

1
Just perfect

He likes them best like this, laid out neatly in the white gowns, on the stainless steel tables. They are still and clean, no disguises, stripped of their fashionable feathers and prepared just for him, like chicken breasts waiting on a cutting board. It is easy, like this, to see their asymmetries, their blemishes, their imperfections.

Never mind the reason why they think they are here, he knows that the real reason is to be corrected, to be made perfect. His task – no, more than that, his duty – is to fix them. It is a vocation, really, to leave them better than he finds them. They are so confused – distracted from the beauty of form by the attachment to function. They do not know what is best for themselves.

But he does.

He leans over this one now. She is so still, so relaxed, so ready. Her breathing is slow and steady, her gaze a little unfocused. He can feel his own breathing quickening, feel the heat rising from his core like a tremble of divine joy.

There is just enough time for a small whisper, a soft encouragement of hope, before the darkness slides her entirely into his honing hands.

He leans over and breathes into her ear, "Just relax. I'm going to do something very special for you now. And when you wake up, you're going to be just perfect."

He takes one of her hands, pats it gently. Her eyes have already closed when he murmurs, "Doctor knows best."

2
Good intentions

New year's resolutions
1. Stop trying to save others.
2. Save money instead.
3. Embrace my extra 4 kg..
 ("How blessed am I to live and love in this temple.")
4. Recycle more.
5. Learn to cook. Anything.
6. Be (even more) patient with mommy dearest.
 ("I am as a hollow reed. Troubles pass through me as the wind...")
7. Open bank statements. Read them.
8. Keep a pot plant alive for an entire year.
9. NB: Teach Oedipus to stop drinking from the toilet bowl!

Affirmation for the year:
"I am a creature of conscious choice – not a victim of circumstance!"

Megan Wright wondered how it was possible that, less than two weeks into January, she had already broken each of her resolutions in some way. She sat in her car for a moment, windows open, savouring the freshness of the morning and sipping on her take-away cup of coffee. The hospital car park was littered with the remnants of the previous night's thunderstorm: small branches and castanet-shaped seed pods of the jacaranda trees which bordered the parking lot, grey stones and gravel washed down from the flower beds on the northern embankment, leaves wrenched from trees and swirled into random piles by the strong wind, and scraps of litter blown against the palisade fences. But the air was clean, the wide African sky washed to a cloudless cobalt blue, and already the sun was hot above Johannesburg.

Megan was just getting out of her silver Renault, balancing the coffee in one hand and her handbag and briefcase in the other, when her cellphone began to ring with Chicago's "When you're good to Mama...". The brightness of the early January morning dimmed a little.

"Hi, Mom," she said, slamming the car door closed with a swing of her hip and setting off from the shaded staff parking across the lot towards the busy main entrance of Acacia Private Clinic.

"Good morning, Megan." Just the way she said it was irritating. "And how are you?"

"I *was* just swell, but I'm guessing that's about to change. Now, what do you want?" Megan wanted to say.

Instead, she said, "Fine thanks, how are you?"

"Oh, *I'm* fine."

Megan already had a good idea what the call might be about. She headed for her usual shortcut across the small island of grass in the centre of the car park. There was an old pepper tree growing there, shading a small stone bench. The gnarled and twisted base of the trunk gave rise to swathes of green leaves, which always gave her spirits a lift. It seemed proof of her hope that life thrived, even here in the disinfected and sterile hospital environment where antiseptics and antibiotics ruled supreme, and death seemed the only organic process.

When Megan did not respond, her mother continued, "... but Cayley's not."

"Big surprise," Megan muttered, taking a quick gulp of coffee and coughing as it burned down her throat.

"What's that?"

"Nothing. What's wrong now?"

Megan was on conversational auto-pilot. Their exchange was proceeding along its usual well-worn but futile path. She might as well let her mother get it all off her chest. Megan leaned briefly against her pepper tree as she passed, as she liked to do every day, imagining some of its solid strength and vitality flowed into her. What she really wanted to do was to stop and hug the tree, but it would not do for Megan Wright, Counselling Psychologist, to be seen doing something quite so eccentric. The doctors might stop their referrals if they thought she was odder than the patients.

A small movement of brown fluff on the grass in front of her caught her attention. It was a baby bird. Its right wing was extended at an odd angle, its feathers ruffled and misaligned, and it was struggling to hold its head up.

"She's not doing well at all. She seems very depressed, hasn't been to work in days," her mother was saying. "She just stays in her room – only comes out to eat and … you know."

"Oh, the poor thing!" said Megan, now on her haunches in front of the helpless creature. She balanced her coffee cup on the bench and gently cupped the bird in her hands. She could feel a rapid heartbeat beneath the downy softness squirming feebly in her fingers.

"Don't panic," she said, soothingly. "We'll get you some help."

"Well, I must say, I'm glad to hear a little sympathy for once!" said her mother, sounding surprised.

"Oh, right," said Megan.

She strode to the entrance of the clinic, past the Emergency unit outside on the right where an open-doored ambulance was parked. Two paramedics leaned against the sides of the vehicle; one was smoking a cigarette and the other had her eyes closed and her face turned towards the sun.

The glass doors of the entrance slid open at her approach, admitting her to the lobby with its potted yuccas and palms, its gleaming brass rails and polished floors, the expectant wheelchairs parked alongside a row of vending machines, and its unmistakable smell – a mixture of strong antiseptic and anxiety. She headed for the clinic's retail pharmacy which was across the way from the intake desks with their serried rows of blue and maroon chairs.

"Megan!"

"What?" said Megan.

She scanned the shelves in the pharmacy. Wedging the phone between her ear and shoulder, and cradling the little bird tenderly in one hand, she snatched a dropper off a rack of medical equipment and a small box of baby cereal off a shelf.

"I really think you have no love for me at all," her mother was saying with a sniff. "Or for your sister."

I am as a hollow reed, troubles pass through me as the wind.

The cashier, a thin woman with the dark rings under her eyes which spoke of shift work, rang up the purchase, looking from the bird in Megan's one hand, to the phone – now back in her other.

"Please hold this for a sec," Megan mouthed to the cashier, handing the phone to the woman and opening her handbag to rifle one-handed through it for some money.

The cashier, who looked weary enough to have seen most things in life and to be unsurprised by the rest, took the phone and put it to her own ear.

"Yes," she said. "Uhm-hmm… Hm-hm-hm… Eish!"

Megan handed over the money, shoved the dropper and cereal box into her bag, and took back the phone – resisting the temptation to leave it with the cashier, who seemed to be doing a better job of consoling Moira Wright than she had.

"Thanks," she said to the cashier, then headed across the tiled foyer to the lifts. Her hands were too full today to climb the curved sweep of stairs which lead up to the higher floors.

"I should say so," came the bitter response from the other end of the line. "Anyway, she's losing weight again. She won't tell me what she weighs, but she promises me she's not under 49 kg."

"Oh well, if she *promises*, then I'm sure you can believe her. It's not like Cayley would ever lie about her weight," said Megan, trying – and failing – to keep the acid note of sarcasm out of her voice.

Megan was slim enough to squeeze into the crowded lift when it arrived, tall enough to lean over another occupant and press the button for the third floor with a knuckle, and stubborn enough to avoid looking at her reflection in the mirrored control panel, sure that the irritation at her family would be clearly written on her face. Almost thirty years of skirmishes with her mother was starting to show in the beginnings of fine lines at the edges of her blue-grey eyes. She shook back shoulder-length hair somewhere between darkest red and auburn-brown, and cradled the baby bird protectively against the jostles of the usual flock of white-coated doctors and orderlies in their regulation greens. A nurse, who was standing behind an aged and frail-looking man in a wheelchair, left off staring at the small dent on Megan's left cheekbone and peered disapprovingly down at the bird in her hand.

"That's not very hygienic," she said.

"No," said Megan with a smile, "it isn't, is it?"

"No it isn't – I'm glad you agree!" said her mother. She had been complaining at length about the treatment Megan's sister had received during her last in-patient treatment at the eating disorders unit of the psychiatric clinic – the same one where she had been hospitalised half a dozen times over the course of the past eight years.

"I do think it's time for you to get involved again, Megan. Personally involved, I mean. Not just referring her on to one of your colleagues. After all, who knows her better than her own family? Who could treat her better than her own psychologist sister?"

I am as a hollow reed...

Megan stepped out of the lift with a final bright smile at the sour-faced nurse and strode down the tiled corridor to her office, cuddling the bird to her chest.

"Mom, you know I can't treat members of my own family – it's unethical. We've been through all this before. Many times. Anyway, she wouldn't listen to me, and I couldn't force her – she's twenty-four, not four."

Megan stepped into the reception of her consulting rooms. Several new pot plants – newly purchased to replace those that had died over the Christmas break – nestled between the soft seats and the side tables stacked neatly with magazines. The smell of strong coffee drifted out from the small kitchenette to the rear of the reception desk where Patience Ndlovu sat, large and placid, labelling envelopes.

"Hi," Megan waved. "My mother," she mouthed, holding the phone up in explanation, and handed over the tiny bird to Patience's big, soft hands. There was a small basket of wrapped mints on the reception counter – a moment of sweetness after the sadness of therapy for departing clients. Megan tipped the sweets out, lined the basket with a clutch of tissues and held it out for Patience to deposit the bird gently into it.

Her mother was still talking non-stop into her ear. "Mom..." she interrupted the flow of pleading, haranguing and self-pity. "Mom!"

"Will you help Cayley or not?" said her mother, in irritated ultimatum. Then, with a throb of melodrama in her voice, added, "Will you save your sister?"

"No, I won't."

Hollow reed, hollow reed!

"Not because I don't want to, but because I can't " Megan spoke slowly, as if by careful enunciation of these words which she had spoken repeatedly to this woman, she could make them stick and be understood. "I can't save her unless and until she decides she wants saving. It's her choice. While she still believes there's not much wrong with her and that we're the unreasonable ones, then there's nothing that anyone can do for her."

"Yes, I remember the joke," her mother said bitterly. "How many psychologists does it take to change a light bulb? Only one, but the light bulb must really *want* to change."

"I'm sorry, Mom, I really am. There's nothing more I can do." And nothing more I want to do either, she thought to herself. "Besides, I gave up being a saviour for New Year. No more lame ducks – apart from my patients, of course. It's one of my resolutions."

"Oh, yes?" muttered Patience, looking sceptically from Megan to the limp bird in the basket.

"You're prepared to help strangers, but not your own family – I don't know where we went wrong with you, Megan, I really don't."

"With me? Where you went wrong with me! I'm not the one who's nuts, Mom."

"What a lovely term – did you find it in one of your diagnostic manuals?"

Megan sighed, took a deep breath and told herself not to rise to the bait. "I have to go now, I have clients waiting. Love to you all."

Without waiting to hear her mother's response, she pressed the red button on her phone and, for good measure, switched the damn thing off entirely. It was still early in the morning, only the second week in January, and already she felt exhausted.

"Sawubona, Patience," she said, putting all thoughts of her dysfunctional family firmly from her mind.

"Yebo sawubona; unjani?"

"Fine thanks, you?"

"Ngikhona."

"So who's lined up for today?" Megan asked, turning the large desk diary around so that she could read it.

"Mr Labuschagne first," said Patience, wiping her nose on a pink tissue and tucking it away snugly somewhere in her ample bosom.

"Then a gap, then Alta Cronjé – hmmm," Megan noted. She was glad of the gap. It would give her time to review her notes on Alta and to have a think about the woman. Something was wrong there, things were not progressing as they should. "Then a Miss Nyoka – new patient?"

"Yes, referred by Dr Malan. Needs trauma debriefing for hijacking."

"Okay, remember to change the year date on the intake forms and indemnity forms, and then make a bunch of copies of each. And then, after lunch..." Megan gave a deflating sigh.

"The Bickers."

"The *Vickers*, Patience." Megan consulted the clock on the wall. Six minutes to go before her day began. "Please, if you could find it in your most kind and generous heart, I ..."

"... would love a cup of coffee. Yebo. But what about the bird?"

"Oh, right. Can you make some of this," Megan said, fishing the box of baby cereal out of her bag and plonking it on the reception desk. "And feed it to the bird with this." She produced the dropper with a flourish. "I guess you'll have to make it quite runny."

Patience just stared at her.

"What?" asked Megan.

"This bird is going to die."

"No, we can save it. Just give it some food and maybe water, and I'll nip out at lunch and take it to the vet. There's one in First Avenue."

"Even a very good vet cannot save this bird: it is not strong. It is going to die, but first it will suffer. I think it's better if I just break its neck."

"No!" said Megan, shocked. "It just hurt its wing, that's all. Probably got blown out of its nest by the storm last night."

She took a worried peek at the bird. It seemed to be moving less than it had earlier. Was it just less panicked than before and resting, or was it weaker?

"Maybe its mother kicked it out, when she saw how weak it is."

"Patience – just feed the bloody bird, okay? Keep it alive until lunchtime and I'll take care of it from there."

"If you say so," said Patience, unconvinced, but already taking the bird and food to the kitchenette. "We better not leave it here, the patients will think you're no good at saving and fixing," she said over her shoulder.

Patience always got the last word in, Megan reflected, and almost always, she was right.

3
Alta

Megan's office was a mix of soothing neutrals, a calm background for the pain and horror which was released daily in the space. Scatter cushions of pale mauve – a colour one of her more sandals-and-candles patients had told her was associated with healing in the world of crystals and auras – added some colour, but the overall feel was light and airy and uncluttered. Her desk stood at the far side of the office, backed by high shelves of books and strewn with files, a few journals and piles of papers. On top of one of these stood a paperweight: a fragile dandelion seed head trapped in timeless perfection inside a heavy glass cube.

Brilliant summer sun streamed through the single window which overlooked the outside parking lot with the pepper tree, and the remaining wall was hung with a large abstract oil painting. A long couch, a two-seater and a single wingback chair were grouped between the desk and the door, together with two small side tables – one topped with a dried flower arrangement and the other with a large box of tissues.

"Mr Labuschagne is here," said Patience, coming into Megan's office and putting a large mug of strong coffee on her desk. She took the moment of relative privacy to bend over and rearrange her bosoms in their double-D-cup bra.

"Problem?" asked Megan, a little fascinated with these adjustments. Her own specimens had room to spare in a B cup.

"New bra. Too tight," said Patience.

"Uh, okay. Does he want any tea or coffee?"

"No, nothing. As usual."

"Give me two minutes to review the file and then you can send him in."

Henk Labuschagne, photocopier repairman and weekend pigeon racer, had so far spent four sessions with Megan, supposedly to deal with his marriage. Every time, Megan had suggested that it would be easier to address the issues in the relationship if both he and his wife were present, but Mr Labuschagne had fervently resisted any attempt to allow his wife to join his sessions. It was time to turn up the heat a little.

He sat before her now, short, with thinning grey hair and a round pot belly, rattling off the inconsequential details of his week. He hardly paused to take a breath, but rubbed his hands nervously over his stained but meticulously clean and ironed jeans. Megan wondered if he was afraid she might ask some hard questions if he gave her half a chance, and if he was consciously or unconsciously keeping her at bay with an endless stream of prattle.

"Henk," she interrupted. "Why do I get the feeling that you're telling me everything except what you really came here to talk about?"

He tucked his chin back in surprise. His mouth opened and closed silently a few times.

"It's okay to tell me, you know. What you tell me is confidential – I won't tell anyone else. And," she gave him an encouraging smile, "I've probably heard it before."

"Well, Doc–"

"Megan," she automatically corrected.

"Megan," he said, and bit at the cuticle of one thumb. "I did it, Doc – I'm ... an infidel."

"Sorry?"

"I've been an infidel!"

Whatever Megan had been expecting, it was not this. She had no idea what he meant. He had joined another religion, engaged in some occult practice?

"I'm not sure I understand."

He looked at her, a desperate pleading in his gaze.

"I've committed an infidelity."

"Ohh," the penny dropped. "You're saying you were unfaithful to your wife?"

"Yes, Doc. With a Chinese ... er ... massager. There by Cyrildene."

"You had sex with someone who worked in a massage parlour in Chinatown?" she clarified.

There was a sheen of perspiration on his forehead now.

"I didn't mean to – I mean my friend Piet said they give great massages, you know – Eastern style. And my back was killing me from bending over the machines all the time, so I thought, 'Why not, hey?' And I got the number from him and I went there, but the girl didn't speak too much English, so maybe she didn't understand what I meant. And I couldn't help it, Doc, honest, when she started touching me and stuff. And she smelled so good, spicy, and she was very pretty. So when she started massaging me I got a–" he looked up at Megan, alarmed.

"You got an erection?"

"Yes – that! And then I was lost, a goner. I couldn't stop, Doc, I just couldn't. It felt too good. But then afterwards I felt so bad. Because Mienkie is a good woman, she's a good wife. And she doesn't give me a hard time, and it's not right what I've done. And now," his voice began to peter off, "I don't know what to do about it..."

"First things first," said Megan, trying to keep her voice brisk and business-like. "Did you use a condom?" Please say yes, Henk, please say yes, or else things are about to get a whole lot worse.

"Yes, she didn't even ask, Doc, just rolled it on my ... you know ... *dinges*. She was very professional. Very good. Verrry good." He paused for a moment and seemed in danger of getting sucked into the erotic memories, then yanked himself back into the guilty reality of the present. "But now I feel terrible! What must I do? Must I tell her what I did? Or mustn't I?"

Suppressing a sigh, she said, "Let's start by looking at the choices you have, and what the potential positive and negative consequences of each of those might be. When you have a clearer idea of those, then it might be easier for you to make a decision."

Then again, maybe not. How nice it must be to be a mechanic. To be able to establish exactly what had gone wrong in an engine and to be able simply to clean the dirty pipe, or reconnect the detached alternator, or replace the faulty fan belt, and pronounce it "fixed". Human beings were a lot more complicated and a lot more messy, and they were never entirely as good as new.

"Tell me how you would feel about telling Mienkie, and what you think would happen if you did," Megan began.

She was soon into the swing of the day and the rhythm of the session. The outside world was shut out as she focused all of her attention on this fearful man sweating his way through the cock-up – a literal one, she realised – that threatened to destroy the love he knew and valued. She had not a thought to spare for her mother or her sister, and even the helpless bird with its tiny fighting heart was forgotten in her total absorption.

Half an hour later, Megan saw Henk Labuschagne out of her consulting room. Patience would sort out the payment and book his next session for the following week. Megan flopped down in the comfortable chair behind her desk and sifted through the pile of patient files which Patience had efficiently laid out for the day's consultations. She wanted to review her session notes on Alta Cronjé and plan what should happen next in therapy with her. She began rereading her notes from their first session together, almost six months previously.

Alta Cronjé, 31 yrs, computer programmer
Married (Johan, 35 yrs, electrician)
1 child, daughter (Marlien, 4 yrs)
Grandfather (maternal) was an alcoholic. No other family history of alcoholism, depression or other psych conditions.
Presenting problem: adjustment problems post-surgery (gynaecological, Dr A Trotteur @ Acacia).
Secondary insomnia (early morning wakings), nightmares, generalised anxiety, labile affect: anger → weepiness, irritability & temper outbursts;

concentration & short-term memory problems (negative impact on work performance → undermining motivation); weight gain (+7 kg), unwillingness to be physically touched, problems in sexual relationship with husb, incl loss of desire and dyspareunia.
→ problems in marriage, husb doesn't fully understand, though has been supportive and accepting of her phys changes.
Low-grade depression, Q'd for suicidiality: reports passing thoughts of death, but no clear intention. Husb & children plus faith (Christian) = strong inhibiting factors. (Joked that would take a bottle of pills with a bottle of French champagne).
Prelim. diagnosis: probable Adjustment Disorder, tending to Mild Depression

Megan read through all the process notes from the regular weekly sessions with Alta which had followed, thinking all the while. Some things had improved for Alta over the course of therapy. She was now functioning better at work, she was able to hug her family members again, and had managed to implement many of the anger-management techniques she had learned in therapy.

But, frustratingly, other symptoms had not faded. On a separate sheet of paper, Megan made a note of the problems which had persisted, resistant to her best therapeutic efforts to eliminate them.

Weight gain (no loss since start of therapy)
Nightmares (themes of threat, torture, powerlessness)
Mood swings
Sense of physical numbness
Sexual problems (loss of libido, battles to relax, dyspareunia)

Alta Cronjé had been operated on in Acacia Private Hospital for a lesion on her genital labia. Prior to the surgery, she had not known both labia were extensively affected and had been shocked by the amount of tissue which had been removed. What she had been through had surely been a crisis and the recovery, especially of her sex life, had been painful, but it did not fully account for the clinical picture Megan was seeing.

Alta had developed post-traumatic stress disorder, despite the treatment which should have prevented this. Either, thought Megan, her treatment approach to Alta had been ineffectual – always a possibility – or something else was at work. Something deeper, perhaps cloaked in amnesia or repression or one of a dozen other defence mechanisms, was driving the ongoing presence of these symptoms. Simply stated, Alta should be much better by now. Perhaps it was time for a different approach.

Megan studied her client carefully when she arrived for the session. Alta was shorter than Megan, and plumper. There were dark shadows, like black arcs, beneath her brown eyes. Her hands fidgeted constantly with a tissue, tearing off small bits and rolling them into tiny balls which she placed in a small pyramid on the arm of the couch on which she sat. When the tissue had been shredded, she sighed with irritation, swept the balls into her hand, walked over the room, and tossed them into Megan's dustbin, before grabbing another tissue from the box on the coffee table and starting over again.

"I think," began Megan, "that we should take some time to recap things before we go on. That okay with you?"

"Ja, sure," said Alta, unenthusiastically. She stared at her busy hands, saying nothing while, aloud, Megan reviewed why Alta had come to therapy, what they had done in their sessions so far, what had and had not improved.

"By now you should be feeling much better than you are. So I'm worried that there is something else underneath all this, something which is preventing you from healing."

"What sort of something?" asked Alta, showing her first sign of interest in the session.

"I don't know. And I don't think you know either – at least, not consciously. So we can talk and talk until the cows come home, but we may never figure out what it is unless we try a different approach."

"What do you mean?"

"I think it might be useful to try some hypnotherapy," suggested Megan.

"Hypnosis? *Nooit!*" said Alta.

Inwardly, Megan sighed. She was sure she was about to hear some of the many misconceptions about hypnosis that abounded and which made her work much harder than it needed to be. But she kept her expression neutral and merely said, "Tell me your concerns."

"Hypnosis! That's mind-control," said Alta firmly. "That's why they tell you at the church never to do it. It empties your mind completely. It drives out the Holy Spirit. And I don't want to end up eating onions and quacking like a duck – no thank you very much!"

"Alta, you've been seeing me for six months now. Do you honestly think that what I want for you is to eat raw onions and quack?"

"Well, okay, no. But what about the mind control?" asked Alta.

"I can't control your mind – not when you're fully conscious and not when you're in trance. No one can. If hypnosis was as powerful as people seem to think, then why would we psychologists bother talking to you and listening to you? I could have just knocked you out in the first session, said, 'right, you feel all better now, wake up and back to normal!' and you would have been fixed."

"Hmmm," said Alta, apparently unconvinced but not as certain as she had been.

"And as for the Holy Spirit," continued Megan, knowing how important it was to work within her clients' worldviews, "if I don't have the power to make *you* change, I surely wouldn't have the power over God! Besides, why would I want to drive away the Holy Spirit? I want you to hang on to anything that helps you feel and get better."

"I'm still a bit scared," said Alta.

"Of what?"

"Of not being in control, of not knowing what's going on, what you're doing to me. It will be like another general anaesthetic."

Megan, who had long since mastered the art of writing while still maintaining eye contact with her clients, made a note on her paper while she said, "Alta, when you're in trance, you're very relaxed, but you're not asleep or unconscious. And you won't be amnesic for what happens. Anyway, I won't be "doing" anything to you – all hypnosis is self-hypnosis, and if at any time you want to stop, all you have to do is open your eyes."

"Really?"

"Really."

"Well, I guess you can try, but I don't think you'll be able to get me to go under."

Megan allowed herself a small smile: the battle was half-won. In her experience, those clients who believed themselves impervious to hypnotherapy made the best candidates and went into trance most easily. She thought this might be because they had good defences and were determined to protect themselves against being taken advantage of, and knowing that their conscious minds were keeping a wary eye on proceedings paradoxically allowed them to relax more fully.

She said, "Let's give it a shot next session and see how it goes, okay? I actually think you'll be very talented at hypnosis – you're clever and creative. The only folks I battle with are those with a lower intelligence, because they battle with abstract thought and symbolic images."

This was true. But it was also a therapeutic double bind that she often used when preparing clients for hypnotherapy. They had either to go into trance, or admit that they were not intelligent – invariably they chose the former option.

"Okay," agreed Alta. "I'll try it. I'll try anything, I guess. I'm so sick and tired of feeling like this, you know? I just want to get better." Her eyes were moist with tears.

"That's all I want for you, too." After a pause, Megan asked, "What's your take-away for today?"

Alta thought for a bit and then said, "Maybe there's something else. Something else wrong with me."

"Yes. And that's a bit scary. But it can also give you some hope – because if there is something, and we can find out what it is, then we can try to fix it."

She ended the session there, telling Alta to book another session with Patience as soon as possible – before some unhelpful soul talked her out of trying hypnotherapy – and wished her goodbye.

She looked down at her notes and inked a large asterisk in the margin next to one of the lines, then circled the asterisk for good measure.

*Fears loss of control – connects to loss of consciousness and experience of gen anaesthetic "What you're **doing to me**"???*

Underneath she wrote: *Next session: hypnotherapy (already prepped), regress to operation and gen ansthc. Check if anything happened which she repressed.*

Then she took a deep breath, and focused on trying to clear her mind before the arrival of her next patient.

4
Last time

Oedipus ran up to greet her, barking and yelping and dancing in circles, when Megan opened the door to her town house. He was a fat and lazy golden retriever ("more doughnut than dog" according to Cayley) who did not stir himself easily, but who always had these moments of evening madness when Megan or Mike came home from work.

Her town house was compact, but gave the impression of space, perhaps due to the fact that it was largely under-decorated. She had moved in a year ago, Mike had followed just a few months later – sort of, he still kept his own apartment in Sandton – and she had never gotten around to adding those little touches which would give it a more homey feel. Issues of *Garden and Home* magazines lurked about in bedrooms, the two bathrooms and the small kitchen, with brightly coloured Post-it notes poking out from pages marked for their inspiring photos of designer spaces. But, somehow, Megan never managed to find the time or energy to connect the dots between inspiration and execution. Tables and chairs and sofas were where they should be, but the walls were mostly bare and the place had an unlived-in feel which both stymied and irritated Megan.

Oedipus was now jumping up against her legs, demanding attention.

"Sit!" she said firmly, then leaned over to give the dog a loving pat. Everyone should have a dog, she thought, if only to have someone so glad to see you at the end of the day. Mike's greeting was less exuberant.

"Howzit," he called from the couch in the living room where he sat facing the television. A back-on-form Tiger Woods was struggling with a shot on a green somewhere in the world, and it looked like Mike's Facebook page was open on the netbook propped on his lap.

"Hi, you," Megan said, leaving Oedipus to go and rumple Mike's fair hair and plant a kiss on his lips.

He craned his neck around to catch a putt on the screen, groaned in disappointment and then smiled up at her.

"Good to see you – finally."

"I know, I know – I'm late. Did you start supper?"

"No, I was working," he said gesturing to his computer, now displaying a page from a conveyancing contract.

"So was I," she replied, vaguely nettled.

Oedipus leapt up on the couch alongside Mike and stared adoringly up with his chocolate brown eyes.

"Charm monster," Megan accused. She dumped her bags alongside the couch, helped herself to a glass of wine from the bottle of Merlot sitting on the low table, and pushed the dog aside to squeeze in next to Mike. Her first sip was a big one, and it was followed by a deep sigh. She felt exhausted.

"Bad day?" asked Mike.

"Not great. It was full, with some hard sessions and a new client. And then there was the bird."

"Bird? What bird?" asked Mike, glancing up from his keyboard to look at her, while sneaking in a quick peek at the golf.

"There was this tiny, baby bird that I found under the pepper tree in the car park at work. It must have fallen out of its nest during the storm last night," she said, now tickling the pale fur of Oedipus's soft belly. Every time she paused, the dog writhed and kicked a paw out to get her attention.

"Don't tell me you–"

"I couldn't just leave it there."

"Yes, you could. That's exactly what you could've done. Should've done. It would have made a nice meal for some cat – all part of the natural order." He keyed a few strokes on his computer and snuck another look at the television.

"I thought maybe we could save it."

"We?"

"Okay then, me. Anyway, I took it to the vet at lunchtime, but it was already so weak and she said there was no real hope, and so she … she–"

"… sent it to the great seed bar in the sky? Oh, my poor Meggy. Mad about all creatures damaged and deranged." Mike set aside the netbook, got up and kissed Megan's forehead. "Come on, let's go make something to eat." He took her hand, pulled her up and pushed her towards the kitchen.

She opened the fridge and stared inside. On the top shelf stood a bottle of milk and another of wine. Scattered below were the dried remains of a ready-roasted chicken from the nearby deli, some wilted celery she had bought with the vague idea of making a Waldorf salad, a tub of liver pâté with a furry grey-white film creeping across the surface, and a few eggs still in their brown cardboard box. Bottles of sauces, gourmet mustards, curry pastes, tapenades and pestos – most of them still unopened and a few already past their best-by date – stood on the door shelves, staring at her like the reproachful evidence of good intentions. Beside her, Oedipus also stared hopefully into the fridge. He gave a sharp bark, perhaps of disgust.

Megan sighed. "*Oefs* à la Megan?" She tossed the mouldy pâté and the limp celery into the bin.

"Scrambled eggs. Again."

"Or you could go out for pizza."

"You know, Meggy-babes, you won't be able to rely on your looks forever. You really need to learn how to cook," said Mike, pinching her bum.

"So do you!" Irked, she slapped his hand away.

Megan knew she was a hopeless cook. Cooking had always been Cayley's thing. Cayley, who cooked perfect food for others, Cayley, who knew the nutritional content and calorie count of every morsel she allowed herself to swallow, but the pleasure of none of it, Cayley, who had never known the sensuous joy of a delicious bite unseasoned by guilt. Cayley, who kept everyone else out of the kitchen, and herself away from the table.

Scrambled eggs and spaghetti bolognaise, learned in some long-distant home economics class at high school, were about the extent of Megan's repertoire. She knew she had to improve her skills – eggs for supper at her age, for God's sake! Like some hard-up, hung-over student in res. It was even on her wretched list of New Year's resolutions, but it irritated her to hear Mike state the obvious, and in a way which implied it was her job to do the cooking, her job to take care of *him*.

"Chauvinist pig," she muttered, whisking the eggs.

"Maybe, but you love me anyway – 'cos I'm so cute and handsome!" And he was – tall, blonde hair, baby blue eyes, and a tight butt.

Megan grinned in spite of herself, denting her left cheek where the odd dimple marked the result of a childhood accident. She stirred the eggs while he put toasted bread on two plates.

"Eat up, cute and handsome, it's all you're getting," she said, sliding the rumbled yellow mess onto the toast and plonking one plate at his place at the oak kitchen table.

They spoke a little about his day. Mike was a conveyancing attorney and they had met when he had handled the transfer of her town house. It was not a field that Megan found particularly interesting, but she knew that Mike was passionate about his work.

"The good news is," he said, washing down the last corner of toast with a swig of wine, "that it looks like we'll get the deal for all the units in that housing development in Blaauwberg."

"That's fantastic," said Megan, smiling and clinking her glass against his. A thought occurred.

"Could you do it from here? Or would you need to be based in Cape Town?"

"Cape Town. I could stay there for the duration, or else fly down for the weeks and return every weekend, or every other weekend."

"Charming."

"What?"

"It won't be too fantastic for us, Mike, we'll hardly see each other."

"You *are* in a bad mood today. Here," he said, pouring her another glass of the red. "Have a little more – atta girl – and then we'll go to bed and I'll kiss it all better. All over."

"You know, sex doesn't fix everything."

"No," he conceded, winking lazily, "just most things."

As soon as she had finished the excuse for supper, he took her hand and pulled her to the bedroom, closing the door firmly in Oedipus' hopeful face. He kissed her softly on her cheek, deeply on her mouth. He tasted of wine and toast and familiarity. He unbuttoned her blouse as he kissed the soft hollow at the base of her throat, and reached in to cup her breasts with warm hands. They tumbled slowly onto the bed where he slid off their clothes with practised speed, but slowed down to slip on the condom with great care.

"Don't want a repeat of the last time," he said.

They went through the usual touches and kisses and strokes and, as usual, it was good, but Megan was left feeling strangely unsatisfied. Tired as she was, she lay awake for a long time thinking about Mike and work and resolutions, before eventually drifting into a restless sleep where she dreamed of Alta Cronjé, lying in an hypnotic trance on a couch littered with dead birds.

5

Trance

"So just *relax*. Lie back, make yourself completely comfortable, take a deep, deep breath and try to find a spot on the ceiling that you can stare at without blinking," Megan began.

Alta Cronjé relaxed back in the couch, her feet resting on a footstool, her arms lying on the soft mauve blanket which draped her lap and legs.

"Now as you stare at that spot, trying hard not to *blink*, perhaps you could imagine that your eyes are like tension magnets, pulling all the stress and tension from all parts of your mind and body up into your eyes, leaving your body so comfortable and so relaxed."

Alta's eyes started to blink slowly.

"And soon you may find," Megan continued in a monotonous, sing-song voice, laying emphasis on the words that acted as subliminal suggestions, "that your gaze begins to glaze over or that your eyes begin to feel tired and heavy. And when your eyelids feel so tired – so tired and so heavy that they would really rather close – then just allow them to *close*. And if your eyelids would prefer not to close, then just allow them not to *close* – whichever is more comfortable."

Alta's eyes took one final slow blink and stayed closed.

"And as you relax even deeper and deeper, focusing on your breathing and my voice and just allowing the rest of the world to drift off and away, perhaps you could imagine, now, that a warm, heavy, soothing sensation is entering your body, through your toes, and as it enters your feet you can just allow them to relax and become warm and heavy and relaxed, all tension melting away..."

Megan's voice soothed in calming tones, in slow sentences which had no beginning and no ending, as she guided Alta in the progressive relaxation up through her body. Megan noticed how Alta's feet turned limply outward, how her arms slumped heavily to her side, how her shoulders dropped and the tension eased from her face.

"… and just allow that warm, relaxing sensation to flow over your face. Find the muscles between your eyes and around your eyes and let them soothe out, smooth out. Find the muscles in your jaw, where you store so much tension, and just allow them to relax so comfortably. And finally find the muscles in your eyelids and allow your eyelids to become so heavy – so heavy, so comfortable and so relaxed – that it's just too much effort to open them, and when your eyes are so heavy and so relaxed that you can no longer open them, just let one of your forefingers lift and lower so that I know."

Megan leaned forward and stared closely at Alta's hands. The forefinger on Alta's right hand twitched and lifted a few millimetres before moving back down.

"Thank you, you're doing wonderfully well. Now, while you allow your body to *relax* deeper and deeper with each breath, and your mind to become soft and deep like folds of velvet, perhaps you could focus on my voice and listen carefully while I give you the protections which will ensure that you are always kept safe in hypnosis."

Megan installed the standard set of commands which would protect Alta, then went through the other usual stages in first inductions, a deepener to get Alta into an even more concentrated trance, the installation of a beautiful "safe place" in the subconscious mind where Alta could rest while in trance, confirmation of *yes* and *no* fingers for signalling and, as they had earlier discussed, the installation of a command suggestion. During hypnosis sessions with Megan, Alta would now respond to the word "sleep" by immediately relaxing and going into trance, or deeper into the hypnotic state she might already be in.

Megan concluded. "Remember, the word 'sleep' when used in ordinary conversation or by anyone else will have no effect on you, only when you know it to be appropriate. So for now, just do that, just *sleep*."

Alta's head lolled to one side on the cushion. Her breathing was regular, deep and very slow, and Megan was satisfied that the trance was deep enough to begin the regression she had planned.

"Well done, Alta, you're doing very, very well. And now, I would like you, if you will, to imagine that you are looking at a calendar. And this calendar has one page for every day, and it is open on today's date, Monday the 12th of January – today's date. But this is a very unusual calendar, because it works backwards, so if you tear off the top page, you will see yesterday's date: Sunday the 11th of January. Do that now, tear off the top page and see how it works." Megan paused a moment before carrying on, "Can you see the calendar? Can you see how it goes backwards, how it takes you backwards? Let your fingers tell me."

She looked down at Alta's right hand and saw the yes-finger twitch.

"Excellent. Now I would like you to start tearing off the pages, one by one. And as you tear them off, you will find yourself carried back in time – in time with the pages. Nice and slowly now, as you relax even more deeply, go back to Saturday the 10th, and then Friday the 9th, then Thursday the 8th." Megan kept her voice in its rhythmic, melodic cadence, keeping Alta lulled into the serene calm which would allow her to return to her traumatic experience.

"And perhaps, as you continue looking at that calendar, the pages begin to tear themselves off, one by one, and you just allow yourself to be carried back, day by day, so comfortably, so easily... And after a while, perhaps right now, those pages begin to tear off and flutter away more and more quickly, page after page. And it's so relaxing to see them going so fast, it's almost a blur... And they go and go and go, back and back and back – through December and November and even earlier... And you go back in time with them... And after a while it starts slowing down, slowing right down until it stops and brings you to that date in July last year when you had the operation. And when you're there, on that day, let your yes-finger lift and lower so that I know."

A pause. Then the finger lifted, almost imperceptibly. Alta was very deep now.

"And perhaps you could read off that date to me, Alta."

Megan waited for several moments. It was usual for people in trance to have a delayed response, particularly when the trance was this deep. When it seemed that no response was coming, she suggested, "You will find talking easy now, Alta. Tell me what date the calendar has brought you to."

After a few seconds, Alta mumbled, "Last year, the twenty-second of July."

Megan checked her notes. This had indeed been the day of the operation.

"Very good. And I wonder if you would just allow yourself to look around, and be aware of where you are. See the lights and the colours, allow yourself to hear the sounds. See who is nearby and just tell me what you're experiencing."

"Pain, so sore," the answer came quickly this time. Alta's body twitched in the seat.

"Just stay relaxed now, Alta so deeply relaxed and comfortable." Her patient's body relaxed again.

"Where are you?" Megan asked.

There was a pause, then, "Recovery room."

"You're in the recovery room, after the operation?"

"Mm."

"And you're in pain?" Megan asked. She kept her voice neutral even though it seemed strange to her that Alta should have felt pain so soon after the procedure. Surely she would have been given medication to keep her pain-free once the general anaesthetic had worn off?

Perhaps this might be the reason why Alta had subsequently been so traumatised, had been so sensitive to touch in the weeks and months that followed. It would not have been the first time that a patient was under-medicated.

"So sore," Alta whispered.

A single tear from the corner of her left eye slid over her face and down her neck, leaving a trail like the thinnest of rivers through the make-up on her face. Megan knew from experience that one tear on the outside usually meant that the client was weeping intensely on the inside, and she hurried to intervene.

"For now, you can just allow that pain to become much, much smaller, Alta, almost as if you were turning down the volume control on your pain. There is no need to feel it now, just turn it right down, and relax deeply and tell me what happens next."

Alta sighed. "The doctor comes to me."

"The one who operated on you?"

"Hm."

"And what does he do or say?"

Alta gave a little gasp, a small gulp of air, then said, "Smiles... pats me on the head."

"He pats you on the head?" Again, Megan kept her tone dispassionate, but silently she thought, "Patronising git!"

"Hm. All done, all perfect now."

"Say again?" Megan leaned forward to catch the softly mumbled words.

"All done, all perfect now," Alta repeated.

"Do you say that or does he say that?"

"He does."

Megan sat back, a little surprised. The words seemed peculiar to her. She would have expected the doctor to say something like, "You'll be feeling better soon" or "I'll come back and check on you later" or "The op went well, you can relax now". But "all perfect now"? It gave her an odd feeling. But it was her job to help her clients, not judge the doctor's bedside manner, so she reframed the words into something more healing.

"So it's all finished and you can go back to your bed in your ward and just relax and know that you will recover very well. All's well now."

She could end the regression at this point, but something was niggling at Megan – some prompting of her therapist's intuition. All practitioners knew it – or at least the good ones did – and although they warned you against it in training and urged you to stay on the straight and narrow path illuminated by theory and research, Megan did not know a single practitioner who didn't, on occasion, follow the lead of their inner voice. She followed hers now.

"Okay, Alta, you've rested now for a while, and you feel very relaxed and comfortable. With each breath that you take, just allow yourself to *sleep* even deeper and deeper, more and more and more relaxed. And perhaps you would just allow yourself to go back to earlier in the day, before the operation. Would it be okay to do that?"

When she got the affirmative signal, Megan continued, "And, again, look around and tell me what you see."

"Lights."

"Lights?"

"Light ... light ... light."

"Okay, and what do you hear?"

"Click-click ... click-click."

Megan thought she understood. Alta was probably experiencing being back on the gurney, being wheeled down a hospital corridor to the operating theatre. But, careful as always not to plant ideas or suggest images with leading questions, she asked an open question.

"And where are you?"

"On trolley ... passage."

"You're lying on the trolley, in the passage – of the hospital?"

"Uhm."

"And you can see the lights passing overhead and hear the clicking?"

"Uhm. Wheeling me."

"They're wheeling you now. And how are you feeling?"

"Muzzy ... fuzzy."

"You're feeling muzzy and fuzzy. Do you know why?"

"Gave me a pill."

"I see. They gave you a pre-op tranquiliser to keep you nice and calm – is that right?"

"Mm."

"And do you feel calm?"

"Mm, feels nice," said Alta, her tone lifting a little.

A smile dimpled Megan's cheek. "Yes, it feels very nice to be calm and relaxed. And then what happens?"

"Get to the operating room. A."

"You get taken into operating theatre A. And what's that like?"

Alta shivered. "So cold."

"Yes, the operating theatres are cold. Who's there, Alta, have a look around and tell me."

"Nurse."

"There's an OR nurse. And who else?"

"Anaesthet– … anaes– …"

"The anaesthetist is there. Anyone else?"

"Dr Trotteur."

"Is he your doctor? Your gynae?"

"Hm."

"Does he say anything?"

"… not to worry."

"He tells you not to worry. And then?"

"Tells the nurse to go."

"The doctor tells the nurse to go?" Megan repeated, checking she had heard right.

"Not needed … 's simple procedure. Doesn't need help… She must go to C, help Dr Williams with Caesar."

"I want to be sure I understand, Alta. The doctor sent the OR nurse away. He told her he didn't need her help with the surgical procedure and she should rather go and assist Dr Williams with the caesarean section in operating theatre C. Have I got that right?"

"Uh-huh."

Megan was no surgeon, but she found this very unusual. Surely it was standard procedure always to have an OR nurse present at an operation – particularly one of the gynaecological kind? A bad feeling was starting to take root just under her chest.

"And what's happening now?"

"She's gone," said Alta. Her left hand twitched where it lay, and a foot moved under the blanket.

"The nurse is gone. So it's just Dr Trotteur and the anaesthetist?"

"Uh," said Alta. Megan was not sure if she was imagining it – or projecting her own rising unease on the woman in front of her – but she thought she heard a tremor in Alta's confirmation.

"Where is the anaesthetist now?"

"m'head."

"He's sitting at your head," Megan repeated and then checked, "And what's he doing?"

Alta mumbled something softly. It sounded like "ko."

"What was that? Say again?"

"… 'uko."

"You'll find it easy to speak more loudly and clearly Alta, because it's important for me to hear. So say again, what is the anaesthetist doing?"

"S'duko."

"He's playing sudoku?" Megan heard the outrage in her own voice and took a deep breath to steady herself.

"Yes."

"And what is Dr Trotteur doing?"

"He's putting the tools straight."

This time Megan was sure she had not imagined it. There was a definite quiver in Alta's voice, and the pitch had risen, too.

"He's arranging the instruments for the operation."

"There's a knife!" Alta shuddered.

"A knife? Could it be a surgical scalpel?"

"Yes," said Alta and seemed to relax just a little.

"Then what does he do?"

"Smiles. Touches me." Alta's chest was beginning to rise and fall faster.

"Where?" Megan asked shortly, "Where does he touch you?"

"… forehead."

Not *that* then. Aloud she asked, "He smiles and touches you on the forehead. Does he say anything?"

Alta said nothing. Her body stiffened, her fingers were curling up into her hands. She was on the verge of an abreaction, but Megan was loathe to interrupt the regression. She decided to get it over with as quickly as possible.

"What happens next Alta, tell me quickly."

"The anaesthetist puts a needle in my arm, and there's a tube… He sticks injection into the tube…" Alta's hands were now balled into tight fists.

"He's getting ready to give you the anaesthetic. Does he say anything?"

"Count backwards, from 100. See if you can get to zero," Alta said in a voice deeper than her own.

"And then?"

"He looks at Dr Trotteur," said Alta, her voice catching on the last two words. Her feet gave a reflexive kick under the blanket.

"He looks to Dr Trotteur to give him the go-ahead?"

"Uhm."

"And then? Tell me now – what happens then, Alta?"

Alta rolled her head from side to side against the cushion of the chair. Her knuckles stood out like white hinges on her fists, her elbows were pulled in tightly against her sides.

"Don't want to," she whimpered, tears now sliding freely down both cheeks.

"Tell me quickly and then we'll go away from here and be safe," Megan urged. Her own heart was thudding in her chest. She was desperate to ease Alta's suffering, but knew that the truth was perhaps just moments away from being revealed.

"What happens then? Tell me now," Megan said, using a strong, commanding tone.

"Doctor leans over me, leans on me, on my boobs. He says … he says–" Alta broke off and pushed herself back into the softness of the chair, as if cringing away in fright. Her legs drew up against her body.

"What does he say?"

"Too much!" Alta gasped.

"He says too much?"

"No…" There was a long pause and then Alta gave a single sob from deep in her throat and said, "Too much of me."

"He says there's too much of you?" Megan was beginning to feel real alarm.

"Whispers."

"He whispers? What exactly does he whisper?"

"Don't want to listen, I want to go, want to go, please," Alta begged.

"We'll go soon, Alta, I promise. Just a few seconds more, and then we can leave. As soon as you tell me exactly what he says." Looking at Alta thrashing on the couch, Megan wondered if she was pushing her too far. She was just about to call it quits when Alta spoke.

In a clear, deep voice she said, "There's way too much of you, my little bitch. But not for long. I'm going to cut it all away and make it neat and perfect. Doctor knows best."

6
Gut feel

"Now, Alta, just *sleep!*" Megan commanded, "It's all over. Just sleep and go back to your safe place and rest there, safe and sound, for a while."

Immediately, Alta stopped sobbing. Her head lolled to the side, she took a deep breath and Megan could see the muscles throughout her body relaxing.

Megan covered her mouth with a hand as she thought frantically. Was this a real memory, or some anaesthesia-induced hallucination that Alta only thought was real? It seemed very real to her, but Megan could not be absolutely sure.

Alta's extreme distress was undoubtedly genuine. How was Megan to help her feel better without interfering with the memory? If it had really happened, Alta might want to pursue a case and then she would need all the details to be clear and accurate. Megan knew that with all the prejudice against hypnosis, and all the disinformation propagated by the so-called "false memory" organisations, she had already perhaps compromised her patient's memory in the eyes of the law.

Inwardly she cursed herself for not taping the session as proof that she had not planted suggestions, or introduced inaccuracies. She knew colleagues who recorded every single hypnosis session on video, but they were mostly male therapists who made the recordings as a "cover-your-arse" to protect themselves against accusations of inappropriate contact with female clients. Although her own consulting room was set up for audio recording, Megan had found that the suggestion that the session might be recorded had made clients even more resistant to the idea of working in trance, so she only used it when really necessary.

She brought herself back from useless regrets and back to the issue of what she could do to help her client. Ordinarily she would have used techniques in hypnosis to diminish the distress associated with the event, or she would reawaken her patient and use a trauma technique to desensitise the memory, but these were methods which would invariably reduce the clarity of the memory. What she did now depended on what Alta would want to do going forward. It was time to finish up this session.

"Okay, Alta, as you rest, I would like you to realise very deeply that the experience you had in the operating theatre is over. It happened many, many months ago. It is not still happening now. See the calendar again. Now use that calendar to come back, day by day, to the present here and now. See yourself sitting safely in this room, today. The operation is over, you are safe and sound, and you are no longer in physical pain. You will be able to remember the exact details of the experience you have recovered when you awake."

Megan moved on to the reawakening and reorientation of Alta to the present, and gave her a few moments to fully wake up. Alta opened her eyes and sat up straight, then she looked at Megan.

For a minute, the two women simply stared at each other, then Alta said, "What the fuck?!"

"Yes," said Megan, keeping her voice calm, "It's very shocking."

"What the fucking hell did that man … that … that monster, do to me? And why?"

"Okay, Alta, take a deep breath and let's just talk for a moment about what you've remembered. About what it may or may not mean."

Alta, who Megan could see had been about to continue venting her shock and rage, was distracted by this comment.

"What do you mean?" she said.

"Hypnosis is not what you see in the movies, Alta. It's not a scene-by-scene accurate video of precisely what actually happened. It's a subjective record of what we remember happening, all mixed up with our feelings and thoughts about what we think happened. It's a subjective perception, not an objective record – do you understand?"

"What are you trying to say – that I imagined the whole thing?" Alta was getting angry again, leaning forward in the couch.

"Not at all. I'm simply cautioning you that, that…" What *was* she trying to say? Was she merely attempting to manage her own anxiety by casting doubts on the veracity of Alta's memory? That would be unconscionable.

"I'm just saying we need to go slowly here, and cautiously. A memory recovered in hypnosis doesn't count as evidence of anything – you need to know that."

"Do you think it happened?" Alta's face was bleak.

"Gut feel? Yes, I do," said Megan. Alta slumped back and was quiet for a few moments.

"So what now?" she asked. She had started crumbling a tissue again.

"That depends on what you want to do. If you want to take this further, lay a charge – of assault, I guess – against Dr Trotteur at the police, or make a complaint against him with the Health Professions Council, then it's important that we don't tamper with your memories. I would support you through that process, though it won't be easy on you emotionally to dredge it all up for others to hear. And I'm thinking it would be a difficult case to prove. But if you do manage to nail him, then you would have done something tremendous to right a wrong and to stop him, because there might be others…"

"He might have done this to other women?" said Alta, looking up alarmed.

"If he has done it to you, then maybe, yes," said Megan. "But it's your choice, Alta. If you simply want to forget all about it and want me to help you dull the memories and heal the pain, you're within your rights to choose that course of action. And I'll support and help you in that, too."

Alta sighed and it seemed to Megan that the breath came from the very depths of her pain.

"Why don't you take some time to think it through? You don't have to decide immediately. Think about what it will mean to you either way, think about what, in a year's time, you will wish you had done now. Maybe chat to Johan about it and see what he thinks. And we can talk it through next time."

"All right," said Alta, pulling her handbag towards her and getting ready to leave.

"Are you okay to go?" asked Megan. Alta nodded. "Call me if you're not coping."

"Maybe I'll take the week off and we can spend some time at the farm, and get my head straight on all this. Just the three of us – Marlien and Johan and me…"

"That sounds like a good idea, it's important for you not to be alone too much right now."

They said their goodbyes and Alta went out to schedule her next appointment in the diary that Patience kept. Megan flopped down onto her chair and blew out a breath she felt like she had been holding for the last half hour. She held up her hands, they were trembling slightly, and she was aware of her heart racing in her chest.

She knew, just knew, that Alta's memory had been real. That somewhere in this hospital there was a very disturbed and dangerous doctor, and a slew of vulnerable women. Whatever Alta Cronjé decided, Megan knew that she would need to take this further.

What she needed first was more information.

That night, little though she felt like it, she set about finding out more. After an afternoon of demanding sessions with three more clients, one of whom had spent the whole hour complaining that therapy was not working for her, yet insisted on making another appointment, Megan was exhausted and wanted only to research the softness of her pillow. But her session with Alta Cronjé was still weighing heavily on her mind, so she booted up her laptop and settled cross-legged on the couch, a piece of salty Siciliana pizza in her free hand.

"Surfing the web?" asked Mike, nabbing the last piece from the box and peering over her shoulder while he ate it.

"Sort of."

"The 'Health Professions Council of South Africa'," Mike read off the screen. "Ooh, mega exciting stuff."

"Just got to look something up," said Megan.

"Aren't you all registered and paid up?"

"It's not for me."

"Oh, a *client*." He said the word with heavy emphasis as he plopped onto the couch beside her. "One of the crazies."

"Don't call them that."

"Is the client a doctor? Or a dentist?" he asked, tickling her knee.

Megan twitched her knee away; she hated being tickled.

"Nope."

"Hmm. A mystery..." said Mike, tickling her other knee and moving his exploring fingers up her thigh until she swatted his hand away.

"So that must mean–"

"Haven't you got something else to do?" Megan asked.

"Well, yes, babes. But I would need you for that." He grinned and wiggled his eyebrows suggestively.

"Mike, I'm so tired that it would technically constitute necrophilia."

"Reminds me of a limerick I once heard," said Mike, a teasing glint in his eyes. "Only poetry I could ever remember. Goes like this: There once was a caveman named Dave, who kept a dead whore in his cave. He said, 'I admit, I'm a bit of shit – But think of the money I save!'"

"That's disgusting," said Megan.

"Oh, lighten up! It's a joke – remember them? Things that make you laugh and smile. Or have you forgotten how?"

Megan ignored him. She had no energy for fights tonight.

After a pause, Mike began again, "So if the client isn't the doctor, that must mean ... that the client has a problem with a doctor. And you're trying to check up on the doctor."

"Dammit!" said Megan.

"I'm right!" Mike crowed.

"No, the website just crashed."

"Oh, come on, Meggy, I think you've got something to say to me." He sang it to the tune of the Rod Stewart classic.

"You know I can't."

"Just a few juicy details. What's the deal with the doctor? Or is it a dentist? I've always figured only dodgy people want to spend their lives with their hands in other people's mouths."

"Mike, just let me finish this, okay?" said Megan, irritated.

She retyped the address of the Council in the search engine, but the system hung for a few moments and then returned the message, "Gateway Timeout". She tested her search engine on other sites, which all loaded without a problem, and then tried the Council's again, double-checking the address as she keyed it in.

"What difference can it make if you tell me? They wouldn't know," said Mike.

"I'd know," said Megan. "It's unethical. I won't be telling you anything, so you may as well stop nagging me."

"Is it a doctor at the hospital – at Acacia?" Mike said suddenly. Megan was so surprised that she glanced up quickly, startled. Mike took this as confirmation.

"It is, isn't it?" he said gleefully. "What's he done? Or is it a she?"

"Mike!"

"Oh-oh, shenanigans in the consulting room, I'll bet! Have they been playing doctor-doctor?" He reached out with open hands as if to examine her breasts. "Should *we*?"

Megan swore. The website had failed to load again, and the links to it from other websites were not working either.

"You could be the naughty nurse, who's just done something *wery badd*..." he teased.

"You really have a one-track mind, Michael Welsh," she said, pushing his hands away.

"So do you. It revolves around work," he snapped and there was no humour in his voice as he got up and left the room, slamming the door behind him.

Megan swore again.

7
Ripples

He smears the butter from side to side, evenly and right up to the edges, not neglecting the corners. His morning ritual of bread and tea is soothing. This mass-produced, ready-sliced bread tastes like nothing, of course, but each slice is perfectly rectangular and white. Nothing else in the day that follows will likely be as neat as this. The anchovette must also be evenly spread – no lumps or swirls can remain to disturb the surface. He picks up a chef's knife – its sharper, curved edge is better for this job than the serrated edge of a bread knife – and cuts off the crusts with four swift swipes. He wipes the mess of butter and spread off the blade and cuts again, twice across, twice down. Nine equal bites. He eats them.

Palesa, who has already washed the dishes, wiped the counters and put his laundry into the washing machine, comes into the kitchen. Her black and white domestic worker's uniform is spotlessly clean and neatly ironed; she knows this is important to him. Her face is beaming with pride as she beckons her son into the room.

The boy is twelve, on the cusp of his mutation to manhood, and he is a delight to look at. His features are symmetrical, his skin a smooth, unblemished brown, his teeth as he smiles are straight, even and white. Oh, that they could all be this way.

"Tsebo got his report yesterday. It is all A's. Even for maths – an A!" says Palesa.

"Perfect!" he says and bestows a smile on the child. "Simply perfect. Congratulations."

The boy grins and squirms, both pleased and uncomfortable.

"What do you say to the doctor?" Palesa prompts her son.

"Thank youveryverymuchforpayingmyschoolfees," Tsebo says. It comes out in a rushed, uneven utterance. The child looks better than he speaks.

"Would you like to see his report?"

Not really, but it seems it must be done. Things cannot always be as perfect as the boy's results, as unspoiled as his skin.

"Go fetch it, Tsebo."

Palesa urges the boy outside, to the room at the back of the house, and begins laying the tray for tea. Pot, cup, saucer, milk jug, and sweetener tablets in the bowl – all white, all placed in their correct places on the linen tray cloth.

He always has his tea directly after his breakfast. Routines are important. He hates it when something, or someone, disrupts his routines and his plans. Glitches and mishaps and disruptions leave lingering ripples in the smooth flow of his days. He drops sweeteners into his tea – one, two – stirs precisely five times, sips.

It is time to choose another and he must do better this time, choose more carefully. He has made some unwise selections in the past and it has come back to disturb his ordered existence. That distressing – abusive, really – phone call today, for example. They usually have a better respect for authority, the Calvinists, but she might be one of the stroppy ones, and she had, he had discovered today, an uncouth husband. He wishes he could cut the disturbing phone call away from his day as easily and thoroughly as he had cut the crusts off his bread. He must not let these flies in the ointment get under his skin.

He picks up the linen napkin, dabs at his mouth, feels, as he always does, that almost imperceptible ridge on the bottom of his chin. No. He will not think about that.

He stares out at the garden, sipping his tea. In future, he must investigate better, know more before he makes his decision. The student had been a mistake, too. He had assumed from her earrings and bohemian way of dressing that she was an arts student – a know-nothing, do-less. But he discovered – afterwards – that she was a law student. Not good enough. He must be more meticulous.

His hand strays back to his chin, strokes the line. It feels longer – could it be growing? No! That is an intrusive thought, an impossible, erroneous one. He will clear it from his mind. But he finds himself walking to the bathroom, standing in front of the basin, pulling the magnifying mirror out on its extendable arm to check.

There, see? It is not bigger. It is almost invisible.

But still, it is there.

"Are you ready?"

A girl, a swing, a fall, a cut. His mind pulses with the images.

He spins around on his heel, bellows, "What did you say?"

Palesa stands in the open doorway, clutching a white sheet of paper. She retreats a step, her face alarmed.

"Are you ready? To see Tsebo's report?" her voice is barely above a whisper.

He slams the door in her face. Stupid woman!

Are you ready? Are you sure? The voice again. It is not real. It is not now. But, still, it is strong enough to carry him back a quarter of a century.

He is little again.

"Are you ready?" the girl asks.

"Oh, yes," he says, climbing onto the swing, eager to get going.

Red paint peels from the seat's rough surface, and splinters prick him as he wriggles, but these things do not bother him. He is about to be pushed by Sara, the oldest child in the home. Sara is big and has thick arms and when she gives you a Chinese bracelet on your wrist, it feels like your skin is being ripped off. Everybody tries to stay on the right side of Sara – and here she is, offering to push him on the swing.

"Are you sure you're ready, Attie?"

She speaks in a strange way, drawing out his name slowly. Her teeth gleam and her eyelids droop over her deep-set eyes when she grins.

"Yes, yes!" He takes a firm hold on the chains.

All the other children draw closer to watch. One of the older boys nudges Sara and whispers something in her ear that makes her giggle. The smallest child in the house, a runny-nosed girl whom everyone calls Beany, peeps around one of the poles at him and smiles shyly.

"Then let's..." Sara pulls back the swing until the seat tilts, "begin!"

She thrusts it forwards, pushing so hard with both hands against his back that he almost loses his grip on the chains.

"Up you go," Sara shouts. "Up..." Shove. "And up!" Shove.

Higher and higher he rises with each thrust. It's like flying! The little ones below gasp as his skinny legs and bare feet sail up into the air, and his head tips back with each lift. Over there is the red-brick house where they all live with their house mother Tannie Liesbet. He soars higher even than the corrugated tin roof winking silver in the late afternoon sun, as high and light as a bird. If he lets go of the chain, he will swoop through the air, free and strong.

And still, Sara pushes him higher.

"Look," she cries to the others, "Pigs can fly!"

"Pig-gy, Pig-gy," they begin to chant the hated nickname.

"This little piggy went to market, this little piggy stayed at home," she pushes in time to the chant, her thrusts like blows on his thin back.

"This little piggy had roast beef, and this little piggy had none." She is yelling the words up at him now. "And this little piggy cried wee-wee-wee all the way home!"

The swing seems to pause at the top of each lift – to stop and hang suspended in the air before it plummets down with an unsteady back-swing. With each pause, his bum lifts off the seat, and with each drop, something cold swoops in his stomach. Sweat trickles down his face, but he dares not let go of the chains to wipe it from his eyes.

"Stop it! Stop it, I don't like it."

She ignores him.

The seat of the swing wobbles and jerks from side to side. Any moment now, it might loop right over the bars which hold it up. The poles creak and strain against bolts already loose in the base of old, cracked cement. What if the whole thing pulls loose and topples over? What if his sweaty hands slip and he falls down onto that hard red earth?

"Stop! Please, please!" he whispers.

The air roars in his ears. Tears blur his eyes. He wants to scream, but every time he opens his mouth, the wind races in and snatches his breath. Far below, Sara and the others chant and laugh. He cannot hear, cannot breathe. His whole being is one whispered scream. Stopstopstopstopstop!

A gonging sounds out, and silences the chant. The children run away up the slight rise of grass to the back door of the house.

The swing veers and rocks. He clings on, whimpering, cursing. As it sways slower and lower, he sticks his feet out, drags them hard against the hollow of red earth and stones beneath the swing, until it judders to a halt. He topples down onto his knees in the dirt, gasping and trembling.

When he can breathe again, he sits up and fists the tears from his eyes. His feet hurt. They are scraped raw front and back, and the nail of one big toe is torn away from the bloody nail bed. Tiny bits of grey and white gravel *pit the grazes on his knees. Worst of all, there's a warm, wet stain across the front of his shorts.*

There's a small noise to his right. He swings around, sees Beany still standing behind the pole. She takes a step towards him.

"Sorry, Attie," she says.

A fierce hotness begins to pulse in him. That she should feel sorry for him – this puny, snot-faced girl, with her too-short dress and stupid voice. She saw what they did to him. And she saw what he did to himself. He wants to yell and run away from here. He wants to smash and break and bruise. Blood beats in his ears as all the world becomes this moment, this rotten place.

"Come here, Beany," he says, taking a ragged breath and forcing his lips to twist into a smile. "It's time for your turn on the swing."

The little girl smiles and clambers onto the same seat, seeming not to mind the wetness he left behind. Dirty girl. Dirty, rotten, stinking girl.

Now he is behind the swing. Now he is pushing – hard and high. It does not take very long for Beany to get panicky. The swing is hardly high at all when she starts to scream like a mad thing, a high-pitched scream of terror which rings in his ears and drills through his head.

"You shut up," he screams. "You dirty–"

"Attie! Stop that!"

He turns for just a second to see Tannie Liesbet charging down the rise toward them, and in that instant, the red swing with the screaming girl swings back down at him and clips him on the chin. His teeth snap together with a sharp click. He flips backwards through the air and lands hard on the ground, banging his head on the red earth. Then he feels and sees nothing more.

When he opens his eyes, he is lying on the back seat of a car. There is blood in his mouth. It tastes tinny and sharp like the two-cent pieces he puts in his mouth to hide from the other boys. It trickles down the back of his throat and makes him feel sick. Tannie Liesbet sits next to him, pressing a cloth against his chin and mouth, and something against the back of his head. Someone, a man he does not know, is driving the car.

"Are you awake now? You banged your head and cut your lip, so we're taking you to the doctor to get stitches," says Tannie Liesbet.

"What?" He feels confused. Her face above him is too big. He tries to bat away the pressure at his chin. "Hurts."

"We're taking you to Dr Biddle – so he can check you out and sew you up again."

"Don't like him ... hurts you."

"Now don't talk nonsense. We always take you kids to Dr Biddle and he sorts you out fine, doesn't he?"

"Gonna puke ..."

"Don't–"

He retches. A thick clot of dark blood, chased by a stream of vomit, spills onto the seat, onto Tannie Liesbet's dress. His throat burns, his head is going to split.

"Ag, sis! Now look what you've done, Attie."

He stares at the black leather of the seat. Blood and vomit run in rivulets down the stitched grooves. The darkness takes him away again

He lies on his side on a hard, high bed in the doctor's office, on top of a green rubber sheet which sticks to his bare legs. A strong smell catches in his throat. He stares at the jumble of silver instruments lying on a metal tray on top of a small table beside the bed.

"What have you been doing to yourself, young man? Getting into all sorts of mischief again, hey? You've got yourself a nice cut here on your chin." The doctor reaches out a thick finger and pokes. He wears a white coat and he smells funny, too.

"Eina!" He pulls his chin back.

"And he's got a cut on the back of his head here, too, doctor," says Tannie Liesbet from behind him at the top of the bed. "And he's been vomiting and passing out."

"Hmmm ... probably got a concussion. Let's see this cut on the back of his head."

The doctor whistles and clicks his tongue against his teeth. "We're going to have a bit of a problem here, because this cotton wool is stuck onto the cut."

"I was trying to stop the bleeding, doctor."

"Well, it worked, but now the blood's dried and the cotton wool is all stuck on. See, when I try to pull it off?"

Sharp pain at the back of his head. It feels as though they're trying to pull off his scalp.

"Eina!"

"That's not sore, not for a big boy like you." The doctor laughs at him. "Come on, sit up now."

He wants to explain that it is sore, but he already knows that the doctor won't listen – those thick fingers are too busy pouring a splash of Dettol into the water in the curved, shiny metal basin on the bed. The water turns milky white and a sharp smell fills the air.

The doctor dips some gauze into the white mixture and rubs at Attie's chin. The cloth hurts, the antiseptic burns and it feels like tufts of hair are being torn out the back of his head where Tannie Liesbet pulls off the cotton wool. His throat pinches closed and hot tears spill over.

"Why are you crying? It's not so bad. Don't be such a baby, now," says the doctor.

Those hurting hands come closer. There is a threaded needle between the thumb and forefinger. He jerks away, back into the softness of Tannie Liesbet.

"Can't we give him an injection, doctor, so it won't hurt so bad?" she asks.

He nods, even though moving his head hurts.

"No, no. It really doesn't hurt that much, just a little pinch. I've sewn up kids half his age who haven't shed a tear. He's just making a fuss to get attention. He's as bad as a girl! Besides, by the time the anaesthetic starts working, we can already be finished here. Trust me, Tannie Liesbet. Doctor knows best."

He waits for Tannie Liesbet to stop the stubby fingers with the sharp needle, waits for her to insist that the doctor take away the pain. But all she does is clutch his head tighter back against her chest and say, "Doctor knows best, Attie, now sit very still or you'll get sewn up skew."

A sharp pain burns his chin like ice, like fire. He feels each hot stab as the needle twists in and out of his skin, each sharp throb as the thread tugs and pulls tight. His whole face aches. He tries to keep his lip and chin still, tries not to start crying again, but he can't stop himself from groaning.

The doctor tuts, ties a final stitch and says, "There you are – good as new! Better actually, since I cut off that ugly mole at the same time. Okay, now turn around and we'll do the cut at the back of your head."

"No," he says, though it hurts to speak and he cannot move his lips properly. "It's too sore."

"Stop being such a baby!" The doctor sounds cross, now.

Those stubby fingers turn his head around roughly and yank off the remains of the dried cotton wool, ignoring the sobs.

Tannie Liesbet pulls his face gently against her chest and whispers, "Shhh now, shhhh... The doctor says it doesn't hurt, it'll soon be over. Just shhh and be still."

"Why do you believe him and not me? It's my head. I know what it feels like. It hurts bad. It feels like my head is on fire. Make him stop!" he wants to say, but they'll never listen, not to him, so he says nothing, merely burrows his face deeper into the softness of Tannie Liesbet's bosom.

She smells like sweet flowers, and he can see a fine dusting of white powder on her skin. She holds him tight to her, and kisses him on the top of his head. He no longer needs to cry. He pushes what is happening at the back of his head to the back of his mind. It is happening to someone else, somewhere else. The doctor is hurting another little boy far away. He, Attie, is here, nestled against the soft pillows of Tannie Liesbet's breasts.

Strange tingles of hot and cold begin to buzz through his body, coming from somewhere deep down. He wants something more, needs something more. He wants to climb right inside Tannie Liesbet, to burrow deep into her soft sweetness. His hands creep from where they clutch her back, move around to her front. Tannie Liesbet gives an odd sort of giggle and pushes him away from her.

"Now just the tetanus shot... and... there you are – all finished and klaar. Won't even leave much of a scar. Didn't I tell you it wouldn't be so bad, eh?"

A burning pain sears down his left arm, but it is nothing compared to the burn behind his eyes – a heat which has nothing to do with tears.

Maybe the doctor notices, because the disgusting man blinks and takes a step back.

"She believed you. She listened to you."

"People listen to their doctors, Attie. That's because doctor always knows best."

Instructions are given to Tannie about bringing him back to have the stitches out. But he is no longer listening to the doctor.

He is thinking.

8
Verdicts

"Any messages?" Megan asked Patience after she saw Zanzi Nyoka out at the end of her session. The trauma debriefing was going well and the client would need only one more appointment.

"Yebo," said Patience, holding up three pink slips. "Cayley called. Plus the Van Niekerks late-cancelled, she's got a tummy bug."

"Good," said Megan. Catching Patience's look of surprise, she explained, "Not that she's sick – I'm just glad to have a free hour, I've got some important admin to do."

"And the transplant board wants to know if you can take another potential recipient evaluation."

"What for?"

"Liver."

Megan considered a moment. She enjoyed the work of assessing whether patients with organ failures were suitable candidates for receiving transplants from donors, but the cases took a lot of time in the testing, report-writing and feedback to the transplant board and she had an idea that Alta Cronjé's dilemma would be sucking up much of her free time.

"No, I think let's decline. But ask them to keep me on the referral list. I still want the work, I'm just too busy at the moment."

"And then a call from my favourite honey."

"Wade?" Wade Alden was Megan's long-time best friend, and had winkled his unique way into Patience's affections over the years.

"I like that boy," said Patience with a wide grin. She handed over the message slips, then fished around inside her massive handbag, brought out a pack of chewing gum and popped one into her mouth. She offered one to Megan, sniffed in response to her refusal and returned the crumpled cardboard pack to its hidey-hole. "He's kind and polite and good for you. And so handsome! You should marry him."

"Patience, you do know he's gay?" It was hard to miss.

"Thcha," Patience clicked her annoyance. "Sex! There's more to love than that, you know. You want a man who can listen to you, who can comfort you when you're sad, who can be strong when you are weak." She took a deep sip of tea the colour of mahogany.

"I'm not weak," Megan pointed out.

"That's your problem, right there – a woman can be too strong," said Patience, as if clinching the argument "That's why you're still alone."

"But I'm not alone," Megan protested, "I've got Mike."

Patience made a dismissive movement with her hand as if brushing off a fly. "How are you going to get a *decent* man, a *strong* man," she continued, "if you're so strong you don't need one?"

Megan just stared at her.

"Besides, that boy can *cook*." She swallowed down the remainder of her tea.

"Look, just give me the number for the HPCSA, won't you?"

"What about–"

"I'll call Wade next, promise."

Patience looked up the number in her dog-eared index book, wrote it on a slip of paper and handed it over, saying, "You think about what I said."

Megan merely sighed. One needed patience for Patience, she thought. Back in her office, she dialled the Pretoria number. It rang for several minutes before being answered by an unenthusiastic voice. Megan asked to be put through to the department which handled complaints and disciplinary matters.

"What Board?" asked the voice.

"Uhm, Medical."

"Pleasehold, s'busy."

Megan held on, wedging the phone between her shoulder and neck, while she sorted through papers on her desk. "Greensleeves" played on a repeat shuffle in her ear, interrupted every few minutes by the voice's, "Stillbusypleasehold."

After twelve minutes – she timed the call, silently fuming about bureaucratic inefficiencies – somebody finally answered the line.

"Good day, my name is Megan Wright. I would like to enquire whether any charges for unprofessional conduct have been laid against a certain medical doctor."

"No, you've come through to the wrong extension, this is the Dental Therapy and Oral Hygiene Board. Hang on, I'll put you back to switchboard."

"Wait!" Megan said, but it was too late, "Greensleeves" was looping tinnily again.

"You holding for?" asked the same bored voice after a long wait.

"Complaints against doctors – medical doctors, not dentists," said Megan as clearly as she could, and with forced politeness.

"Same Board, pleasehold…"

After another interminable round of being shuttled between the music and the switchboard, the line rang.

"Medical and Dental, Mrs Mdluli speaking, how can I help?" said a tired female voice. Megan repeated her spiel.

"Why do you want to know?" asked Mrs Mdluli.

"I'm thinking of making this doctor my doctor," Megan improvised, "and I want to be sure that he's good, that he's had no problems before."

"What's his name?"

"It's Dr A. Trotteur," said Megan and spelled the surname.

"Hang on, I'm just looking him up on the system." Megan could hear the sound of keyboard clicks in the background.

"Here we are … an obstetrician-gynaecologist?"

"That's the one," said Megan. She pushed the telephone hard against her ear, eager to hear what Mrs Mdluli had found. There was silence on the other end of the line.

"Hello?" said Megan, fearing she had been cut off.

"Yes, I'm still here."

"Well? Have there been any complaints against him?"

"The Board does not disclose whether there have been complaints against practitioners, as these may be inaccurate or unfounded," said Mrs Mdluli, sounding like she was repeating a piece of legislation for the umpteenth time. "I can tell you that there have been no verdicts against Dr Trotteur."

"None?" asked Megan. She had been so sure there would be something.

"No. No verdicts," said Mrs Mdluli. Megan thought she heard a slight emphasis on the last word.

"No verdicts," she persisted, "but have there been any complaints laid? Any disciplinary hearings held?"

"I'm sorry," said Mrs Mdluli, and she sounded it. "I can't tell you anything more. Is there anything else you want?"

"No, but–"

"Goodbye," said Mrs Mdluli and the line went dead.

Megan replaced her handset and stared at the telephone, wondering. Wade was always good for encouragement and advice. Now seemed like a good time to return his call.

"How goes the world of advertising?" she asked.

"Magnificently, fabulously, wonderfully – but wait, that's not all!" When Megan gave only a feeble laugh, he asked, "How are you, sweetheart?"

"Crap," Megan said. She tucked the receiver under her chin and began playing with the paperweight on her desk, passing it from hand to hand, feeling its heft. She loved the contrast of the fragile dandelion seed head and the sharp-edged cube of solid glass. Usually the beauty of the delicate puffball, the promise of regeneration and new life were what stood out for her, but today it was the encircling heaviness of the glass that registered.

"That bad?"

"Yes, I'm tired most of the time, fighting with Mike lots of the time, and really worried about a client for the rest of the time."

"Oh, my poor baby!" said Wade and the real concern in his voice brought a lump of self-pity to her throat. That was another thing he was good for, thought Megan, sympathy. Patience should add it to her list of his attributes.

"Anything I can help you with?"

"Nah. I'm just really worried, I've got a feeling a doctor did something really bad to a patient, but when I tried to check, the official at the Health Professions Council just said there were no verdicts against him. She said it like that – "no verdicts". I don't know, I just get a sense there's something there, but I don't know what to do."

She could talk to Wade about work. He never pressed for names, was not curious about the gory details, and he was a bottomless well when it came to keeping secrets.

"Why not go there? In person, I mean. You could turn on the charm and use your spidey-psycho powers to winkle the information out of her."

"Hmm… That's actually not a bad idea," Megan said, putting down the paperweight and sitting up straighter.

"I'm full of them. And here comes another one – trust your intuition, girl."

Sitting in the small and cluttered room at the HPCSA offices in Pretoria a few days later, though, Megan reflected that intuition seemed a very insubstantial basis for her visit. Mrs Mdluli was an older woman, of about fifty, with short greying hair framing a round face set in grim lines. She seemed just as resolute about not divulging any further details as she had on the telephone.

"All the guilty verdicts of our hearings are public record. They're published on the website. But I'm not permitted to disclose any further information about this member," she said, tapping the buff-coloured file on the desk in front of her. The file looked thick. Surely it could not be so thick unless a number of complaints had been laid against Trotteur, even if none of them had resulted in the elusive guilty verdict?

"So there *is* further information which you could–"

"Which I could *not*," said Mrs Mdluli firmly.

Megan was beginning to feel desperate. It was infuriating that the information she sought was a mere arm's length away, and yet was out of reach. She wondered what would happen if she just snatched the file and made a run for it. A hearing of her own, no doubt, one which *would* result in a damned verdict.

"I wonder," she began, unsure if she were following the promptings of intuition or insanity, "I wonder if I could perhaps make it worth your while to share some of that information."

Mrs Mdluli stared at her.

"I mean, really worth your while."

"Mrs Wright, are you trying to bribe me?" asked Mrs Mdluli, her face unreadable. Was she insulted, or tempted?

"Er…"

"You people!" Mrs Mdluli virtually spat out the words. "You think just because I'm black, I'm corrupt."

"No!" protested Megan, "I just–"

"All blacks are lazy and dishonest and potential criminals – is that it?" Mrs Mdluli leaned forward across the desk, fury in her dark eyes.

"No, really, it has nothing to do with race," gabbled Megan. "I'm sorry, really sorry, Mrs Mdluli. I'm just desperate. Please, just listen."

Mrs Mdluli said nothing, her lips were tightly pursed, but she sat back fractionally in her chair.

"I have a patient, and I think, from what she remembers, that she was seriously abused by Dr Trotteur. Emotionally tortured and physically maimed. And I think he did it deliberately. I'm scared that he may have done it to other women, that he might do it again. And I need to know whether other women have laid complaints. I'm sorry I tried to… But I just don't know how else to get the information I need. If I'm right, he must be stopped – surely you can understand that."

The official stared at Megan for a long moment, then she said. "I'm afraid I can't help you. I am not permitted to disclose confidential information. You must please excuse me, I need to go to the bathroom. I will be back in five minutes, please ensure you are gone by then. And I remind you, you are not permitted to read this file," she pushed the buff folder a few centimetres in the direction of Megan, "Not under any circumstances – do you understand what I mean?"

She got up from behind the desk and walked out the office, clicking the door closed behind her.

For a moment, Megan was immobilised by surprise, but then she seized the file and opened it, paging quickly through the papers filed inside it. From what she could see, they consisted of notes of preliminary disciplinary hearings, official forms which looked like charges and, towards the bottom of the file, letters to the Board complaining about Dr Trotteur. She was quickly scanning these, shooting glances at the office door every few seconds, when her eyes were caught by a bullet-pointed phrase, "that Dr Trotteur did, unnecessarily and with no medical basis, surgically over-tighten the opening of my vagina and cut out my clitoris".

They were real words, in the grammatically correct order, but still they made no sense. Megan reread the sentence slowly. She felt suddenly nauseated and swallowed down the bile rising in her throat. She could feel a cold sweat beading her top lip. A sudden, loud noise in the corridor made her look up quickly, clutching the file to her chest, but it was just two people walking down the passage. She could see their shadow moving past the frosted glass of the office door. She needed to hurry. Cursing that there was no photocopier in the office, she leaned forward and snatched a piece of notepaper and a pencil from the desk in front of her. As fast as she could, she jotted down the names, addresses and telephone numbers of the two women who had laid formal complaints. She was running out of time, there was no chance to note more of the details in the file – at any moment, Mrs Mdluli might return.

Megan closed the file, replaced it on the desk and, grabbing her bag and stuffing the paper into it, exited the office. She had taken only a few steps down the corridor when Mrs Mdluli passed her, walking in the opposite direction. The eyes of the two women met for a moment. Megan silently mouthed the words "Thank you," and Mrs Mdluli gave a small nod, without pausing in her stride back to her office.

Megan almost ran down the corridor, pushed open the door of the fire escape stairwell and flew down the stairs, out the lobby and towards where her car was parked in the hot sun of Vermeulen Street. She was still two car lengths away from it when her stomach convulsed. She bent over a rubbish bin and threw up, retching until there was nothing left but dry heaves.

9

Surely not

"I'll have the carrot cake with cream cheese icing, please, and a caffè latte," said Megan, handing the menu back to the waitress.

"Uhm," said Cayley, "just give me a minute." She seemed to be reading and carefully considering every item on the menu. "I'll have the ginger rooibos tea to drink – no milk or sugar – and..." She returned to scrutinising the menu.

The waitress tapped her yellow pen against her front teeth. Megan looked around. They were trying out a new coffee shop in Parkhurst's main drag for their regular coffee morning catch-up. Too many uncomfortable wrought-iron chairs and tables were crammed into a cobbled courtyard with a few unhealthy-looking, potted olive trees giving scant shade. The brick walls were hung with words roughly wrought from wire: *peace, forgiveness, dream, love!* It was all a little chi-chi and underwhelming, except for the prices, which were impressively steep.

The waitress cleared her throat and looked at Megan. Megan looked at her sister.

"Cayley?"

"No, nothing for me, I think," Cayley said, passing the menu back to the waitress who gave a barely suppressed sigh and walked back to the shadowed interior of the restaurant.

"So, how's life?" Megan asked.

"Same shit, different day," said Cayley, "but I might be getting a new job."

"Oh, yes?" said Megan, trying to sound enthusiastic rather than cynical. Her sister had run through at least half a dozen jobs in the previous two years. Nothing lasted long in Cayley's life – except her obsession with food and her body.

"Yes, it's quite exciting actually. There's this catering company – Juicy Morsel. It's owned by one of mom's friends, and they've said they'll take me on as a ... well, not a chef, but a catering assistant, I guess you could call it. Helping with the food prep, and plating up at functions and stuff. They do corporate shindigs and weddings, twenty-firsts, all sorts."

"Mom got you a job. At a catering company?"

"Why do you say it like that?" said Cayley, sounding defensive.

"Like what?"

"Like you think it's a bad idea."

"Isn't it?"

"You're so negative, Megs, it's a good job. I'll enjoy it, earn some money, pay off my Edgars account. What's the problem?"

"The problem is, Cay, that you have an eating disorder..."

"I do not–"

"... and a job," continued Megan, ignoring the interjection, "which involves thinking about and working with food all day, will only feed your obsession with food and eating and weight!"

"I'm not obsessive."

The waitress had arrived with their orders. She put their hot drinks down in the middle of the table, and an enormous wedge of cake, topped with cream cheese icing and a mini marzipan carrot, in front of Megan.

"That looks really good," said Cayley, longing written over her face as she stared at the cake.

Here we go again, thought Megan. "I'm sure it is good. Are you sure you don't want a slice? I can easily call the waitress back."

"No, I couldn't," said Cayley, "but I wouldn't mind just testing a crumb to see if it's moist. Carrot cakes can be very dry, you know. It's hard to get them moist without making them claggy."

She crumbled off a small piece of cake, sniffed it, and then put it in her mouth as though it was the rarest of exotic foods.

"Mmmh. It's very moist. Maybe they used crushed pineapple. Some recipes include it and it stops the cake from being dry. This one's really good." She ate another small piece.

"Here," said Megan, reaching over to grab the serviette-wrapped utensils from Cayley's setting, extracting the fork and stabbing it into the top of the cake. "Let's share – help yourself."

"No, I mustn't – I've already eaten today," said Cayley, but moments later her hand, like some shy creature not fully part of herself, crept across the table top again and broke off another small morsel. She looked up to see Megan staring at her.

"This way it doesn't count," she said with a mischievous smile. "If you break it up and eat only the crumbs, all the calories would have oozed out by the time it gets to your mouth. It's been scientifically documented, it's officially called 'calorie leakage'. I saw it on *Discovery*."

Megan smiled, but it was a sad smile. She was all too aware how their chat had narrowed, as it always did, down to the sole focus of Cayley's relationship with food. She looked down her sister's slight frame to where her thin arms rested on the table. They were covered with lanugo – the anorexic's telltale light fuzz of downy hair.

"Cayley, is there any point in telling you that you do not need to worry about calories?"

"None at all," said Cayley, sneaking another bite. "Why aren't you eating? Don't tell me the mega-mentally-healthy Megan has started worrying about *her* weight?"

"I think you do enough of that for the both of us. Here – you have it," Megan said, pushing the plate of cake over the table, "I'm feeling a bit queasy, actually." The whole issue with Alta Cronjé and Dr Trotteur was really bothering her – enough, apparently, to turn her stomach, especially when she thought about that letter in the file, that poor woman.

"*Babelas?*" said Cayley, beginning to tuck into the chunk of cake.

"I am not hung over."

"Maybe it's food poisoning," Cayley teased, sucking icing off her fingers. "With your cooking I wouldn't be surprised."

"Lately, I've been so busy and so tired that we've been living on take-aways, so I guess it's possible that I picked up a bug. But I haven't had a runny tummy or anything, and I don't feel sick all the time – just at odd moments." She sipped at her coffee, but it tasted bitter and smelt strange.

"Maybe you're pregnant," said Cayley, and, at Megan's horrified look, said, "Kidding!"

As they both laughed, Cayley looked around, caught the waitress's attention and ordered a slice of Black Forest cake – "What the hell – in for a penny, in for a few pounds!"

They spoke for a while about their parents ("Mom's taken up scrapbooking now, so the whole house is covered with ribbons and stickers and home-made calendars, Dad's AWOL as usual – Atlanta, I think."), Megan's work ("When are you going to settle down and get a real job, Megs? Kidding!"), and her relationship with Mike ("Sounding a little rocky, there, sis.").

"Anything to report on your love-front?" asked Megan.

"Nah, all the good ones are dead, married or gay. And for the rest – arseholes aplenty. Tell me this, sis, if they can send a man to the moon, why can't they send them all there?"

Cayley's cake arrived and she began to eat it quickly, gobbling down forkful after forkful, without pausing for breath or even appearing to taste it. Absorbed as she had been in eating it, she seemed surprised when she noticed it was finished, and a dull flush suffused her face. A heaviness settled across Megan's chest as she watched her sister. She knew what was coming next.

"Excuse me just need to go to the loo."

"Cayley, please don't do this," said Megan urgently, laying a hand on her sister's arm.

"Do what," said Cayley, all innocence. "I just need to pee, okay?"

"Cayley. Please."

"Oh stop ss-mothering me, Megs. One overbearing, over-controlling mother is more than enough."

She stood up, spun around and flounced off in the direction of the toilets, her short skirt swinging above her impossibly thin legs. Megan watched as her beautiful sister's course across the courtyard drew admiring glances from the men and envious looks from the women.

If they only knew, she thought. But I am not going to follow her. I am not going to storm into that bathroom and yank her head out of the toilet bowl. Not again. I am going to sit tight. I gave up rescue missions for the New Year. I cannot rescue someone who insists she is not lost or stuck. I am going to sit here and drink my coffee and think about something else, about… Unbidden, Cayley's throwaway phrase bubbled up from whatever subconscious depths Megan had shoved it to: "Maybe you're pregnant!"

It bubbled up again late that night, and it was the words – surely not true, surely not even possible – and not Mike's uneven snores, that kept Megan awake in the darkness.

10
Imperfection

He can feel the pressure rising, building inside him, expanding, stiffening the muscles in his back and tensing his scalp. It is getting harder to contain.

All around him, all he sees is imperfection. Flaws and blemishes and uneven, unbalanced defects.

That man over there, with the front tooth missing from his puckered mouth; that woman, the thick make-up, the long, heavy fringe failing abysmally to conceal the port wine birthmark blotting her forehead and temple; that child gripping the can of cola – already fat, rolls of flesh bulging over the belt of her jeans.

The children, in particular, bother him. He believes as a matter of principle that they should be given the chance to outgrow their imperfections – their purple-budding acne, their uneven teeth, their swellings of puppy fat. But with such bad beginnings, what hope do they really have of emerging from the cocoon of childhood without deformity? Already they are incubating ugliness.

It is a defective world. It causes him pain – an actual physical ache that seems to press against his chest from the inside and squeeze and squeeze inside his head.

He pushes his fingers hard against his eyeballs until the phosphenes cover his visual field. He tries to expand his chest, to breathe against the compressing weight that robs him of breath and makes him dizzy. He rubs his chin.

He needs relief. He needs the release – the grounding – that only a scalpel moving through flesh, cutting into and away, can bring.

And he needs it soon.

11

Zuma's law

Patience stuck her head around the door to Megan's office.

"Mr Labuschagne is here," she said.

Megan glanced down at her watch, she still had a minute. "Okay, I'll see him in a moment, just come in for a sec."

Patience stepped inside and, at Megan's gesture, closed the door behind her.

"Do me a favour, won't you," Megan asked. "Will you get the names and numbers of all the gynaecologists in the hospital? Make a list for me. And while you're at it – ask around to find out who's good."

"Gynaes!" said Patience, perking up with immediate interest. "Is there something you want to tell me?" She was visibly swelling with curiosity.

"No," said Megan firmly, "nothing like that, Patience. I just need a check-up, okay?"

"And you don't want to go to your usual doc? To Dr Khumalo? You said you liked her."

"I thought it would be easier to see a doctor here at Acacia."

"Hmmm," said Patience, patently unconvinced.

"Just do it for me, okay?" said Megan. Patience's eyes narrowed.

"Please?"

Patience gave a shrug which Megan took for assent.

"You can send in Mr Labuschagne – I'll get the doctors' names from you after his session."

An hour later, she stared at the list of five names. The last one immediately caught her eye, but she made herself ask Patience what she had gleaned about each of them.

"This one – Dr Weinberg – I have written him at the top, see? Because the nurses tell me he is the best one. Very gentle, very good. They say he has the most natural births." Patience gave Megan a significant look. "Do you want me to make an appointment for you?"

"Hang on a sec, what about the others?"

"Dr Gebhardt is no good for you."

"Why?"

"They say it is a funny thing, but every one of his patients has a pelvis too small for normal delivery and she must have a Caesar."

"I don't need to know about their birthing skills. Patience, I need a gynae."

"That *wabenzi* Dr Maseko also," said Patience, ignoring the interruption. "The doctors who make too much money – you must stay away from them."

"And Dr Williams?"

"They say she's good, but she's not taking any new patients now, she's about to go on leave to have her own baby."

"What about this one?" She pointed to the last name on the list.

"Dr Trotter?"

"Trotteur, I think," Megan pronounced the name with what she thought was the correct pronunciation. It looked French.

"They wouldn't say much about him. But they didn't say nice things, like they did about Dr Weinberg."

"Did they say anything bad?"

Patience gave Megan a sharp glance. "They didn't say anything specific, but Sister Mercy called him *indoda engalungile*."

"There's a sister called Mercy?" laughed Megan, momentarily distracted.

"Yebo. But you're a shrink with a receptionist called Patience."

"Sorry. Anyway, what they called him – a dodi-whatsit – what does that mean?"

"It means you should go see Dr Weinberg," said Patience, adjusting her bra-straps with an air of finality.

For a moment, Megan was tempted to schedule an appointment with Dr Trotteur. She wanted to see him, to assess him for herself. But only an idiot would walk directly into a situation she knew was potentially dangerous. She also did not want to cue the good doctor on to the fact that she was investigating him. It was better to find out what she could – quietly, subtly and indirectly.

"Make me an appointment, will you? As soon as he can squeeze me in," said Megan.

"They'll want to know what it's for," said Patience, still looking curious.

"Nice try, Patience," said Megan with a smile.

Patience shrugged and ambled back to the front office, sticking her head back around the door to announce that Alta Cronjé had arrived for her appointment.

"Send her straight in," said Megan.

Alta's appearance had improved. Her hair was freshly washed, the shadows under her eyes seemed less pronounced and her face was not quite as pinched. She was not tearing tissues.

"You're looking better than when I saw you last," said Megan, after they had exchanged greetings. "Did your break at the farm do you some good?"

"Ja, it was great to get away, you know? It's so quiet there and peaceful. It was just Johan and Marlien and me, and we just took it easy. I slept better."

"That's great," said Megan, and waited. Until Alta had decided what she intended to do, it would be unethical to tell her about the other victims, because it would be sure to influence her decision.

"I told Johan."

"About what happened that day? What you remembered in hypnosis?"

Alta nodded.

"And?"

"He went mad. Nuts. Chucked a lamp on the floor and shouted. And then … it was horrible…"

"Did he hurt you?" It was always touch and go how male partners would react to the rape or abuse of their women. As often as not, their rage found focus in blaming the woman herself.

"No, man! Hell, you always think the worst, hey? Must come with the job. No, he's never laid a hand on me. Well, not like *that*, anyway. But he started crying, Megan, like sobbing – hard. And I felt so bad for him, that I wound up comforting him! *Jinne*, it's a terrible thing to see a big, strong man cry."

"He was really shocked and upset," said Megan, falling back on the old therapeutic technique of reflecting back to the client what she had just said.

"Ja, and then when he stopped crying, then he got really angry, I mean, *woes*. Wanted to jump in the car then and there and drive back to Joeys and kill that doctor. Said he wanted to cut off his balls first and see how he liked it!"

"He felt powerless about what had happened to you, helpless that he couldn't prevent or fix it. He wanted revenge."

"You're right there. I swear, if we'd been in Joeys, the doc would be dead by now. It was only because we were on the farm, and I told Johan that he couldn't leave me and Marlien alone – it's not safe, there have been so many farm murders – and so he calmed down a bit and stayed put. But we could only talk properly the next day."

"How did he respond then?"

"He still wanted to kill the oke, and painfully. Me too, actually. But I made him think and see that that will only get *him* locked up for murder. 'Cause that's how it works in this place – the real killers and rapists walk free. But the good citizens who put one foot wrong – they get caught and locked up. Murphy's law. Ha!" she gave a cynical laugh. "Or maybe Zuma's."

"Is he calmer now?"

"Worried he's gonna come here one night and do something to the doctor?" said Alta with a grin. "No, he's calm now. But we both want to do something to take this further. Charge the doctor, or whatever."

"Are you sure?"

"Ninety per cent sure," said Alta, huffing a breath up into her fringe. "We're just worried that it's his word against mine. And it's too late to get a second opinion about whether the surgery was necessary because the ... the part that was supposed to be diseased is gone, isn't it? There's no, like, evidence."

"Well," said Megan slowly, thinking carefully about her next words. "I've been doing some digging."

"And?" said Alta sharply, leaning forward and looking intently at Megan.

"I ... found out that there have been several other complaints laid against Trotteur, two of which resulted in charges being brought by the Health Professions Council of South Africa – the Board that governs and disciplines doctors."

"What for?"

"Pretty much the same as happened to you," said Megan. "He mutilated them, Alta, there's no other word for it. I didn't get the full details, but on one of them, he tightened the vagina way too much and ... and cut off her clitoris."

"Fuck," said Alta.

Megan gave her a moment to take in what she had just heard.

"So how come he's still practising? How come he's not locked up in the *tjoekie*?" Alta was getting angry now.

"There has been no verdict against him," Megan explained. "When a complaint is laid, they investigate a bit and then hold a disciplinary hearing if they think it's warranted. If there's enough clear evidence against the doctor, then he gets a verdict against him and a fine or maybe a suspension, or if it's really serious he's deregistered and can't practise anymore."

"A fine! Deregistered – for what *he* did?" Alta looked appalled.

"I don't know what they would do in a case like this, there was nothing like this on the list of verdicts. Maybe they would be obliged to report it to the police, if there was a guilty verdict, and then there might be a criminal case, or the victim could bring a civil claim. In any event, it never came to that with Trotteur. I'm not sure why – maybe there was insufficient evidence. I'm not even sure it came to a proper hearing stage."

"Can we find out?"

"I can try," said Megan.

"Because if we're going to get him, we need more evidence. And if other women have tried to get him locked up, and it hasn't worked, then we need to find out why their cases didn't hold. So we don't make the same mistakes. I want to get him, Megan. I want to nail this bastard, this butcher."

"Okay, I'll see what I can find out, leave it with me," said Megan. "In the meantime, let's shift our focus back to you. Tell me what else is happening in your life, because you are so much more than this one trauma, Alta. You are a whole person – a programmer, a wife, a mother. A funny, clever, creative woman. Don't let's reduce you to this one thing that happened to you; don't let him win."

"You're right," said Alta. "Do you know that Marlien had her birthday while we were on the farm? She turned five – my little baby is five years old!" She fished her cellphone out of her handbag, tapped the screen and then held it up so that Megan could see the photograph of the little girl. Her hair was the same shade of brown as her mother's, but her smile was more carefree than any Megan had ever seen on Alta's face.

"She's gorgeous! And she's not such a baby anymore?"

"No, she's a proper little girl, she's growing up so fast. She'll start big school next year. You know, I've been wondering…"

"Tell me."

"She doesn't need me so much now. And Johan is better with her since she's a bit older – I think he was scared of breaking her when she was so little. But now they can kick a ball and play a game together and stuff. So I have more free time and I thought, maybe, that I might volunteer. Like a counsellor, you know? Do a course and help out other people who are having problems, who just need someone to talk to. But maybe it's a stupid idea," she said, looking almost shyly up at Megan, as if for approval.

"I think it's amazing that you'd like to help others. And I think you'd be good at it."

"You do?"

"I do. But I also think that before we introduce Lifeline or Childline to the helping talents of Alta Cronjé, we need to make sure that you're as healthy and strong as you can be. Because it's hard to hear other people's pain when you're still dealing with your own issues."

Which just about disqualifies every psychologist I've ever known, Megan thought. Including myself.

12
Probing

There were three other women in Dr Weinberg's waiting room on the second floor of Acacia Clinic, all of whom had large bellies bulging out front and expressions of glazed placidity on their faces. They sat quietly, smiling benignly at each other, occasionally stirring to gently rub their baby bumps. One was knitting – something Megan had not seen in years. Megan, by contrast, battled to sit still; she alternated pacing the small confines of the room with sitting uncomfortably in one of the pink chairs lining up against the pink-painted walls. It was like being inside a rosy womb. A patient – not pregnant, from what Megan could see – emerged from the consulting room, and one of the waiting women was called in.

Megan thought about her objective for the consultation with Dr Weinberg: to get more information about Dr Trotteur. She tried to come up with a subtle and plausible way of fishing for this information, but none occurred to her. How did one unobtrusively weave into casual conversation questions about a medical colleague deliberately botching operations? *So tell me, Doc, have any of your colleagues maimed and tortured patients lately?* She would just have to wing it when the time came, she decided.

There was another exchange of patients – one into the consulting room and one out – and a young woman, not obviously expecting but wearing a suspiciously loose-fitting top, came in and reported to the reception desk. There was only one patient ahead of Megan now. She reached over to the pile of magazines on a side table covered with lacy cloth in the ubiquitous pink. Perhaps reading would help settle her nerves. She shuffled through the magazines, trying to find one which would interest her: *Living and Loving*, *Your Baby*, *Your Pregnancy*. A phrase on the cover of one of them caught her eye: "Are you or aren't you? Symptoms of pregnancy".

She found herself turning to the article and scanning the list of symptoms printed in a pink text box. Did the whole world go pink when you were pregnant? *Tender breasts* (not that she'd really noticed); *dizziness* (nope); *nausea* (check); *missed period* (check – maybe); *fatigue or exhaustion* (check with a vengeance); *increased need for urination* (immediately she felt the need to go); *food aversions* (check)... A definite pattern was beginning to emerge. She felt her anxiety spike and her stomach clench, but maybe that was just symptom number ten: *heartburn and indigestion*. The whole thing sounded like some horrible disease – she did not know why the contented women sitting alongside her looked so smug.

"Mrs Wright?" The receptionist was indicating that she should proceed to the consulting room.

Megan looked with some surprise at the third, obviously pregnant woman who had not yet gone in. Perhaps she had no appointment, perhaps she just came to the rooms from time to time to bask in the glow of bountiful fecundity.

Dr Weinberg stood up behind his desk to greet her and shake her hand. He was a slight man of about her own height, with silver hair and sharp eyes behind rectangular steel-rimmed spectacles.

He read through the patient history forms which she had completed and then asked, "So how can I help you today?"

"Oh, just a check-up. No real problems."

"How long has it been since your last pap smear?"

"I can't remember," Megan lied. She knew exactly when it had been because every year she scheduled her annual pap smear in the week before her birthday, but that had only been a few months ago and she needed a valid reason for the visit, and enough time to ask some questions. "A couple of years, I think."

"It is most important to have a pap smear regularly – that means annually, Mrs Wright," he chided gently.

"It's Miss, but please, call me Megan."

"Right, Megan," he began. She noticed he did not invite a similar informality with his name. The old doctor-patient power imbalance still held sway. "Anything else bothering you?"

"Not really … except…"

"Except?"

"Well, I've been very tired recently – though work's been hectic and it could be that. And I've been nauseous, even though I haven't been ill."

"Have you missed a period?"

"I think I'm late, by two to three weeks, but I'm not sure. My cycle is usually quite irregular."

"When was the first day of your last period?"

"About six weeks ago, I think. I don't keep records." She felt like a small girl confessing her guilt on some crime, and it irritated her.

"Hmm," said Dr Weinberg, pushing his spectacles up his nose. "Let's do the check-up first and then we can do a pregnancy test. This way, please."

He escorted her into the adjacent examination room through an inter-leading door. A nurse in a blue uniform was waiting there, smiling reassuringly. While Dr Weinberg returned to his office, closing the door behind him, the nurse handed Megan a floral patterned gown. It was pink.

"Everything off, please, and put the gown on so that it opens to the front. You can put your bag and clothes here." She indicated another of the pink chairs against the wall opposite the examination table, and then left to give Megan some privacy.

Megan stripped, hung her clothes over the chair and slipped into the gown; the cotton was cool against her flesh. She hopped onto the examination bed, positioning herself on the disposable linen-saver, and pulled the white blanket over her. An ultrasound machine hummed beside the bed, a tray of gleaming metal speculums with a half-squeezed tube of K-Y Jelly rested on a stand alongside, together with a container of thin wooden spatulas and a box of disposable gloves. A stainless steel lamp with a long, bendy neck was clamped onto the side of the bed. All the equipment needed for probing and inspecting her deepest parts were present and ready.

Dr Weinberg came into the room, followed by his nurse. After he had taken her blood pressure and pronounced it satisfactory, he asked her to open the gown so that he could perform a breast examination. With her arms up above her head and then down by her sides, he firmly palpated each breast, working in circles from the outside inwards towards the nipple. It was uncomfortable to the point of mild pain. Did Dr Khumalo usually press so hard?

"Do you check your breasts regularly?" Dr Weinberg asked.

They must teach them in med school to ask this question, Megan thought, because they all do it, every time.

"Oh, yes, definitely. Every month just after my period."

She had long ago learned to lie to avoid the lecture which otherwise inevitably followed, a lecture which prolonged the trial of lying exposed and cold on an uncomfortable surface, with a strange man's hands pressing hard on your naked breasts, while pretending it was all normal and perfectly pleasant. In reality, every time she felt her breasts, all she felt was a network of lumps which worried her and inclined her to fall back on repression – one of the more useful defence mechanisms.

"I see you have a nurse present when you do the examination?" she said.

"Oh yes," he said, "always."

"Do all doctors, gynaes I mean, work that way?"

"The male ones do – or they should. It's considered ethical and careful practice. It puts the patient's mind at ease, but it's also for the protection of the doctor."

"How so?" Megan asked.

"As obstetricians and gynaecologists, we have to be very careful," said Dr Weinberg, positioning her right arm behind her head and palpating the area under her arm. "We are examining very intimate areas and we can expose ourselves to charges of improper conduct, so the nurse is the witness that we did nothing inappropriate."

"Do you always have a nurse present in your operations as well?"

"Oh, yes. Well, mostly she is needed to assist, of course. But also – more can go wrong in an operation than an examination, so we need someone to be present and conscious, witnessing what we did."

"Surely the anaesthetist...?"

"He's at the other end of the operation – the head – while we're at the tail, so to speak." He smiled and closed her gown. "All fine there, let's do the pelvic exam now. Please bend your knees."

Megan bent her legs, spread them open and stared at the ceiling. Dissociation was the defence mechanism called for in this part of the examination – a splitting off of the conscious self so that it was free to drift off to a peaceful place far away from the vulnerable body displayed like a frog on a dissecting table.

"Just relax now," said Dr Weinberg.

Megan always wished she had the guts to reply, "I'd like to see you relax while someone inserts a cold metal implement into your most private part, cranks you open, and then has a spotlight-lit inspection while someone else looks on!" But she merely took a deep breath and tried consciously to relax her muscles while the chilly speculum was pushed inside her and opened.

"That all looks fine," said the doctor.

There was a small pinch, which Megan knew to be the pap smear being taken. She saw Dr Weinberg pass the spatula to the nurse, who smeared it onto a glass slide, sprayed the surface with something from an aerosol can, and then put another glass slide over the top of the sample. She felt the speculum being closed, the discomfort of its withdrawal.

Now she could feel his fingers entering her, moving up and around – presumably to feel her cervix, his other hand pushing down on top of her lower pelvis. Unbidden, images of Alta Cronjé's ordeal flashed through Megan's mind.

"Relax again, please."

The gynaecological examination was surely the ultimate in patient vulnerability, and it was worse being examined by a male gynae. Without medical training, how could a patient be sure that every touch was justified, every inspection not voyeuristic, every squeeze not actually a grope? She grimaced at the nurse, who smiled reassuringly back.

"All done," said Dr Weinberg at last and Megan could not repress a sigh of relief. He closed her knees, peeled off his latex gloves and tossed them into a waste bin. Then he handed her a small plastic bottle with a green lid.

"There's a bathroom in the next room. Please would you give me a urine sample and then leave it here for the nurse to test. We can talk in my office when you're all dressed."

She did as he had instructed and returned to the office where he was making some notes in her file.

"It all looks fine. You can call for the results of your pap smear in three days," he said. Just then, the nurse entered the office. Dr Weinberg looked questioningly at her.

"It's positive. Congratulations!" she beamed at Megan, and then left, closing the door behind her.

"What?" said Megan. "What was that?" The sudden cold swoop in her stomach was definitely not indigestion.

"Your urine test was positive – you're pregnant," he said in a neutral voice.

"Are you sure? I mean really sure?" she heard herself say in a high voice. "We use condoms, and it tore only the once. It hardly seems possible. I can't believe it!"

"We'll confirm it with a blood test – here are the forms for the path lab down the passage – but these days the urine tests are very accurate." He studied her carefully.

"Are you all right, my dear? It sounds like this was unplanned."

"I'm a little shocked, I think," said Megan, rubbing her hands over her face. "I'm just battling to take it in."

"Here are some brochures," he said, passing her a couple of leaflets, "on the options open to you now."

Options?

"Have a think about it, give it a few days for the news to settle in, discuss it with your partner, and then come in for another appointment and we can decide what to do next."

"Okay," said Megan slowly. "I'll do that." Her mind was racing, thinking ahead to the implications for work, what her mother would say, how Mike would react. *Oh God, Mike.*

"Was there anything else, Megan?" Dr Weinberg made a final note in her file and closed it.

She tried to stop the swirling in her head, tried to force herself to focus on the other reason why she was here. Denial – that was the defence to use just now, to block out what she had heard and to focus only on the real purpose of her visit.

"Yes, actually. Uhm, while I'm here, I just wanted to ask you … your opinion … about one of the other gynaes here – uhm, Dr Trotteur."

Dr Weinberg arched an eyebrow but gave a broad, white smile. "Why? Are you planning on changing doctors again – so soon?"

"No, no – nothing like that. It's just that sometimes one has to refer a client to a gynae and one would like to be sure that he's … beyond reproach."

"Beyond reproach? What does that mean?"

"You know, competent and compassionate and ethical."

Megan was finding it hard to find the right words. The only word that seemed to be in her brain and on her tongue was *pregnant!*

"I mean, if there was anything against him, any complaints or question marks, then I'd like to know before referring a client to him."

"Have you heard something against him?" Dr Weinberg asked.

"I can't really remember. Maybe just some hospital gossip."

He stood up and looked down at her, a reproving eyebrow raised.

"Dr Trotteur," (he pronounced it Trotter, as Patience had), "hasn't been at Acacia for very long. But ... I know of no formal complaints against him." He spoke slowly and it sounded to Megan that he was choosing his words very carefully. "In any event," he finished more quickly as he escorted her out of his office, "I hope you'll return to me for your care. Goodbye, Miss Wright." Megan noted the return to formality.

She made her payment and then walked down the corridor in a daze, clutching the path lab form and pamphlets in her hand, wondering about what he had not said, and about what he had. *Pregnant!*

A few doors down, her glance was drawn to a brass nameplate beside a closed office door. "Dr A. Trotteur, Obstetrician/Gynaecologist", it read. She stared at it for a long time, then took a step back away from it and continued down the corridor.

"I'm pregnant," she thought. "I really am."

13

Any moment now

"I'm pregnant."

The words hung in the silence, heavy as fear, light as hope.

"You're what?" Mike asked, his face blank, his blue eyes round.

Megan cursed herself inwardly. She had meant to soften him up with a glass of wine and a hug, lead him gently into a conversation about their future and draw out a sense of his intentions. Instead, she had opened the door to him and just blurted out the two words that had been playing pendulum with her feelings all day, swinging her from terror to elation and back again.

Now Mike closed the door, hung his keys deliberately on their hook and placed his briefcase on the table. Oedipus leaped up against his legs, but Mike ignored him. He stood directly in front of her, looked her straight in the eye and said, "What did you say, Megan?"

"I'm pregnant."

He stared back at her. The silence between them drew breath and expanded, seeming to push back against her chest.

"Sorry," she added, though she hardly knew what she was apologising for. For being fertile? For being a woman?

Mike stepped around where she stood, paralysed by a growing dread.

"I need a drink before I can deal with this," he said, heading to the kitchen. "Maybe two."

She trailed behind him, Oedipus trotting behind her, watched as he poured a glass of wine first into a glass and then down his throat. He poured out a second glass and turned to her, grim-faced.

"How could this happen?" Denial again, thought Megan.

"That time when the condom broke ... I think."

"But one time – c'mon!"

"That's all it takes, Mike," she said aloud. Inside she was having a different conversation with herself. Any moment, any moment now he'll pull me into his arms and hold me. He'll kiss me on the forehead, and tell me not to worry, because everything will be all right – more than all right. And then he'll smile that great big smile that splits his face and radiates joy, and he'll swing me around in the air and whoop, 'A baby! We're going to have a baby, Meggy!' Any moment now.

Instead, Mike stayed where he was, leaning up against the kitchen cupboards opposite her. He tilted the wine bottle towards her in silent invitation to join him, but she shook her head, her eyes locked on his face.

"What?" he challenged. "You're not drinking alcohol now?"

She said nothing – she was not about to be diverted into a side issue.

"So," said Mike, topping up his glass and returning the bottle to the fridge. "What are you going to do about it?"

"What am *I* going to do about it? Don't you mean *we*?"

"Well it's your body – isn't that what you women are always saying?"

"*You women?*" she echoed faintly. The slightest ripple of anger was beginning to stir her becalmed numbness.

"It's your body," he repeated, "so it's your decision."

"But it's *our* baby, Mike!"

"It's hardly a baby, Megan, don't let's be dramatic here. It's just a cluster of cells."

She stared at him. She felt as though she was seeing him truly for the first time. Some of this must have shown on her face, because he said, "What did you expect – happy congratulations? Sorry, no can do. I'm supposed to be taking up that promotion in Cape Town, remember? What do you expect me to do – just turn it down? And what about you … your career? How are you going to balance this?"

"Oh please don't pretend your horror is on my behalf!"

"It's a fuck-up, Megan, and no two ways about it."

"So you think I should …?"

"If it were up to me, I'd say end it. Right now. But it's not up to me, this is your–" he stopped abruptly.

"… my baby?" Megan finished for him.

"It'll be you who has to … you know .."

Rationalisation – all the defences were having their boxes ticked today. She did not wait to hear what it was that *she* would have to do – she already had a pretty good idea. She would have to do it all, probably, whichever way she chose. She walked out of the kitchen, whistled for Oedipus, grabbed her cellphone and the lead hanging next to Mike's keys, and headed out.

As they walked briskly through the streets of the townhouse complex, Oedipus anointed his usual spots in the neighbourhood and kept Megan moving in between. The walking helped her think.

A cluster of cells. Maybe so, but a cluster of cells which seemed to have pushed the rest of her life out of focus and into the blurry background. The fact of a life – rooted newly, but deeply, inside her – was all that was clear now. A strangely important heaviness anchored her to her life. Difficult, maybe; inconvenient, certainly. But also solid and real.

Her phone rang. Perhaps it was Mike, ringing to call her back, to make nice. But the screen displayed a different name.

"Hi, Wade."

"Howzit, sweetheart. What's up?"

"I'm pregnant!"

The briefest of pauses, then the words she had craved to hear all day. "Oh, Megan, how wonderful!" The kindness, the genuine joy in his voice undid her and she started to sob, walking blindly behind Oedipus and tripping over the uneven paving.

"What are you blubbing for?"

"Mike doesn't want it."

There was silence for a long moment. Wade had never said a bad word against Mike, though Megan suspected that he was tempted now.

"No problemo, because your little one will have me as its one and only fairy godfather." The words were light, but his tone was fierce, protective.

"We... I haven't decided what I'll do yet, Wade."

"Honey, this is me you're talking to. Of course you'll have it. And it will be fabulous."

How did he know her so well?

"And I will be there for you – all the way. Do you hear me?"

"I love you, Wade."

"Love you, too, sweet cheeks. Call you later?"

"Please."

Oedipus stopped and sat on Megan's feet. She realised they had walked the entire circuit of the complex and were back outside her front gate. It clicked open as she reached for the buzzer. Mike stood in the frame of the front door, appropriately neither inside nor out. His eyes questioned her.

She sighed. "There's the logic, Mike, and then there's the pull."

He tugged her against his chest and held her there. But he said nothing.

14
Choices

He stares at the board nailed above the hissing coffee machines
    Americano, Latte, Espresso, Cappuccino
    Short, Tall, Grande
    Chai, Macchiato, Red Steamer, Frappuccino
    Choices, choices. An action as simple as buying a cup of coffee has become endlessly complicated.
    "Yes?" says the woman behind the counter.
    "I would like a cup of coffee, please," he says.
    "Filter or espresso?"
    "Filter," he says, and adds, "with milk," before she can ask how he wants it.
    But still she finds a question: "Full cream, semi, skinny or soy?"
    "Full cream."
    "Flavour?"
    "Coffee," he says contemptuously and watches with derision as she actually turns to consult the board where the absurd flavours are listed – hazelnut, mocha, coconut, salted caramel, gingerbread – to confirm the unfamiliar varietal, before she gets it.
    She gives him a look, a tight smile. He sees that her teeth are uneven – she has an overbite and her right incisor has edged forward and a little over the left, like pertly crossed legs. It bothers him. He wants to reach out and thrust the erring tooth back into its proper place. He realises that she is offering him yet another choice.
    "What was that?"
    "Short, Tall, Grande?" she repeats.
    "Medium," he says, refusing to capitulate to the absurd lingo. She gives him another look, this time without the lopsided smile. Be thankful for small mercies, he thinks.

"That'll be with wings – take-away," she says. It sounds more like an instruction than a query, but he is more than happy to comply. He is eager to get away from this place – the noise of shouted orders and fizzing machines, the hot push of people in the queue behind him, the mess of milk puddles and coffee grounds on stainless steel.

While he waits, he looks at the confectionary displayed in the glass-fronted counters: cheesecake, chocolate cake, pecan pie – all available by the slice. It strikes him as significant, these phrases – a slice of cake, a slice of the pie, a slice of life. It is the slicing, the cutting into and off of, which is important, not that which is chopped off or left behind.

A cup of his preferred choice – tall, white, Americano with wings – is shoved towards him and he carries it to the counter where he must further tinker with it. First, he pulls a handful of serviettes from the dispenser and wipes the offending spill of sugar and scatter of empty packets into the hole in the counter for litter. If only all that offends the eye could be disposed of so easily.

He is just about to add sweetener to his cup, has just ripped open the little blue sachet, when someone jostles his elbow. The white powder falls in a moving line across the foamy surface of his coffee, the curled rim of the cup, and the just-wiped countertop. He turns to face the offender, recognises him immediately.

"Oh, hello," says Dr Weinberg.

"Hello Gavin," he says.

"Getting your caffeine fix?"

"I suppose."

He stares at Weinberg, who is pouring sachet after sachet of sugar into his cup and stirring it with a plastic stick which looks like a long, white needle. Whatever happened to teaspoons? His critical scrutiny seems to unsettle Weinberg – he often has that effect on people. He likes it.

"So, have you been up to something you shouldn't have been?"

"What on earth do you mean?" Is it his imagination, or is Weinberg looking at him very keenly?

"Someone was asking about you the other day," says Weinberg, taking a slurp of coffee which leaves a line of foam on his upper lip. The steam fogs the lenses of his spectacles. "Practises here at Acacia and may refer to you, and wanted to know what you're like with patients – sorry, 'clients'," he puts a sarcastic emphasis on the word. "Whether there have been any complaints."

He turns away, ostensibly to tear another sachet of sweetener, but really he needs a moment to soothe the spasm that he can feel momentarily twisting his features.

"Who?"

"Who what?"

"Who was asking?"

"A patient. No names, no pack drill. Practises here at Acacia and seems to give more credence to hospital gossip than she should."

His heart begins to beat faster but his features, now back under his control and long schooled to reveal what he is not feeling, crease and wrinkle to convey bewilderment.

"I can't for the love of me think what that could be about," he says.

"Probably nothing. But keep your nose clean."

Is there a warning in the words?

"I'll do that," he says, pulling back his lips to reveal his own, even teeth. Weinberg nods back, unsmiling, and walks off.

"And more," he thinks.

15

Storm

Rainbow rolls, fashion sandwiches, tuna sashimi with edamame, eel maki.

Megan gazed unseeingly as the small plates with their plastic domes rotated around the turntable; her thoughts were far away. It was hot and muggy in the sushi restaurant – Mike's choice – where the air-conditioning was failing to tame the sweltering February afternoon. Outside, where the smokers' tables spilled onto the piazza, heat shimmered off the paving and mosaic floor art, and a few withered plants baked in their terracotta pots. But hulking above, storm clouds – dark and bulky as thugs – were beginning to muscle out the sun.

She wished it would rain. The enervating heat had sapped her energy and slowed her thoughts to a sluggish torpor. According to "What to Expect When You're Expecting", your body's temperature ran higher when you were pregnant. Too bloody right, Megan thought, pulling her hair off her sweaty neck and securing it into a rough bun with a scrunchie. The book also said that the little tadpole inside her was as big as a small strawberry and now had arms, legs and a beating heart. Bigger than a cucumber maki, not yet as big as one of the California rolls now sailing past her gaze.

"Hello, gorgeous! Miss me?" Mike slid into one of the high stools at the sushi bar beside her.

Several replies vied for escape at Megan's lips:
No.
Where were you?

Don't you know it's rude to keep a lady waiting alone in a restaurant?

But, in the interests of preserving peace, as well as reducing the levels of her stress chemicals – she had read about that, too, in the book – she merely said, "Hi there."

"Oh, excellent – they have butterfish today," said Mike, extricating a black plate topped with slivers of white fish from the passing parade. "Jeez, it's hot. Have you ordered some wine already?"

Megan tapped the glass of mineral water in front of her. "No hooch for me," she said.

"I'll just have to drink for the both of us," said Mike, scanning the wine list he had just been handed by the waiter. "A bottle of the Vergelegen Chardonnay, please."

He snapped open his bamboo chopsticks and stirred a nugget of jade wasabi into his bowl of soy sauce, then snared a slice of the pale fish, dipped it in the sauce and dropped it into his mouth. Megan watched him eat. He really was good-looking. His blue shirt brought out the colour of his eyes, and his hair – in need of a trim – flopped rakishly over one eye. He looked like a cool surfer in search of a beach.

She looked away. Outside the light had turned the peculiar acid yellow of an impending Highveld thunderstorm. Perhaps it would hail. She hoped Oedipus would take cover under the portico at the back door; he was not the most intelligent of dogs.

"Excellent," Mike enthused again, after he had eaten the last piece and sipped deeply from the glass of wine now at his elbow.

He turned his attention to the turntable in search of the next morsel, and Megan returned her gaze to the neat slices and perfect cross-sections on display. It was very soothing, very relaxing to watch them approach from a distance, pass slowly by for her perusal, and then disappear off down the line again. It was almost hypnotic – sushi conveyor belts could probably be used as a trance induction method, she mused.

"What's the matter? You not eating?"

"Hmm? Oh, no, I can't."

"Heat killed your appetite?"

"No. It's sushi – I can't eat it."

"But you love sushi," he insisted, pouring soy sauce into a salmon hand roll and taking a large bite.

"Mike, I'm pregnant. You can't eat raw fish when you're pregnant. It can have parasites and bacteria."

Mike mumbled something, but a deafening crack of lightning muted his words. The long electric rumble of thunder which followed seemed to usher in the cool breeze which Megan had been craving.

"You can have one with a prawn, can't you? They're cooked," said Mike, pointing at a coral prawn, bisected along its underside almost all the way through to its spine, and draped open over an oval of pressed rice. The transverse coral lines looked like ribs on some flayed creature. "Or a yaki-whatsit." He gestured to a skewer of grilled chunks of chicken, now drifting past on one of the turntable plates.

"Yes, but look," said Megan, nodding to where the three sushi chefs in the central preparation island were filleting and slicing fish with long, sharp knives and sculpting balls of rice with their fingers and palms. "They use the same knives and boards for preparation, and they don't seem to wash their hands between touching the raw fish and the cooked food."

Mike caught the waiter's eye and indicated with an impatient gesture that he wanted his wine replenished.

"Now you're just being ridiculous," he said.

Was she? She didn't think so. It seemed stupid to take the risk of getting ill when you would not be able to take medicine to get better. There was so much stuff you had to avoid for the sake of the developing baby: not just sushi and alcohol, but also camembert and Roquefort, coffee, X-rays, hair highlights, headache tablets – she could have used one of those right now. The oppressive heat seemed to be pushing in on her skull, squeezing her brain. She cricked her neck to loosen the tension locked into her muscles there, and ordered a Greek salad from the hovering waiter.

"I saw Dr Weinberg again today."

No response.

"I figured I may as well stay with him, it's more convenient than driving all the way out north to see Dr Khumalo."

"I thought Doc Khumalo was a soccer player." Mike smirked. "And who's Dr Weinberg?"

"Mike, are you deliberately trying to piss me off, or are you so far stuck in denial that you won't even allow yourself to remember that he's my gynae? You know, the one who'll be delivering *our* baby come September?"

Mike said nothing, lifted a plate of shredded crab salad off the turntable, inspected it and dumped it back on the belt. He checked his phone. Outside, the rain finally broke. Hard heavy drops pockmarked the piazza, sending shoppers scrambling for cover. The outside diners grabbed their plates and glasses, and ducked inside, laughing and shaking water from their hair. Steam rose off the paving and the heady scent of rain on parched earth drifted in to where Megan sat.

"I have to work in Cape Town next week, on the Blaauwberg project," said Mike, his chopsticks toying with the pale pink shavings of pickled ginger.

"The foetus is about so big," she held her thumb and forefinger apart to show him. "He calculated that I'm seven-and-a-half weeks along." Megan had to raise her voice to be heard above the rain now drumming on a roof somewhere above them.

"I'll be working flat out, and I'll have to be there for the following week, too."

"The first scan will be at nine weeks. Will you be here for it? They'll give us photos from the scan, even a DVD if we want," said Megan. She said it to the dissected segments of fish and flesh passing her line of vision.

Mike spoke to them, too. "So I thought I'd just stay there over the weekend. Save the cost of another flight and get some work done."

Megan swivelled in her stool and turned to face him "So this is how it's going to be? Like this? Really?"

Mike looked at her and shrugged. "Your choice," he said, downed the remains of his wine and signalled for the bill.

16
Anxious

Megan scanned the list of the day's scheduled appointments.

"Who's this? I don't recognise the name," she said, pointing to the entry in the first slot of the day.

"Mr Thomas," said Patience. "New client."

"But haven't I already got a new client today? Here," said Megan, tapping the last slot where the name, Dr Smith, was listed. It was one of her rules that she saw only one new client per day. First sessions were more demanding and tiring than follow-ups. They also often ran overtime and she liked to schedule them at the end of the day so that they would not make her run late for other clients.

Patience shrugged. "He said it was urgent. And your first appointment had cancelled, so I put him in."

"All right. Buzz me when he's here and has filled out the forms."

"Yebo," said Patience. "And I have to leave early today. My cousin in Newcastle…"

She rummaged about in her blouse and produced a crumpled black and white photo of a suited man posing earnestly beside a straight-backed chair. The man looked young, the photo – a formal, studio shot – looked a century old.

"Fine. It's fine – just let me know when you go," said Megan, grabbing her coffee and heading into her office.

She sat behind her desk and sipped her coffee. It still tasted peculiar to her, oddly metallic, so she set it aside and spent a few minutes sitting still and thinking. She tried to prepare her mind for the day ahead, for the clients she would be seeing, but soon her thoughts strayed to Mike, the fight they had had the previous night, how they had lain afterwards, back to stiff back in the suddenly vast bed. From there, it was a short mental hop to baby beds, antique cots with brass fittings and snowy bedding. She was thinking about tiny white Babygros when Patience announced her client. It seemed a long journey back to the reality of the consulting room.

Mr Thomas looked to be in his early forties. Megan's first impression was of a very attractive man. He was tall, slim, clean-shaven, with thick dark-blonde hair swept back from a high forehead. His features were even and attractive. The irises of his eyes, which were the dark brown of aged port, did not quite touch the rim of his lower lids, giving his eyes an enigmatic appeal. He wore dark grey trousers with a blue shirt open at the collar, the sleeves rolled up casually to just below his elbows. His hand, when he reached out to shake Megan's, was cool and dry.

"Mr Thomas, er…" said Megan, shuffling through the completed intake and indemnity forms which he handed to her, trying to find his first name.

"Please, call me Tony," he said.

"Hello Tony. You can call me Megan."

"Where should I sit?" he asked.

"Wherever you're most comfortable." It was her standard reply. She liked to study her new clients in these first uncertain moments and to form hypotheses about them depending on where and how they sat.

Tony Thomas sat, as most clients instinctively did, in the chair facing the door, with his back to the wall. Facing the opening of the cave, Megan thought wryly, ready to fight or flee the threat of anticipated therapeutic challenges.

"You have a lovely office," he said, looking around the room. "The colours are very … calming."

"Thank you," said Megan. "Before we begin, can I just get a few details?" She launched into her usual list of questions: about his age (45), family structure (single, never married, no children, parents deceased), and occupation.

"I'm an artist."

"Really?" said Megan, interested. "What kind?"

"Photography, mostly," he replied. "But I also do some sculpting from time to time."

"Should I have heard of you? Are you famous?"

"No," he gave a modest laugh and ran his hand through his hair, smoothing it. "No, I'm not well known at all. I do mostly landscapes, but celebrity portraiture is where the fame is – Annie Leibovitz, David Bailey, Lord Lichfield."

Megan finished drawing the simple genogram that was the first entry in any client's file, thinking how nice it would be to chat to a man whose idea of high art was not the perfect putt or drop kick. Mentally chastising herself for these wayward thoughts, she raised her eyes to give him her full attention.

"So – what brings you here?"

"A friend recommended you. But I must be honest upfront – I was reluctant to come."

Megan held the silence, sure he would continue.

"I'm a very private man. The thought of spilling my guts to someone, the thought that others would know or find out…" He looked at her intently with those dark eyes, as if trying to assess her trustworthiness.

"Maybe it would help to know that psychologists are ethically and professionally bound to maintain the strictest ethics, particularly that of confidentiality. We are not permitted to share any details of your treatment, even the fact that you are in treatment, with anybody without your express and written consent. We're not allowed to do or say anything which might breach your anonymity and confidentiality."

"No exceptions?"

"That's a good question. There are actually three exceptions to the confidentiality rule. By law, we are obliged to report if and when a client is actively intent on killing themselves, or on harming or killing someone else, or where we discover ongoing abuse of a child." She paused to let him process the information before continuing, "Does that reassure you?"

"Yes, that seems safe. I'm sorry to be so…"

"Not at all. It's important for you to be comfortable, to be able to trust me and this process."

"It's hard for a man to admit he has problems and needs help."

"It is. Why did your friend suggest you come?"

"To talk through … some issues," he began hesitantly, shrugging and looking a little embarrassed.

To Megan, it hardly sounded like it merited an urgent appointment, but she knew that when people got up the guts to make the call to a psychologist, they often did so in a now-or-never state of mind. By the time they sat in front of her, however, their problems often seemed less critical and they felt silly about discussing them.

"What sort of issues?" she pressed.

He tilted his head, thinking. "I have a bit of a temper, it gets me into trouble sometimes. Oh – not beating up people or road rage or anything like that," he said quickly, smiling in response to her raised eyebrows. "It just interferes with how I relate to people."

She waited.

"And … I apparently have 'unrealistic expectations'," his fingers sketched quotation marks around the phrase, "or so I'm told."

"Who told you so?"

"More than one ex," he said, with a self-deprecating smile which made his eyes twinkle with a sherry-coloured light.

"So, it sounds like you've had some relationship problems, partly due to difficulties in managing your anger and your expectations," Megan reflected. He nodded.

She continued probing for a while, asking for details and examples, and making a note of the issues which would be targets for therapy. She would teach him strategies for anger management, then explore his typical patterns of interaction in romantic relationships.

It seemed a simple enough case, but she had practised for long enough to know that no "case" – no person – was simple at all. With this particular client, for example, she would need to track back through his past to find the real source of his anger, the origin and true function of his exacting standards. But there would be time enough for that in later sessions once she had built a relationship based on trust with him.

"Don't go too deep, too soon – you'll scare off the punters." Megan could still hear the voice of her first supervisor. It had been sound advice.

She sketched out some preliminary goals and the framework of a treatment plan with Tony Thomas. He seemed relieved to have a plan of action.

"I'm so glad I came today. I was in two minds, you know, but then I decided to meet with you and I feel so much better." He grinned. It really was a charming smile.

"I'm glad. Though there's still a lot of work ahead."

"I know, I know. But I feel I understand and can put things in a much better context now. I know what I'm up against – so thank you, really, thank you."

A little embarrassed, she let him out to the reception where he eagerly booked a succession of appointments with Patience after saying his goodbyes to Megan.

Tony Thomas's calm air and pleasing manners could not have been more different to that of her last client of the day whom Patience ushered in at precisely 17:30 with an adjustment to her petticoat and a reminder to Megan that she would be leaving early and would not be there to book follow-up appointments at the end of the session.

Dr Arthur Smith hesitated on the threshold of her office for a moment before taking two deliberate paces inside. He was thin and of medium height, dressed in a navy suit worn with a plain white shirt and a conservative grey tie. His grey hair, cut short, fell evenly on either side of a defined middle path. His eyes, which scanned the room in a series of quick glances, were an icy blue and his mouth was set in a grim line.

"Dr Smith," said Megan, reaching out a hand to shake his. "May I call you Arthur?"

"I suppose." The pale eyes came to rest on her.

"Won't you sit down, wherever you'll feel most comfortable."

Arthur Smith immediately sat down in the tall wingback chair with its back to the door. The power-seat, Megan noted to herself, usually taken by either the supremely confident wishing to dominate the process, or the desperately insecure seeking a little more protection in the chair's high back and armrests. She wondered which Smith would turn out to be. Of course, he could always be both. It was not unusual for both personality positions to coexist uneasily in the psyche of one troubled individual.

Megan sat in the two-seater nearest him, tossing onto the adjacent couch a cushion which was in her way. She headed the top page of her notepad with his name and the date and started as usual.

"Before we begin, may I just get a few details?"

"If you must."

He pulled his gaze back from the couch at which he had been staring, and turned his head to look at her. He seemed almost to study her, from the top of her auburn hair pulled back from her face, today, with tortoiseshell clips, to her strappy black sandals. He frowned at these Megan felt faintly uncomfortable. If he planned on being so unenthusiastic and uncooperative, why had he come?

Diligently she noted her feelings on the paper. *Countertransference: irritation, feeling judged.*

"It helps me understand you better if I know your family context," she said. "How old are you, Arthur?"

"Fifty," he said.

Abruptly he stood up. He moved jerkily over to the couch and arranged the jumble of scatter cushions into a straight line – a mauve cushion on each end, the tan one precisely in the middle.

"It was bothering me – the mess," he said, sitting back down in the wingback.

"I see," said Megan. "Is there anything else in the room that bothers you?"

"The picture," he said, jerking his chin twice in the direction of the painting which hung directly behind her desk.

"Would you like to ...?"

"Yes." In a moment he was out of his seat and adjusting the painting, stepping back to check that it was hanging straight.

"There you are – perfect," he said with a kind of grim satisfaction.

No, there *you* are, she thought. It was her turn to study him as he settled himself back into the chair. She wondered just exactly what she was seeing: extreme anxiety – possibly even obsessive compulsive disorder? Or a further attempt to dominate the session by controlling the space, to dominate *her* by implying that she was untidy.

"Do things like that often bother you?"

"I'm here, aren't I?" he snapped tersely.

"Right," she said slowly. "We'll come back to that in a minute. First, I do need to get the basic details. I see from this," she said, holding up the intake form which he had completed in neat black capitals, "that you're a doctor?" He merely nodded.

"Any speciality?"

"I cannot see how that's relevant. I suppose you want to know if I'm married, have children, that sort of detail, too?"

He rubbed the knuckles of one hand hard against his chin. This time, it was she who nodded.

"I was married to the same woman for twenty-four years. We have two children – a daughter of twenty-three and a son of twenty years."

"You say you *were* married?"

"Maureen passed away five and a half years ago. Cancer."

"I'm sorry to hear that. How old was she at the time?"

"Is it really necessary for you to know all this?"

"Yes, Arthur, it is."

"Fine," he said, crossing his legs first one way and then the other. "She was fifty-two years old."

Megan noted the details.

"I suppose you're doing the sums, writing up all sorts of Freudian theories now – why I married a woman older than myself, what that says about me, that I married a mother figure," he almost sneered the words.

"Did you?"

"No!"

"Right, then," said Megan, looking back down at the genogram in front of her.

"And did Maureen work?"

He paused, then said, "She took care of me. And the house, of course. I like it to be neat and tidy. I have a domestic worker now."

"So let's talk about that," Megan said, then paused.

The noise of an approaching helicopter had been growing steadily louder. The helipad for the air ambulance was located at the farthest end of the car park and was visible from her window. Arthur Smith was totally distracted. He walked jerkily over to the window and watched the landing.

"Is it always so loud?" He raised his voice to be heard above the racket.

"Pretty much, but it doesn't happen often."

Megan studied him while they waited until the noise had died down and then brought the session back on track. "Why is it important that things are neat, tidy, ordered," she pointed at the row of cushions on the couch, "and straight?" she pointed at the painting. "What happens inside of you when things are messy, uneven, untidy?"

She listened very carefully to his answers, but Arthur Smith seemed intent on yielding the bare minimum of information. By the end of the session, she was still not sure what she was dealing with. He might just be a deeply anxious man suffering in the self-imposed trap of obsessive compulsive anxiety disorder, overcome by a compulsion to impose order on a world which threatened him with its entropy and unpredictability. But there was a chance he was something altogether more problematic and troubling. She could not rule out that she was seeing a man with obsessive compulsive *personality* disorder, a man who wanted to control others, to force them to fit his template of how the world should be. A man who might resort to intimidation, even abuse, to maintain the illusion of control which protected his fragile sense of self.

Megan was suddenly aware of the complete silence outside, that she was alone in her offices, alone with this man with the hostile eyes.

"I think we'll leave it there for today," she said.

He looked surprised.

"Next time I think we should explore if you have any rituals – any behaviours or habits which you feel compelled to do to help discharge some of your anxiety. So you can think about that before our next session."

"You think I'm anxious?"

He had a peculiar expression on his face, somewhere between humour and derision. He rubbed his chin again.

"Yes, I do," she said. She stood up abruptly, feeling a compulsion of her own: to open the door and get out into the corridor as soon as possible.

They moved into the reception room, Arthur stepping aside to let her precede him. She sensed a quick movement behind her and felt the hairs on her neck rising. She took a long, quick stride away from him, stepped behind the counter, and spun around to face him. She had seen, as soon as she entered reception, that the sliding glass door to the corridor was closed, the latch of the Yale locked – clicked into position to prevent anyone from wandering into the rooms while she was consulting.

"You can pay for today next time," Megan suggested.

She felt an urge to run to the door and fling it open, but Arthur stood at the end of the counter, between her and the door.

"I'd prefer to pay now," he said.

He reached into a breast pocket of his jacket and withdrew a black leather wallet. Extracting a silver-coloured credit card, he held it out to her, but just as her fingers touched it, he jerked it back out of reach. The sudden movement made her jump.

"Cash," he said, counting out notes instead and tossing them onto the counter in front of her. "Cash is king."

Every instinct told her to get out. Now.

"Goodbye, Arthur," she said, stepping firmly towards him in the hope of shepherding him towards the door. He took a step back, but only one small one, and then stopped.

"Aren't you going to make another appointment for me?" he asked, his lids narrowing over his cold blue eyes.

"Yes, of course, I forgot – I don't usually…" she babbled.

She opened the large desk diary, paged to the next week, chose an empty morning slot at random and said, "How about next Wednesday at 9:30?"

He shifted his weight from one foot to the other, and back again. Then he reached over, took the diary from her hands, thumped it closed and put it back down on the counter.

"I don't think so, Megan," he said, straightening the diary so that its edges were perfectly aligned with those of the counter. "I'm not sure I want another appointment. I was determined to meet you, to see for myself… But I'm not sure you can help with what's wrong with me."

Normally, Megan would encourage a reluctant client to give therapy a few sessions before they decided whether it was likely to be beneficial. Normally she would have tried to talk a client out of coming only once, to dissuade them from sliding back into avoidance and denial. But this didn't feel normal. She wanted nothing more than to get away from him.

"Right. Fine," she said, grabbing her handbag and keys, and pushing past him to the door, fumbling the catch open with trembling fingers. "You can call my receptionist if you change your mind."

He walked up behind her just as she slid the door open and stepped outside into the corridor. It was deserted, the lights dimmed to their after-hours setting. This wing was home to the offices of specialists who consulted during office hours, far away from the hustle and bustle of the hospital wards. Arthur Smith stepped out to stand beside her, pulling the door closed behind him and giving her a sideways glance.

Megan stepped around him to lock the door, keeping the keys fisted in her right hand. "The lifts and the exit are that way." She indicated down the corridor.

"I'll walk with you," he said, his pale eyes glittering in the subdued light of the corridor. "You shouldn't be here alone at this time of day."

She set off, walking briskly and feigning a confidence she did not feel, in the direction of the lifts. His legs kept easy pace with her stride. She kept her eyes on the ground and noticed that he never stepped on the join line of adjacent tiles. Each step fell precisely in the centre of a tile. Was that intentional?

As soon as she reached the bank of lifts, she jabbed the down button. After a brief moment, Arthur reached forward and pushed the up button.

She stared at him. "Are you going up a floor?"

"No." He tugged at his chin. "It just bothered me ... the one light."

The lift doors opened and Megan stepped in immediately, taking up position right next to the panel of buttons. With her left hand, she punched the button for the ground floor. She held her right hand behind her back, threading the sharp keys between her fingers in a makeshift knuckleduster, trying to do it without allowing them to clink.

Arthur stood too close to her, examining her face. The doors slid shut slowly and the lift seemed to pause in the absolute silence before beginning to sink slowly down. Arthur looked from the display of lights above the doors to Megan, and then to the panel of buttons. She felt the skin on her scalp tighten. He took a sudden step right up to her, his ice-blue eyes blazing in his taut face, and spoke. His voice was loud and urgent in the metal cube, "I must–"

The lift stopped, the doors opened, and a young couple holding the hands of identically dressed twin toddlers stepped in, bringing with them a burst of noise and motion.

Arthur shrank back to the corner of the lift. Megan smiled at the family in weak relief. She stuck close to them when they exited on the ground floor, merely nodding a greeting to Arthur when he said goodnight. She watched as he strode across the foyer, paused at the automatic sliding doors, looked back over his shoulder at her for a moment and then stepped outside.

17

Revenge

Megan bent over the bunch of roses she had just been handed and inhaled. No fragrance – they were perfectly shaped hothouse blooms the colour of antique lace with the faintest trace of dusky pink in their swirled centres.

"They're lovely, Alta, thank you."

"Just, you know, to say thank you. I'm doing so much better, and I wanted you to know how grateful I am," said Alta. She looked better, too. The tightness had left her face, she seemed to be taking more care with her appearance and she was smiling happily. It was for the reward of seeing previously depressed patients smile like this that Megan did the work she did.

"I'm glad," said Megan, freeing the roses from their cellophane binding and putting them into the vase which Patience had just brought into her office, "though you know you don't need to give me thank-yous or presents, don't you?"

Therapists were not supposed to encourage their clients to show their appreciation. To Megan, it had always seemed to be both better manners and more sensible simply to receive gifts with good grace, rather than to meet a client's kindness with a psychodynamic interpretation that her gift was an unconsciously manipulative attempt by the psyche to ingratiate itself with the Kleinian "good breast".

It also meant she could keep the flowers.

"So, what have you been up to this week?"

"I thought that was my line," said Megan, with a smile.

"No, I meant with, you know…"

"I know. I've been asking around, but I haven't found out anything specific. Nobody seems to want to say anything. I've booked Monday off and I'm going to visit the two women who laid complaints with the Board. Actually, I've only managed to contact one of them – I've set up an appointment to see her. The other woman's phone number gives me a 'no longer exists' message. But I have her address – it's in Lenasia, so I thought I'd just take a chance and swing by there. I'll chat to them both, find out what happened to them, why their hearing didn't proceed and, of course, whether they'd be prepared to try again."

"That sounds good," said Alta. "I've thought a lot about it, and Johan and I have discussed it. And I've decided I'm definitely going to go ahead with a complaint."

"I see," said Megan, trying to let her face show neither her satisfaction nor her concern.

"I've started working on a letter – can I bring it for you to look at when I'm finished? I'm not sure about the language and stuff, maybe you can help?"

"I'll be happy to take a look. So, do you want to talk about that today? Or is there something else you'd rather do?"

"What I'd like to do," said Alta with a wide, mischievous grin, "what I'd reeaaally like to do is to kick a cop!"

"Huh?"

"Kick a cop! Poke a popo, push over a pig!"

"What...?" A giggle was building inside Megan. Some clients were so much easier to like.

"So I'm driving here, right. And you know I've got some serious stuff to worry about without some fat pig of a cop adding more worries to my life, right? And at this bloody stop street here – down the road from the hospital," she pointed south, "I sort of pause and cruise through, because it's a boom opposite and no road on the right, so the only other cars come from the left and I'm turning left, so it's hardly dangerous. I don't even know why it's a stop street instead of a yield sign. Wait! No, I do know. It's so some fat lazy pig of a popo can meet his ticket quotas without having to get off his arse and catch the real criminals out there. So he jumps out and waves me over, right? I swear, Megan, there was a moment there when I was really tempted just to put my foot down and run him right over, squash him flat as a pancake."

"But you didn't? Please tell me you didn't."

"Of course not! Hell, what do I look like – a crim or something? No, but then he hangs all over my window, half sticking his stupid head inside my car, checking my licence and stuff. And then – get this – he wants a bribe! *Jislaaik*, I wanted to kick him so badly – just here," she indicated the centre of her shin, "and hard!"

"He asked for a bribe?"

"Not directly. No, he says he's so hungry and it's so hot here in the sun and maybe I could help him buy lunch, how 'bout it? I mean, have you ever?"

Megan was beginning to enjoy the story immensely. It was a delight to see Alta so animated and feisty. Who knew there was such a thing as crooked cop therapy?

"So what did you do?" she asked.

"I said to him, 'Better yet,' I said, 'maybe I could buy you a box of condoms for when they send you to the *tjoekie* for bribery and corruption! How 'bout *that*, officer?' I swear he swelled up even bigger and wrote me up probably the biggest fine he could – R900 – for that! But it was worth it. The *doos*."

"It made you feel better to challenge the injustice."

"Well, I felt a little bit better then, but I was still *moerig*, right? So I couldn't just leave it like that."

"What did you do?" asked Megan, delight vanishing in the face of rising anxiety.

"I went to the CNA down the road and bought some big sheets of cardboard, and some fat khokis and duct tape. Then I made a few posters. Like 'Crooked Cop Ahead', 'Cop at the Stop Street!', 'Poke a Popo!' and – hell, I couldn't resist it – 'Kick a Cop Today!' Then I drove back around the block and stuck them up on the lamp posts coming up to the stop street to warn other decent motorists like me – ha!" she laughed. "So then I stop at the stop street, wait a good few seconds before moving off and turning left and I drive past the fat bastard again, waving and smiling like the queen."

Alta heaved a deep, satisfied sigh, "Hell, it felt good!"

18
What remains

"Thank you for agreeing to see me, Mrs Cole."

"Technically, I suppose it's Miss Cole, now. Or Ms. Maybe just call me Stacey."

They were sitting in the living room of Stacey Cole's Norwood house. From the lead-paned bay window behind Megan, sun streamed into the room, turning the Oregon floors a golden pink. It should have been a beautiful room, but the space between the wooden floors and the pressed steel ceilings was clogged with clutter. Uneven columns of books and magazines teetered alongside baskets of laundry and old take-away food containers. Piles of paper, unopened post and old newspapers were strewn across every surface. Megan could see that the passage leading from the room was similarly congested with mounds of clothes, stacked shoeboxes and black plastic storage bins. The whole house seemed filled up and weighed down by the clutter.

Everything was covered in a layer of dust. It puffed up in a cloud when Stacey flopped heavily onto her sofa, and the motes sparkled in the sunlit air. On the floor next to the chair where Stacey sat, stood an unopened box containing some appliance – it looked like a bread-baking machine – and rows of empty wine bottles were lined up in front of the decoratively tiled Victorian fireplace which dominated the room.

Stacey Cole seemed weighed down by herself. She was quite short, yet probably a good 40 kg overweight, Megan estimated. Her eyes, some dull indeterminate colour, were lost in the swollen face and the hand which pointed to a tray bearing a blue patterned tea set, was dimpled with fat.

"I made tea," Stacey said, her voice as lifeless as her eyes and unwashed hair. "Help yourself." She leaned forward with some effort and took three Romany Creams from a serving plate.

"Thanks," said Megan.

She poured herself a cup, more out of politeness than desire; the tea was probably already cold. She took a sip – it was. She set the cup down carefully on a side table crowded with used coffee mugs and four framed photos. The largest of these, in an ornate silver frame, showed an attractive woman, dark hair glinting in the sun, looking with loving eyes into the face of a smiling young man. The woman was wearing a long white dress, embroidered with lace and crystals, the man wore a tuxedo.

"That was me. It's the *before* picture," Stacey gave a harsh laugh and bit off half of a biscuit, watching as Megan carefully replaced the photograph. "I know. It's hard to believe, isn't it?"

Megan leaned over the tea things and handed Stacey her business card.

"I'm here because I know that you laid a complaint against Dr Trotteur and I'd be very grateful if you could tell me more about your experience."

"How'd you find out?"

Megan hesitated, then opted for the truth. "Inappropriately," she said. "Possibly even illegally. I looked at a file that I wasn't supposed to."

"Why? What's it to you?" Stacey brushed crumbs off her chest. They landed in her lap.

"As you see, I'm a psychologist. One of my clients, a young woman, was, I think…" she searched for an appropriate word, "maltreated by Dr Trotteur."

"*Maltreated*. That's a nice word for what he does." Stacey ate another biscuit. "What's he done to her?"

Megan was reluctant to give details. This was not her story to tell, yet it was a big ask to expect this damaged woman to give details of her own ordeal without sharing some confidences in return.

"I think ... he mutilated her. Unnecessarily removed almost all of her labia."

"That all?"

"All!" repeated Megan.

"She got off lightly," said Stacey in a voice bleak with bitterness. She must have seen something of Megan's shock on her face, because she sighed and continued, "Sorry. I don't have much compassion left for others – too busy feeling sorry for myself."

"What happened to you? What did he do?" Megan asked softly.

"What did he do? Let's see... First, he told me exactly what he was going to do, whispered it right into my ear before the anaesthetic kicked in. He said – I haven't forgotten the words, you see, can't forget the words, actually – 'I'm going to neaten you up, dear Stacey. Cut away all the unnecessary stuff down there and leave just the essential bit. Because that's all you are, aren't you? Just a hole. But I'll make that right and tight, too. And if I find that your uterus is dirty and stinky, I'll clean up there as well. Doctor knows best'."

"Oh, Stacey..."

"Next, he cut off my labia and my clitoris, and removed part of my perineum," she nodded when Megan flinched involuntarily. "Then he did a thermal ablation of my uterus – do you know what that is?"

Megan shook her head, horrified into silence.

"They crank open your cervix and pour very hot saline water into your womb. It burns the lining, destroys the endometrium permanently. No more messy periods after that. No more chance of messy babies, either."

"Oh, God, Stacey."

"Then he stitched up my vaginal opening *really* 'right and tight'. No more messy sex either." She paused, looked down at the brown crumbs in her lap. When she looked up again, Megan could see that tears were coursing down her cheeks.

"I should have listened to my intuition. The first time he examined me – in his rooms, before the operation – he pulled the speculum out roughly and said, 'You're not very tight – you have a lot of sex, I can tell.' It gave me the creeps, but I thought I was just being silly, a prude. I even signed a consent form, giving him permission to tighten my vagina. And of course you sign forms that if they find something malignant while operating, they can cut it away right there and then.

"I guess you could say he cut away .. what's his word for it? *Excised*, that's right. He excised my husband, too. What's the use of a woman who can't have sex, a wife who can't have children? Who can't do anything much but pile on the mess, inside and out."

Megan could feel tears in her own eyes. "Stacey, I'm so sorry. So very, very sorry." The words seemed worse than inadequate.

"Well, that makes two of us. Because *he* certainly wasn't sorry."

"You confronted Dr Trotteur?"

"Of course, once I had figured out what had happened to me, the extent of the damage, the permanent pain. He reminded me that I'd given consent for the procedures. He insisted that it had all been necessary, that the excised tissue had been malignant. But when I insisted on proof, he couldn't give me any. Said the lab had lost the results and he hadn't kept a copy. Said I'd imagined him whispering to me before the operation. All lies, of course. So I laid a complaint against him at the HPCSA. Figured once I had a ruling in my favour there, once he was stopped from practising, then I could lay a criminal charge of assault or negligence or whatever. Maybe even a civil claim."

"What happened?"

"It took ages to get the hearing, almost a year, and then it basically boiled down to my word against his. No 'evidence'. And when I told them what he'd said, and it took everything I had to say those words out loud, you could tell they thought *I* was completely delusional. Or maybe I'd been imagining it because of the drugs. They couldn't believe that of a *doctor*, one of their own. I could see it on their faces.

"Meantime, my husband had left, the divorce had come through, I'd lost my job. Huh!" She gave a sour smile. "I was a personal trainer. Can you believe it? Look at me now. But I couldn't work anymore, I could hardly get up most mornings. I got the house after the divorce, but I got the mortgage with it. And I had nothing left, didn't know where the next bond payment was going to come from. Then *he* called me, offered to settle."

"Trotteur?"

"The same. He offered me a settlement. R250 000 to shut up and go away and sign a contract waiving my rights ever to institute any claim – professional, criminal or civil – against the good doctor in the future."

"You took it?"

"I took it. I was penniless and desperate and it seemed the only way I could keep the roof over my head. So I withdrew the complaint. But," she looked at Megan with fierce eyes now, "not a day has gone by since when I haven't regretted it. I sold myself. I sold bits of my body. I sold my sexuality, my fertility, my marriage, my self-respect. And not even for very much. And now you come and I find out I've sold out other women, too."

"They might not have decided in your favour anyway," said Megan, "even if you had refused the settlement, pursued the case."

"That's what I tell myself at night, when I can't sleep. Funny thing, though, it's not as consoling as a bottle of red."

19

Sacrifices

Megan was still thinking about Stacey Cole as she made her way around a sunny Johannesburg and onto the Golden Highway that would take her south to Lenasia. She had been unable to phone ahead for this visit. The telephone number of the second complainant which she had copied down at the HPCSA offices seemed to be discontinued – either that or she had copied it down incorrectly. She was grateful now that she had risked the extra seconds to note their addresses, too.

During her training and internship, she had been to clinics and training sessions in community halls in Lenasia on a couple of occasions, but the area was still largely foreign to her. Ridiculous how when you lived in this city, you only lived in certain parts of it. She drove past the enormous Trade Route Mall, past banks and B & Bs, and lamp posts covered in posters for the latest Bollywood extravaganza, following the directions of her GPS. She passed madrassas and temples and mosques where clusters of robed men spoke animatedly to each other on the pavement.

Outside a corner café whose windows advertised *samoosas, curry 'n rice, bunny chows* and *Russian & slap chips*, a gang of young men – some no more than boys, to judge from the soft fuzz on their cheeks – slouched in low-slung jeans, hoodies and unlaced hi-rise sneakers. As Megan slowed to take the corner, one of them, a tall, round-shouldered boy wearing a black peak sideways on his head and a T-shirt emblazoned with an Andy Warhol-style print of Osama Bin Laden, crooked his right hand into the shape of a gun, pointed his forefinger at her and fired off an imaginary round. She looked away quickly, but not before she caught his sneer.

Eventually, she pulled her Renault up outside what she hoped was the Reddys' home, in Galjoen Street. The house was small, made of yellow brick and topped by a red corrugated iron roof. A path led from the pedestrian gate to the front door, bisecting a garden blazing with the vivid pinks, oranges and yellows of dahlias, and a white Nissan was parked in the driveway. It all looked like a child's drawing of a little house – apart from the high palisade fencing and the metal plate attached to it depicting a snarling German shepherd and the cautions: *Danger! Gevaar! Ingosi!* She was still in Jo'burg after all.

Megan checked her car was locked and then pressed the buzzer next to the pedestrian gate.

"Can I help you?" came a woman's voice, soft and polite.

"Is this the Reddy household?"

"Who wants to know, please?"

"Sorry. My name is Megan Wright. I'm a psychologist from Acacia Clinic, and I'd like to speak to Nirvana Reddy – if she lives here."

"Nirvana?"

"Yes. Please."

There was a long silence. Megan saw a net curtain twitch at one of the front windows, then a man's voice spoke through the intercom.

"I think you'd better come in."

The gate buzzed. Megan pushed it open and walked up the path, keeping a wary eye open for the guard dog. The front door swung open just as she reached it. A man and a woman, both probably in their late forties or early fifties, stood aside to let her in.

"Please, this way," said the man, leading her into a small sitting room.

Megan was aware of gleaming, ornately carved wooden furniture with plush red upholstery crested by crocheted antimacassars. A newspaper lay folded on the marble-topped table between the sofas.

"Please, have a seat," said the man. "I am Prashant Reddy and this is my wife, Priyanka." Slightly built and balding, he wore a pair of pressed navy trousers and a crisp white shirt. His face seemed to have settled into lines of resigned suffering.

Megan shook their hands, then sat down. Priyanka Reddy said quietly, "May I offer you some refreshment?" Even smaller than her husband, and with finer features, Mrs Reddy wore a sari of a plain deep blue, and a red sindoor dot on her forehead.

"Just a glass of water – thank you."

The woman left, taking small quick steps, and Megan looked around the room. A brightly patterned carpet was soft under her feet and shiny brass-framed pictures of deities hung on the walls.

In a walled alcove at one end of the room was a small shrine. A deity whom Megan thought might be Krishna, was depicted in a relief-carved wooden panel. The god wore an ornate, gilded headdress and was playing what looked like a flute, one leg casually resting in front of the other. He appeared to be looking down at the offering of fruit and rice placed on the shelf at his feet.

Megan's eye was caught by what might have been another shrine, set up on a low table in a corner of the room. Water bubbled and trickled over pebbles in a small water feature behind which was angled a large, framed photograph of a lovely young woman. White candles placed on either side of the frame lit up a face with high cheeks, full lips, a soft smile and deep brown, sloe eyes.

"That is our daughter, Nirvana," said Mr Reddy, following Megan's gaze.

"Nirvana is..." began Megan, unsure of how to ask what she was beginning to suspect, to dread.

A fly buzzed behind Megan, trapped between the net curtain and the window, randomly butting against the glass in an attempt to get free Mr Reddy got up, walked over and opened one of the windows wider, setting the fly free just as Mrs Reddy came silently into the room, bearing a glass of water on a silver tray. She placed the glass carefully onto a white lace doily on the table between them, then sat down alongside her husband on the sofa opposite.

"Thank you," said Megan, taking a grateful sip.

Her mouth was dry, and the water was very cold. Beads of moisture collected into tears on the outside of the glass. Megan's eyes again moved to the portrait of their daughter.

"You have come to see Nirvana, Dr Wright," said Mr Reddy.

"It's Ms Wright – I'm not a doctor. And yes, I came to see Nirvana."

"I am sorry to tell you that she passed away, almost a year ago now."

Megan swallowed, searched again through the inadequate words, and could only come up with, "I'm so sorry for your loss. I never met her, but she looks like such a beautiful, vibrant young woman."

"She was," said Mrs Reddy in a voice that was little more than a whisper. "She was so very beautiful. And so full of life."

"May I ask … how she died?"

"It was an accident – a car. She was coming out of her place of work, coming home. She had just finished her degree, you know, a BA LLB. She was going to be a lawyer, had just started her articles," said Mr Reddy.

"Such a waste. Such a waste of a life," said Mrs Reddy. Her fingers were busy in her lap, folding pleats into the fabric of her sari.

"Her whole life was ahead of her," said Mr Reddy.

He stared at the still image of his daughter and silence settled on them like a shroud. Water bubbled in the corner, a clock ticked relentlessly on a shelf. A car with a souped-up engine and growling exhausts roared up the road and passed the house. Megan had no desire to intrude on their grief, but she needed more information.

"She left work and then had a car accident on the way home?"

"No, no," said Mr Reddy, seeming to return from some distant place. "She didn't have a car – we couldn't afford to give her one. No, she was walking to the taxi rank, crossing the road, when she was … hit."

"A car knocked her over?"

"May he rot in hell," interjected Mrs Reddy, bitterness vying with the grief that suffused her face.

"Priyanka," Mr Reddy chided.

"Don't you Priyanka me. She was young, clever, beautiful – inside and out. She was truly good – a gift to this world. A gift!" she said, turning to Megan.

"You say you're a psychologist? Well explain it to me, then. What is the meaning of it all? What is the point? You try and try to have a baby. You pray to the gods, make sacrifices, and then you are graced with such a blessing. And you love and care for her, from the day she is born. From before! You feed her only what is good for her, hold her when she is sick, rock her when she cries. You plait her hair and brush her teeth and guide her to say her prayers. You help her with her homework and console her when she is teased. And always, always, you try to shield her from danger. A thousand, thousand times you teach her, 'look right, then left, then right again.' And finally one day she is an adult. Finally she is mature and wise and strong and you think it is safe to relax just a fraction, to let go just a mite. And then, bang!" Mrs Reddy slammed her hand hard down onto the armrest. "She is snatched away from you. What is the point? What was it all for?" Mrs Reddy sobbed in pain and rage. Her husband gently pulled her to him, and she wept into his neck.

"We loved our daughter very much, Ms Wright," he said simply.

"Yes," said Megan. "The loss of a child is a grief beyond words."

There was a longing in her own hands to move across her body and cover her belly, as if by doing so she could protect the life within. She had no answers for Mrs Reddy. Every day she heard more about cruelty, abuse and unkindness, bore witness to more pain. Better than most, she knew just how arbitrarily brutal life could be between its rare moments of beauty. Was she mad to want to keep this baby, to bring it into this world?

Mr Reddy stroked his wife's hand with infinite tenderness, then said, "Forgive me, but I am still not clear as to the purpose of your visit."

"Of course, I haven't yet explained. I'm here because I wanted to find out more about Nirvana's treatment with Dr Anthony Trotteur."

Mrs Reddy's head jerked up off her husband's shoulder.

"I believe that Nirvana instituted a complaint against him with the Health Professions Council. I currently have a client, also a patient of Dr Trotteur's, who intends doing the same because of what happened to her. And so I wanted to get more information from other patients who might have suffered at his hands."

"Another monster," said Mrs Reddy, sitting up and dabbing at her eyes with a corner of her sari.

"If it's not too hard for you, could you tell me what happened to Nirvana?"

"I can do that," said Mrs Reddy.

"Will you please excuse me," said Mr Reddy. "I think I'll go make myself a cup of tea." He left the room and Megan could soon hear the chink of china from somewhere down the passage.

"He doesn't like to talk about women's business," explained Mrs Reddy.

"Do you know why Nirvana consulted Dr Trotteur?"

"Oh yes, I knew. For many years my daughter suffered from endometriosis."

"Endometriosis – that's when the lining of the uterus grows outside it?"

"That's right. It caused her great pain in her pelvis and lower back, and when she had her period, she was in agony. She was worried that one day it would interfere with her fertility. Not that Nirvana was married – she wanted to finish her studies first before she settled down. She was very modern." Mrs Reddy sighed, then continued, "For years our family doctor had just treated her with painkillers and anti-inflammatories, but Nirvana decided she wanted to get it sorted, once and for all. I thought she would go to our local clinic here, the LenMed, but she always wanted the best and she said the best in Jo'burg was to be found in the northern suburbs. Anyway, the Acacia was closer to her work, so she went there."

"How did she choose Dr Trotteur? Was she referred to him by someone?'

"No, but he was the only one who had an appointment available on the day she could get off from work." Mrs Reddy paused. A grimness had hardened her features. "It was just chance, random."

"And the treatment didn't go well?" Megan prompted after a moment's silence.

"No, it was a disaster. The doctor said he couldn't properly diagnose the condition from an ultrasound. He said she needed to have a laparoscopy. They make a small hole, you know, at the belly button and then put in a miniature camera so they can see what's going on inside. So she scheduled one of those at the clinic. He said that if there were cysts, or scars from previous cysts, then he could remove them at the same time, also with the keyhole surgery, because she would already be under the general anaesthetic."

"And, what happened?"

"When she woke up, she found he had cut her right open," Mrs Reddy gestured with a slashing movement up her abdomen, "and he had given her a total hysterectomy! Removed her whole womb and both her ovaries. He told her the endometriosis was too severe to remove and she would never conceive anyway and so he just took everything out!"

Megan sat listening in quiet horror as Mrs Reddy continued, "She was young, she still wanted children! Afterwards she was devastated, she told me that she felt she wasn't a woman anymore. She had such problems with her hormones, she had to go on hormone replacement therapy. And her pain was worse than ever.

"I don't understand why he would do that. Why would someone intentionally maim and destroy someone who had done them no harm?"

There were answers to that one – textbooks and journals and studies full of them – but none which would satisfy Mrs Reddy.

"I have a question that you may find strange, Mrs Reddy. Did Nirvana mention whether he, whether Dr Trotteur, said anything to her before she went under the anaesthetic?"

"Oh yes, he did. She told me what he said, and I'll never forget those words. He said, 'Don't worry your pretty little head. I'll remove all the dirty, stinking bits. Trust me, doctor knows best'."

Mrs Reddy looked sharply at Megan, asked, "Do you believe in evil, Miss Wright?"

"My field deals with health and illness, not good and evil," Megan hedged. But Mrs Reddy did not appear to be listening anyway.

"I do," said Mrs Reddy. "I do believe in evil. I find it easier, these days, to believe in evil than good."

Megan could find nothing to say to that. In the quiet, she heard the buzzing of the fly again. It had returned and was bouncing against the large windowpane. Mrs Reddy took a section of newspaper from the table and, rolling it up, walked over to the window, lifted the netting and swatted the fly. The buzzing stopped abruptly. She tore off a corner of paper, wiped up the remains of the fly, and dropped it in a small dustbin.

"Prashant may not hurt a fly, Miss Wright, but I am beyond caring about them. 'As flies to wanton boys are we to the gods, they kill us for their sport'. Isn't that what Shakespeare says? I used to spare flies, and make sacrifices," she gestured to the gifts of food at Krishna's feet, "and observe prayers. But none of it made a difference in the end. I don't make sacrifices to the gods anymore – they've had enough from me."

Mr Reddy came back into the room, carrying two cups of tea. He handed one to his wife and sipped slowly on the other.

"Did Nirvana want to take the matter further?" asked Megan.

"We are simple people. I am a teacher of mathematics and my wife is a teacher of English at the high school. But Nirvana was a law student. She believed in justice, due process, in charges and hearings and findings. I'm afraid I tend to believe that doctors stick together and protect one another – the old boys' club, they call it. I thought it was futile. But she was a fighter," said Mr Reddy. "Well, I don't know how it all would have turned out, if she hadn't passed over."

"And the complaint against Dr Trotteur, the one she instituted at the Council – that fell away with her death?"

"What was the point in continuing? Besides, we couldn't face that, we were ... broken," said Mrs Reddy.

"I understand. And there was probably the other legal stuff still to get through."

Mrs Reddy frowned her confusion. "I'm sorry – I don't follow."

"I thought, I mean – wasn't there some kind of case against the driver who collided with Nirvana? Manslaughter or something?"

"There might have been, if our dear police service had been of any use."

Now it was Megan's turn to be confused. "I'm not sure I understand."

"We never knew who the driver was, Miss Wright. Nirvana was killed in a hit-and-run."

20

Snooping

"You owe me for this."

"You did promise to be the fairy godfather," Megan reminded Wade.

"Yes, but darling, there are limits."

They were shuffling along in the queue to register for the tour of Acacia Clinic's obstetrics and maternity unit. Most of the women ahead and behind them were heavily pregnant. Megan was beginning to get used to the sensation of bellies, surprisingly hard, nudging against her back.

"Name?" asked the woman behind the registration desk. She wore a skirt and jacket in the hospital's official maroon and navy, her grey hair was swept into a smooth chignon and pinned on her lapel was a badge that read "Ms Louise Kelly, Client Liaison Officer".

"Wright. Megan Wright."

"Here you go," said Ms Kelly, handing Megan a security badge on a lanyard and a nametag which read, "Mrs Wright". Megan pulled the lanyard over her head, and attached the name tag to the white jacket which she wore over a navy shirt and white linen trousers. She had chosen her outfit carefully.

"And you must be Mr Wright." Louise Kelly smiled brightly and handed Wade his badge and tag.

"So they tell me," said Wade, running his fingers through his already tousled chestnut hair and winking one of his hazel eyes at her. "But you've spelt it wrong, love. Here, let me just…" He took the pen out of her surprised hand, scratched out the W and pinned the tag to his chest. A look of confusion briefly disturbed the woman's face, but she rapidly recovered her poise.

"Do please help yourselves to some tea or coffee while you wait."

Wade eyed the bowls of instant coffee powder and the cartons of long-life milk with disfavour, but Megan made herself a cup of weak black tea.

"Thank you all for coming," said Ms Kelly loudly when she had registered all the visitors and called in vain, twice, for the Fowlers. "I hope you will enjoy today's tour of our wonderful obstetric and maternity unit. Please feel free to ask any questions you may have at any time. Here at Acacia, we have a holistic approach to women's health and I'm sure you will be impressed by our state-of-the-art facilities and patient-centred services. We are committed to giving you the best, safest birthing experience possible.

"We'll start our tour with a peep at the obstetric wards for both pre- and post-delivery, then we'll stop by our neonatal ICU unit and finally we'll end with everyone's favourite – a visit to the nursery. Please would you all put your cellphones on silent and put them away – calls and photographs are not permitted on this tour. And please may I ask, for the sake of our patients' security and privacy, that the group stay together at all times."

Megan could feel Wade's sideways glance at her as she stowed her phone in her bag.

Ms Kelly clapped her hands, said, "This way please," and headed through the security doors into the unit. Megan and Wade lagged behind, allowing the excited mothers- and fathers-to-be to jostle for prime position immediately behind the guide.

"Here we have our private rooms, each with its own TV, en suite bathroom and wall safe."

One by one, the visitors peered inside the rooms. Apart from the drip stands and the mobile plastic cots standing alongside the beds, they looked more like plush hotel rooms than hospital wards.

"Of course we allow – encourage, even – rooming-in of infants because we pride ourselves on offering family-centred maternity care."

"Do you have family rooms where fathers and siblings can sleep over?" asked one of the more eager-looking fathers.

"Not at this time," said Ms Kelly, still smiling brightly. "We find that mommies who have just given birth need their rest. But please note," she said, waving a manicured hand at the CCTV cameras mounted high on the pale lilac walls at regular intervals, "our stringent security. Not only will you and your little one be safe here, but we will strive to make your delivery an unforgettable experience."

"In a good way, I hope," said Wade out of the corner of his mouth, while Megan wondered how the birth of your baby could possibly ever be forgettable.

"We at Acacia know that every birth is special and we make every effort to accommodate each mother's unique birthing needs."

"So do you have an active birth unit?" asked a tall woman in a yellow dress standing in front of Megan.

"Of course, with the added options of assisted birth and pain relief if the mother desires it or the doctor deems it necessary."

"So we can bring in private midwives? Have a water birth?" asked the same woman.

"Not at this time, but I can assure you that our midwives are more than competent. Here – let me introduce you to the lady who heads up the team," said Ms Kelly, beckoning over a stout woman in a nurse's uniform. "This is Matron Mabuza."

"Ooh, look at all the yummy mummies. You are going to have nice babies here," Matron Mabuza said, rubbing her hands together, as if eager to get started delivering them.

"Here, on your left, are the shared obstetric wards, for mothers who have delivered," continued Ms Kelly.

Megan peeked in. There were six beds, in some of which lay pyjama'd women, holding or feeding babies. One woman in a floral-patterned gown was walking slowly and carefully, as if in great pain, across the ward. Without exception, they looked exhausted and slightly shell-shocked – nothing like the glowing icons of maternity in Dr Weinberg's pregnancy magazines.

"Rather you than me, babes," muttered Wade.

"The wards to your right are for our gynaecological surgery patients, fertility treatments and sadly, miscarriages," said Ms Kelly, a sympathetic little moue temporarily displacing her smile.

"The yeas," said Wade, gesturing to the left, "and the nays," he pointed to the right. Megan elbowed him in the ribs.

"If we're lucky, we'll catch a glimpse of the *doctors*," Ms Kelly said the word in an almost reverential way. "They should be on their rounds soon."

"The gods are descending," said Wade in a dramatic whisper, waving his hands in the air, but keeping them behind the tall woman in yellow. Megan stuck her hand in the air, attracted Ms Kelly's attention, and asked, "What's Dr Trotteur like?"

Ms Kelly looked momentarily disconcerted. She exchanged the briefest of glances with Matron Mabuza, then said brightly, "All of our gynaes are top-notch."

Beside her, Megan heard Wade inhale deeply. "Aahh, the smell of medics closing ranks in the morning," he breathed.

"Let's move on, shall we? This way please."

Megan nodded at Wade, who pushed his way to the front of the group, linked his arm through Ms Kelly's and asked, "What is your policy on breastfeeding?" He spun her around and they set off down the corridor, the crocodile of visitors trailing behind.

Megan peeled off from the group and slipped into one of the rooms on the right-hand side of the corridor. There were eight beds in the ward, six of which were occupied. In the bed closest to the door, a thin-faced woman lay silently staring at the ceiling, tears running down her face. Squashing her immediate instinct to go over and try to help or comfort, Megan scanned the room.

At the foot of each bed hung a slim wire basket which held that patient's file. X-rays, charts and curling rolls of labels poked out of the folders. A small whiteboard was stuck on the wall at the head of each bed, on which was written the name of the patient and – Megan was pleased to see – the name of the patient's attending doctor.

Dr Weinberg, Dr Gebhardt, Dr Maseko

Megan read the names off the boards above the occupied beds on the one side of the ward, then walked down the other side. At the second-last bed, the board read: *Mrs Marshall, Dr Trotteur*. Megan walked over to the bed and, picking up the medical file as if she had a perfect right to inspect it, spoke confidently: "Hello, Mrs Marshall. And how are you doing today?"

From what she could understand from the file, it seemed to Megan that Mrs Marshall had been hospitalised for a threatened pre-term labour. A drip was attached to her arm, but otherwise she looked the picture of pregnant health as she read an issue of *Heat* magazine. Angelina Jolie's lips pouted at Megan from the cover. Mrs Marshall looked up at Megan, a little surprised and obviously trying to place Megan in the rotating succession of doctors, nurses and other hospital officials who popped in and out of the ward over the course of a day.

"How are things going, mmh?" asked Megan. She whipped a pen out from an inner pocket of her white jacket, feigned an entry in the chart, and returned the pen to its place.

"Okay, I suppose," said Mrs Marshall, lowering Angelina onto the bedclothes. "They've managed to stall the labour."

"Excellent, excellent," said Megan. "And I see that your gynae is Dr Trotteur. Are you satisfied with him? Any problems?"

"Why do you ask?" said Mrs Marshall, sitting up straighter and looking a little concerned.

"No particular reason. We just, er, strive to monitor customer satisfaction in our quest for … continuous improvement here at Acacia, so I like to pop in from time to time and check all is well," said Megan breezily. "So – Dr Trotteur?"

"He seems fine. But I've only met him the once – they just assigned me to him when I was admitted. My gynae is actually Dr Williams, but she's on accouchement leave herself, now."

Disappointed, Megan turned and was slipping the file back into the wire basket when a movement in her peripheral vision – a brief flash of white at the door to the ward – caught her eye. But when she looked up, the doorway was empty. She turned back to the patient.

"I see. And has Dr Trotteur been okay, er, so far?" she pressed.

"So far, so good," Mrs Marshall shrugged.

"Humph."

There was a derisive grunt from behind Megan. A nurse had arrived at Mrs Marshall's bedside. She brushed past Megan and stuck an infrared thermometer into Mrs Marshall's ear.

"Do you–" Megan began to ask the nurse, but just then a white-coated male doctor entered the ward. Megan held her breath and stared hard. Could this be him? The doctor headed for the bed next to Mrs Marshall's and the woman lying there pushed herself up on her pillows and said, "Good morning, Dr Gebhardt," just as Megan read the board above her bed: *Mrs Naicker, Dr Gebhardt*.

Megan could not completely suppress a short sigh of frustration. She was getting nowhere. The nurse had noted Mrs Marshall's temperature on her chart and left the ward. Megan decided to follow her and find out what opinions lay behind that grunt.

At that moment, another white-coated man stepped into the ward. Astonished, Megan stared into the face of Dr Arthur Smith who stopped dead in his tracks as soon as he saw her. It was always an awkward moment, bumping into a client outside of the isolated, protected womb of her consulting room. The rule for psychologists was to take their lead from the client. Greet only if you are greeted, so as not to blow the confidentiality of the client who prefers that others not know that he knows you. Dr Smith's face remained blank, but Megan thought she saw a glint of anger – or was it fear? – in his ice-blue eyes. He gave no hint of acknowledgement, merely spun on his heels and walked out of the ward.

Megan's mind was racing. Why had he been in this ward – was he a gynae, then? She did not remember his name being on Patience's list of the hospital's obstetrician-gynaecologists. She was sure, in fact, that it had not been. Was his name even Smith? She remembered how he had insisted on paying with cash. Had he snatched away his credit card so that she could not read the name on it?

"Good luck then, all the best," she said to Mrs Marshall and hurried out of the ward after "Dr Smith". The corridor, however, was deserted except for an orderly pushing a noisy tea trolley and a nurse sitting behind the desk at the nurse's station located midway along the corridor. When Megan saw that it was the same nurse who had taken Mrs Marshall's temperature, she walked quickly over to her.

She greeted the nurse first, then said, "It seemed, back there," Megan inclined her head in the direction of the ward, "that you … I mean, I wondered what you could tell me about Dr Trotteur."

"You just missed him, he was here just now," said the nurse.

"He was?" Megan looked both ways down the corridors, but saw no one. Even the orderly with the tea trolley had disappeared. "What do you think of him?" Megan asked, her voice barely above a whisper.

The nurse looked at Megan suspiciously. "Who are you?" she asked.

"I work here, at the hospital. But not *for* the hospital. I'm trying to help women who have been hurt by him."

The nurse looked at Megan for a long moment, seeming to assess her. Then she glanced around to check that no one was near. She picked up a clipboard and, with her head down as if reading it, muttered softly, "The midwives don't trust him. He is rude, arrogant to the nurses."

"And to the patients?"

"Sometimes his work is perfect. But there are stories about the other times."

"Stories? What stories?"

The nurse's voice dropped even lower, Megan leaned forward and strained to hear her as she said, "Sometimes … sometimes he doesn't even wait for the results of the biopsies. He just cuts. He is rough with the patients when they are unconscious."

"But why don't the nurses speak up? Complain about him?"

"They are scared. He shouts at them, complains. They say that once he even–"

"Mrs Wright?" Louise Kelly's voice rang loudly down the corridor. Megan cursed under her breath, stuck a smile on her face and turned to face the determinedly cheerful woman.

"I wondered where you had got to. I must please insist that you stay with the group."

"Sorry, sorry," Megan lifted her hands placatingly. "I was desperate for the loo – you know how it is when you're pregnant. And when I came out of the loo, you'd all disappeared and I couldn't find you again. I was just asking the kind nurse here if she knew which way you'd gone, when you appeared."

"Come this way, we're just finishing off at the nursery, looking at all the beautiful babies," said Ms Kelly. She seemed appeased by Megan's explanation, but she nevertheless watched Megan like a hawk for the rest of the tour, giving her no chance to question any other of the staff.

Wade, who was waiting with the rest of the group outside the large glass window between the newborn nursery and a small visitor's viewing area, looked up at Megan with raised eyebrows when Ms Kelly returned her to the flock. Megan shrugged. What had she found out really? Nothing definite – just whispers and rumours and silence.

Ms Kelly rabbited on about complimentary mother and baby goodie bags filled with freebies such as newborn nappies, breast pads and cream for cracked nipples. Wade looked mildly appalled. He and Megan stared through the glass pane at the swaddled newborns lying like small pink and brown sausages in their blue plastic cribs.

"They look like monkeys," said Wade, "or toothless old men."

"They do not," said Megan, gazing at the tiny shell-like ears, the fingers waving aimlessly like the tentacles of sea anemones, the scrunched faces and the searching mouths. The crib closest to the window held two babies lying face to face, one in a pink and the other in a blue Babygro. Both had a shock of red hair on the top of their heads and seemed impossibly small.

"Our latest twins," announced Ms Kelly proudly, for all the world as if she had personally pushed them out into the world.

The twin in blue was moving his face from side to side. His lips brushed the tip of his sister's button nose and he instantly clamped his gums down and began sucking fervently. The infant in pink opened its mouth wide and began yelling – a hearty wail which tugged oddly somewhere in the region of Megan's breasts. Both twins were now bawling and turning purple with the effort of their loud protests. Ms Kelly reached out a hand and turned down the volume on the intercom that connected the nursery to the viewing area.

Wade threw an arm around Megan's shoulders and gave her a squeeze.

"Let's hope yours also comes with a mute button," he smiled.

21
Paperweights

It is her hair that strikes one first – thick, russet and lustrous. It is burning copper where the sunlight strikes it, impossibly hot next to the cool of her eyes. Are they more blue or more grey? He must pay better attention during his next session. Because he has decided that he will have another session, maybe many. It might even be fun, getting to know Ms Wright, he thinks, as he sits in his darkening office, watching the night steal away the last light of the day.

Of course, what struck him immediately after the contrast of fire and ice was the dent high in her left cheekbone. A small hollow which dimples when she smiles and which attracts his critical eye repeatedly. A dent is not so easily fixed, it cannot merely be excised and incinerated.

How frustrating that it is the therapist who gets to ask him the questions, that he cannot simply ask her, "What caused that indentation in your cheek? Why have you not had it filled in?" Or other, more interesting questions: "Where else are you not even? What else needs fixing?"

She thinks she can fix him. Ha! She has no idea, no clue as to what she's dealing with. She thinks she's so clever, listening and diagnosing and plotting how to change him – the him he has presented her with. But he has had a lifetime to practise and hide, to lie and pretend. She does not stand a chance, doesn't know that it will be he who is studying her.

He found her easily enough after his conversation with Weinberg. Someone, a female, who has a practice at the clinic, refers patients to doctors and calls patients "clients". Got to be a psychologist, he reasoned. Proper doctors called their patients what they were. Only shrinks called patients "clients". There were two psychologists with practices at the clinic, and only one of them was female.

A thought intrudes, a question which must be answered. What was she doing in the maternity unit? When he saw her – the shock! Could she possibly have been snooping around about him or might she actually be pregnant? How he would like to have her on a steel table, under his fingers, under his scalpel – her blood oozing red pearls when he slices into her pale flesh. His fingers running through her burgundy curls and parting her lips.

To his surprise, he feels himself hardening. He is not usually aroused by correcting the patients who pass beneath his hands. It is a task that must be completed to relieve the pressure, not a desire that must be satisfied to appease the appetite. But this tumescent throbbing is pleasurable, an unexpected bonus.

He adjusts himself, turns his thoughts from the flesh of Megan Wright, fingers his paperweight. He almost laughs when he thinks of her paperweight – a pretty, frivolous thing stuffed with an ephemeral dandelion clock. His is better, a reminder of his sacred work, of what can be improved, removed. He places the paperweight, with its sensuously rounded dome, on top of tomorrow's files – a ritual he follows most nights. Sometimes he likes to keep it in his pocket, where he can fondle its cool, smooth curves. Tomorrow morning he will need to store it in its secret place in the drawer, away from unenlightened eyes, just as he will need to hide his true self, before letting the world in to see the good doctor.

He feels a tickle along the silver scar on his chin. Could it be growing? No. He must stop these thoughts. They are from a time long past. It has been many, many years since he has allowed others to see Attie.

Perhaps he will give Megan a glimpse. Perhaps.

What, however, is perfectly clear is that he will need to figure out a way to see her files. What ungrateful bitch has been whining about his improvements to her? What is she planning? And, something that tickles his curiosity more than his concern, what has Ms Wright been writing so assiduously about him in those notes of hers?

22
Debates

"You have … three … new messages."

Megan pressed "1" for her messages, as directed by the automated voice. As she listened, she moved around her office, plumping up the cushions distraught clients had mangled, sweeping crumpled tissues into the waste bin, and filing notes from her last sessions.

Wade's voice, at cheerful top speed, spoke into her ear: "Okay, I thought chilled baby marrow and cucumber soup to start – you know, keeping it light and fresh. And then – keeping it easy – roast rosemary chicken with boiled baby potatoes and a salad on the side. And – keeping it delish – pavlova for pud. If you have any objections, shout quickly, else my apron and I will be at your place at five. Kiss-kiss!"

"God bless you, Wade," said Megan fervently, deleting the message. The only thing worse than having her family over to dinner, was having to cook for them. When Wade had volunteered to do the honours, Megan had accepted with alacrity. It would be great to have him there, too, for moral support. She had an inkling that it was going to be a difficult evening.

Next up came her mother's voice: "Just double-confirming that we'll be there by six-thirty tonight. Well, Cayley and I will. Your father will be working late, as usual, but he said he'd try for eight o'clock. So don't cater specially for him. But do make an effort to cater for Cayley, dear, please. For my sake if not for hers. Nothing too heavy or rich – you know she either won't eat it at all or she'll … do the other. Maybe some fruit, or some salad. She's being quite good about her eating at the moment – I think working with food is actually helping her. Please, Megan, I don't think I could handle another–"

But the voicemail time limit ran out at this point, cutting off Moira Wright's plea.

"Me neither," Megan said to the phone, and began shuffling through a pile of files that were stacked on her desk.

"It's me!" rang out Cayley's high voice. "Just checking if I can bring anything for tonight – you know I'm a better cook. No? Sure? Well, if you insist. Oh, and while I think of it, don't mention my new job or ask about it in front of mommy dearest. Bit of a drama there. See you later."

Megan sighed, deleted the last message and called out, "Patience? You there?"

"Where else?" came the response from the front office.

"What is this pile of files on my desk about?"

Patience came into the office. She was banging the top of her head hard with the flat of her hand.

"Why are you doing that?" asked Megan, distracted.

"New weave. It's too tight," said Patience.

"And hitting your head helps? Isn't it painful?"

Patience shrugged and sighed in a way that suggested a woman's martyrdom to the dictates and discomforts of fashion was not something that could be either denied or resisted.

"What about the files?"

"Oh, yes. What are these for?" asked Megan, pointing to the six files in a stack on a corner of the desk.

"Monday."

"Monday?"

"Yes, those are the client files for your Monday appointments," said Patience, poking at her head now with the sharp end of a pencil.

"And you took them out and put them on my desk today, Friday, because…?"

"I'm efficient," said Patience with a face suggestive of the innocence of angels.

"And also because…?" said Megan, who was not fooled.

"I might be late Monday morning."

"Thank you for your 'efficiency'," said Megan with a lopsided smile that dimpled the dent in her cheek. She took a quick look at the names on the files to see what, apart from the absence of a receptionist, awaited her on Monday. The name on the last file startled her.

"*He* made another appointment?" she asked, holding up the file so that Patience could read the name.

"Dr Smith? Yeso, last appointment of the day."

"I really didn't think he'd come back. I'm not sure I want him back. And I definitely don't want him scheduled at the end of the day again. Hmmm..."

Megan pondered her options. Her gut was telling her to steer clear, to make some excuse not to see him, but she was not sure she should trust her gut. She, better than most, knew that people could act weirdly, even scarily, out of pain.

"Call him back, will you? And reschedule – to a midmorning slot on a day and at a time when you're sure you *will* be here."

Patience sniffed a little defensively. "Why?" she asked.

"Because," said Megan, picking up a pen and turning the file around to face her, "he's one of these." She drew a pair of round-framed spectacles on the top right-hand corner of the file, then handed it to Patience who stared at the small sketch, obviously puzzled.

"Harry Potter?" Patience asked.

"Watch out!" corrected Megan.

Patience strolled out with the file and Megan heard her greeting someone in the front office. In a moment, she was back again.

"Mr Thomas is here."

"Send him in, please, Patience."

Megan switched her cellphone to silent mode, placed it on the desk alongside her paperweight and stood up to greet a smiling Tony Thomas. He wore khaki chinos with a pale blue shirt, and seemed to have picked up a tan since she last saw him. It looked good on him, bringing out the sherry glint in his eyes and the white of his smile.

She began the session by outlining for him the various theory, practice and skills-training they would have to cover in anger management counselling, but before she had got very far, Tony interrupted.

"I'm sorry, Megan, I can see you've done a fair bit of work preparing for today's session. It's just that – so have I."

"That's great – tell me more," encouraged Megan.

"I've done some reading. I bought the *Anger Management Workbook* and a book called *Taming the Tiger Within*," he smiled, "And I'm working steadily through them. They have lots of practical exercises and suggestions."

"I see," said Megan. "And are you finding them useful?"

"Yes. Well, reasonably useful. I mean, breathe deeply and count to ten, visualise yourself lying on a deserted beach. It's not rocket science, is it?"

"I guess not. So you've decided to do the work by yourself?"

"No, no – that's not what I meant," said Tony, holding up his palms as if to reassure her. Megan noticed that his fingers were long and slender – pianist's hands, they used to be called.

"I still need you, definitely. But not for the basic stuff, you know? That I can do on my own. I need you for the deeper stuff, the hard bits that I can't access without your expert assistance."

Megan was aware that she felt flattered, and dutifully made a countertransference annotation in her notes. "The deeper stuff?" she asked.

"I was thinking it might help to know the source of my anger. Where does it stem from?"

"Insight is always valuable, but I feel obliged to warn you that it doesn't automatically lead to behaviour change. Knowing why we feel and think and behave the way we do is one thing. Changing it is quite another."

"So I shouldn't put away the workbooks yet?" Tony said with a smile that animated his regular features.

"Not just yet," agreed Megan. "All that breathing and

counting can come in useful. But of course I think it would be useful to talk about the origins of your anger, doing so might even release some of the rage. And, if necessary, we could also consider doing hypnosis at some stage." She braced herself for the usual protests, but Tony merely looked interested. "There are some wonderfully creative and safe ways of discharging anger in trance. And it's also a great way to learn how to relax."

"Sounds good." said Tony, rubbing his hands along the length of his thighs. "So tell me, Megan, why do I sometimes get so angry?"

"Okay, well, firstly, anger is always a secondary emotion. It comes after – and usually in response to – some primary emotion. When we're hurt or threatened, we immediately and automatically convert those scary feelings to anger. We feel more comfortable showing the world our anger, less vulnerable side. Anger has an energy to it, a power and some impetus. Sadness and fear, on the other hand, tend only to make us feel impotent and helpless. So to know why you're full of anger – so full that it spills over when you're bumped – we need to know about when in your life you've been badly hurt, or frightened, or experienced some kind of trauma."

Tony thought for a few moments, then said, "I was in an armed robbery a few years back. And I had a car accident."

"Would you say you've been this angry only since then? Or, if you think carefully about it, were you already angry?"

"I guess it's not new," admitted Tony. He ran a hand through his thick hair.

"Then we're probably looking at your childhood. Should we start with your family?" When Tony nodded a little reluctantly, she continued. "Tell me about your parents."

"You want to know about my mother – I should have guessed," he laughed "It reminds me of a joke I heard. A patient's been in psychotherapy for years. One day he says to his therapist, 'You know, I thought I'd been completely analysed, but yesterday I experienced the most remarkable Freudian slip'. The therapist nods and waits to hear more.

The patient says, 'I was having dinner with my mother, and I meant to say: Please pass the butter, but instead I said: You miserable bitch, you've ruined my life!'"

Tony laughed with abandon. Megan gave a slight smile and asked, "Is that true of your mother? Tell me about her."

"So you're a believer in nurture, are you?" He folded his long arms across his chest. Megan lifted her eyebrows in query.

"It's the old nature versus nurture debate, biology and genetics versus learning and experience. You believe in the importance of the family experience."

"You sound like you've studied the subject."

"That's me busted!" He grinned. "I did do a year of psych back in my varsity days, and some reading since. I find it a fascinating subject, and it's great to have someone knowledgeable that I can debate these concepts with."

Megan smiled back, then said, "Um, where were we?"

"You were about to tell me about the critical importance of nurture in shaping who we are."

"I think it's important, yes, but not that it's the sole determinant of how we turn out," Megan said, wondering even as she said it why she felt like she was defending her beliefs; usually her own views were opaque to her clients. The people who came to see her were typically so focused on telling their own stories and expounding their own beliefs that they hardly spared a thought for hers. She needed to shift the focus back onto the client, where it belonged.

"Where would you locate yourself on the nature-nurture continuum?" she asked.

"I suppose at the deterministic end." He said it almost contritely, and with a gentle smile that charmed even as it apologised. "Biology is destiny – isn't that what your guru, Freud, said?"

He most certainly is not my guru, Megan wanted to say, but did not. "I think his actual words were 'anatomy is destiny', but it probably amounts to the same thing. It seems that you believe your genetics, your biological make-up decides your character, and therefore your life path?" She answered his question with one of her own in true analytic tradition.

"I believe that many of our choices are already decided for us by a combination of your DNA and necessity."

"Necessity? Would that perhaps be a necessity of circumstance, of life experience?"

"You won't trap me so easily," he said, wagging a finger at her, but softening it with a friendly smile. "We cause, we bring about certain 'necessities of circumstance', to use your phrase, as a direct or indirect consequence of who we are and how we behave, surely? And that, in turn, is biologically determined. Look around you," he said, gesturing to the objects in the room. "Could that painting have been created by someone with only athletic ability?" He twisted around on the couch to look at her desk and the shelves behind it. "Could those books have been read or understood by someone lacking a superior IQ? And those seeds," he pointed to the paperweight, "could only ever become dandelions, no matter how much they longed to rise above being weeds. It's like developing photographs. The latent image is always the one that will come to the fore – a photo of a landscape will never be one of a portrait. We are what we are."

"So you don't believe in individual free will?"

"No, not really. But I can see that you do."

"Did I say that?" Megan challenged.

"You didn't need to – your passion shines through," said Tony. "I am afraid that I'm more cynical than you. Perhaps it seems strange to you that I'm even here, willing to place myself in your therapeutic hands, given that I'm not convinced therapy even works, that it can change what is hard-wired in the individual."

"Therapy can help individuals become the best, strongest and healthiest they can be. It can empower them to choose to change." Now Megan felt she was defending the whole profession of psychology, not just herself.

"That's one way of bringing about change, perhaps – to strengthen the good. I'm not convinced that it works very well."

"You think there's another way? A better way?"

"A quicker way, certainly, would be to weaken the bad, to reduce the unhealthy, destroy the destructive and thereby allow the healthy to flourish."

"By becoming destructive in your own right?" Megan argued. His argument reminded her of a bit of graffiti scrawled behind one of the doors in a toilet cubicle at varsity: "Fighting for peace is like fucking for chastity!", but she could hardly say that to the client in front of her, no matter how provoked she felt.

"Couldn't it be argued, Tony," she said, "that we are what we do? If I choose to break down, to destroy, then I am a destroyer, not a healer."

"Even if the ends justify the means? Even if it helps the individual or serves the needs of the broader society?"

"Even so."

"Well," said Tony, leaning back into his chair with a crick of the neck and stretching his long legs out in front of him, "I can see that I've come to the right place. I have a therapist who not only believes that change is possible, but who is ready to begin changing me in a non-destructive way."

Was that what the whole debate had been about? Had he only been playing devil's advocate – testing her to check whether she believed it was possible for him to change under her guidance?

"You're right about the first part, but not the second. Only you can begin changing yourself. Are you ready to start?"

"We're out of time for today," said Tony, looking at the clock. "Sorry, I know that's supposed to be your line. Should we start with my mother in the next session?" He grinned mischievously at Megan.

She could not help grinning back. "Yes, let's do that."

23

Family way

The dinner party, Megan reflected afterwards as she brushed her teeth and rubbed vitamin E oil onto a belly that was still disappointingly flat, had not been as bad as it could have been.

It had been worse.

Wade arrived early and cooked a feast of food in his inimitable style. When he heard the doorbell ring, he poured a large whiskey into a nearby measuring cup.

"Is that for the chicken?" asked Megan.

"Nope, it's for the Dutch courage."

"I can't drink," said Megan.

"It isn't for you, sweetie. You forget how well I know your family," said Wade wryly and downed the drink in one gulp.

Oedipus made a general nuisance of himself – leaping up against Megan's mother when she arrived, drinking from the toilet bowl in the guest loo to Cayley's squealed disgust, and then laying his head on everyone's lap in turn, begging for titbits and leaving behind spots of drool, or possibly toilet water.

"Oedipus Rex! Kitchen!" Megan ordered when he began his second circuit, and the dog retreated, sending doleful looks back at her.

Cayley, as usual, was preoccupied with the food. First she asked if there was any cream in the soup and on hearing that there was, she pushed it aside. Next she peeled the skin off her chicken breast with the delicacy of a surgeon exposing an organ for surgery – an image which, given her current preoccupations with Trotteur, did nothing to improve Megan's own appetite. Megan was happily surprised to see, a little later, that all of Cayley's chicken was finished, but then the ecstatic beating of a furry tail under the table indicated where it had gone. She got up, caught Oedipus by the collar and dragged him to the kitchen, shutting the door behind her.

Cayley nibbled on a few lettuce leaves (no dressing) and then proceeded carefully to wipe cream off two strawberries and a quarter of kiwi fruit with her serviette, before chewing them very slowly. The decadently chewy meringue she left untouched on her plate, a silent witness to her own self-discipline and Megan's thoughtlessness.

Moira Wright, wearing a flowing dress more suited to a royal wedding than a casual family dinner, had alternated between pleading and cajoling Cayley to eat, and bemoaning her husband's absence, breaking stride only to berate Megan's lack of decorating ability.

"This place looks no better than the day you moved in. You've probably still got some unpacked boxes stashed somewhere. And those curtains are dreadful, Megan, way too short."

Speaking for Cayley, who was ominously silent on the subject, Moira bragged about her daughter's new job at the catering company, how she had been receiving glowing reports on her performance. Cayley and Megan exchanged speaking glances over the chicken carcass and when Wade, trying to be polite, asked Cayley to tell him more about her work, Megan kicked him under the table and shook her head meaningfully.

Though Moira had spent much of the evening complaining about her husband, how hard he worked at Mathews, Madonsela and Gaines where he was an audit partner and carping about how he was never home and how much she missed him, once Richard Wright arrived, she plonked his plate of food down in front of him with an injured air and then set about studiously ignoring him.

Wade tried valiantly to keep the conversation flowing and made an effort to engage Megan's father in a discussion about the latest King Commission report, but Richard Wright was plainly uncomfortable with Wade and said very little beyond commending the Shiraz and downing several glasses of it.

When Megan cleared the plates from the main course to the kitchen, tossing a few scraps to a mournful-looking

Oedipus, she checked her phone for messages. There was a missed call from Mike, the first in several days. Perhaps he was really beginning to miss her, to rethink his attitude to the baby. When she listened to the voicemail message, however, Megan knew that she had been mistaken, perhaps even a bit deluded. True, he did say that he missed her, but he sounded cheerfully drunk and there was the noise of music and loud voices in the background, as if he was at a party or a pub. A woman's voice kept calling, "Come back here, Mikey."

Mikey?

He made no mention of the pregnancy. Ignoring the burning behind her eyes, Megan deleted the message with a savage press of a button, chucked her phone into the bread bin and carried the coffee pot into the dining room, while Oedipus trotted hopefully behind her.

Eventually, realising that there would be no contentedly quiet moment in which to tell her news without fuss, Megan tapped her fork against her water glass and announced that she had something important to tell her family.

"You're getting married to Mike!" exclaimed her mother gleefully.

"You're getting married to Mike," said Cayley, without a trace of enthusiasm.

"No," said Megan. She took a deep breath. "I'm having a baby."

"So you *will* be getting married!" her mother trilled.

"So you *will* be getting married," said her father flatly. It sounded like an instruction, a threat even.

Cayley's eyes grew rounder and wider. "You're getting married and you're having a baby?"

"No. I *am* having a baby. I am not getting married. I may not even be staying together with Mike."

"But what about a wedding? What about–" began her mother.

"Now, Megan," said her father, "bringing a child into this world is a serious thing. To do it single-handedly is irresponsible. This needs to be thought through properly." It was like he thought she was nineteen, rather than twenty-nine.

"I have thought it through, Dad. I do want this child. But

I'm not going to compound the situation by marrying someone when I'm not one hundred per cent sure about it. Even if Mike had asked me."

"Do you mean to tell me that that fellow hasn't even done the decent thing?" said her father.

"Can I be your birthing partner? Can I?" Cayley interrupted.

"Shut up, Cayley," Moira snapped. Cayley looked flabbergasted.

"Wade is going to be there with me at the birth," said Megan.

"Don't be ridiculous, Megan, that needs to be the child's father, it needs to be Mike," insisted Moira.

"It should really be a midwife or a nurse." Richard Wright eyed Wade. "One cannot be too safe."

"What exactly do you mean by that, Mr Wright?" asked Wade and Megan could feel her own hackles rising.

"But *I* want to do it," said Cayley like a petulant child.

"Want doesn't always get, Cayley. If you haven't already learned that, then now's a good time to do so. I have asked Wade and he has agreed to be my doula," said Megan.

"Wade is going to be your doo-fucking-la? *Wade*? I'm your sister!"

"And I'm your mother!"

"And who's going to be her husband and the child's father? That's what I'd like to know," demanded Richard.

"Look, if it makes you happier, I'll gladly–" started Wade.

"Shut up!" said Cayley and her father in unison.

"Hey! Don't talk to Wade like that," said Megan firmly. "He's my oldest and dearest friend."

"Oh, defend *him* – why don't you. Take his side, hold his hand while you give birth to my niece or nephew. I suppose I don't matter at all, I'm not important."

"Cayley, of course you matter," said Megan, trying to soothe her sister, though her palms itched to slap her instead.

"Pregnant!" Cayley cried, toppling over her chair as she stood up. She ran to the nearby guest toilet and soon loud, retching noises carried over to where they sat silently.

"Hope it wasn't my cooking," said Wade.

24

Unethical

Megan settled herself at her desk, pulled her hair back into a ponytail, and opened Dr Arthur Smith's file. She fitted the small ear buds into her ears, pressed the *play* button on the digital recorder in front of her, and adjusted the volume.

"So, how have you been since we last met?" she heard her own voice ask.

"Fine, thanks, how are you," came Dr Smith's reply.

"You know, Arthur–"

"Art," he corrected her. She would have to try, consciously, to remember to call him that. It did not come naturally – the name did not fit him somehow. It was too casual, too American ad-exec for this compulsively neat and tightly-wound man.

"You know – Art – this is the one place you don't have to answer 'fine, thanks' when asked how you are. Here, with me, you can actually check inside and then tell me how you really feel."

"I am fine," his voice insisted, "I'm just worried."

In her internship, she and her fellow interns had joked that FINE was an acronym for "Fucking incapable of normal emotions". In that sense, maybe Arthur (Art!) *was* fine, but in the normal sense of the word he had looked anything but. He seemed thinner and behaved even more agitatedly, shuffling about in his seat, flicking his gaze repeatedly to her cushions, and tapping his hands on the armrests of the chair. He had arrived precisely on time, to the second, for their appointment, hardly pausing in reception before coming into her office. Reminded of something, Megan stopped the playback, unplugged herself from the headphones and went into the front room where Patience was photocopying intake forms and information sheets.

"I meant to ask, Patience, Arthur Smith – did you–"

"Art," said Patience. She pronounced it *Att*, so Megan did not immediately understand what she was saying.

"What?"

"Art, he likes to be called Art Smith," said Patience.

"Oh, Arrt," said Megan.

"Yes, Arrrt," said Patience, elongating the r-sound, and muttering under her breath, "*Mlungu!*"

"Whatever," said Megan, "Did you make a copy of Dr Smith's medical aid card when he was here yesterday?"

Patience's face creased into apologetic folds. "I forgot – sorry for that. He came in so quick. Then, after, he was hopping and tapping so much I forgot."

"Hopping and tapping? What do you mean?"

"He was hopping from one foot to the other foot all the time he was standing here, and tapping on my basket, now this side, then that side," said Patience demonstrating on the sweet basket while frowning at the impudence of the behaviour.

"Did he make another appointment?" Megan was half expecting, given the nature of the session, that he might just have fled.

"Yebo."

"Please make a note to get his card copied next time – I want to check his identity with the medical aid."

"Good idea," said Patience. "That man is strange."

Megan did not respond to this unscientific diagnosis, but privately she concurred. It was Arthur Smith's unnerving behaviour that had prompted the idea to confirm his true name and identity in the first place. It had also driven her to record his session. She found his near constant fidgeting and fretful mannerisms so distracting that she battled to focus on what he was saying, and had thought that a review of his words might prove useful. Also, if she was being honest with herself, the fact that there was a recording of the session made her feel somehow safer. If he jumped up and knocked her about with an even number of blows on either side of her head, then at least the police would know who to arrest. Guiltily, she chided herself for being ridiculous.

Her room was already set up for audio recording. She occasionally recorded sessions when doing hypnosis with a client where childhood sexual abuse was suspected – she had no desire to be accused by some "false memory" apologist of implanting memories with leading questions or comments which could be interpreted as hints or veiled suggestions.

Wade, who was no mean handyman, had fashioned a metal bracket large enough to house the small digital recording device, and had screwed this under one of the side tables in the office. The tiny, super-sensitive microphone nestled in an arrangement of dried flowers which sat on top of the table and Megan usually placed a box of tissues on top of the thin cord that ran from the microphone to the back of the recorder.

It was not that she tried to hide the recording device from her clients – indeed, they always signed permission forms before she ever recorded them. She had just found with experience that when clients could see the device, they became all too aware that they were being recorded. They wound up focused on the recorder, started speaking self-consciously and censored their stories. It was easier just to have the whole setup out of sight and out of mind – that way they spoke much more freely.

Yesterday, though, she had been grateful that the equipment was set up and hidden. For Dr Smith, she had only had to retrieve the recorder from the drawer, make sure that there was at least an hour's recording time available on the memory chip, and slot it into the bracket under the table. She then switched the side tables around, so that the one with the recorder and flowers and tissues was placed next to the wingback where Dr Smith had sat the first time. It was a bit of a gamble, but clients almost always sat in the same chair session after session, and she was prepared to bet that he, too, was a creature of habit. Two minutes before the session was due to begin, she had started the recording.

It might be considered unethical to record a patient without his knowledge and consent, but she had decided to go ahead and do it anyway. If he found out and reported her, she could always fall back on the general phrase on the intake slip – which he had signed – that granted her permission to use any necessary techniques. She had been sure that Dr Smith would react adversely – have what Cayley would call "a major freak-out" – if she had suggested the idea of recording him. Her conscience had pricked her but, later, his troubled response to their meeting on the ward had confirmed her decision.

"What are you worried about?" she heard herself ask, when she resumed listening to the recording.

"I'm worried about seeing you, almost bumping into you, in the labour ward." His voice sounded nervous, even scared, in her ears.

"Yes, I was surprised to see you there, Art. Are you a gynaecologist?"

"Why are you so concerned about my speciality?"

"Why are you so concerned about my finding out about it?" came her counterquestion.

As she listened to the recording, Megan stared at a miniature Zen garden on her desk. It had been a gift from Mike at a time when, presumably, he had still cared about whether she was stressed or calm. It was a square, black-lacquered, shallow tray filled with fine white sand and three miniature "rocks". She picked up the tiny rake and began dragging it lightly through the sand, leaving curved parallel lines in its wake. The activity and the creation of balanced natural perfection was meant to be soothing, and she could use all the soothing she could get while listening to Arthur Smith's increasing agitation.

"I work here, in this hospital," he said. "People know me. And I don't want anyone to find out I'm seeing you. That's why I wanted to come at the end of the day, when there are fewer people about. Now your receptionist tells me there are only mid-morning slots available! When I saw you in that ward, I thought you might say something, that others might find out that I'm your patient."

"Art, I'm ethically bound to keep all aspects of your treatment confidential, even the fact that you're seeing me at all," Megan heard herself reassuring her client. "But what would be so dreadful about others knowing? What's your fear?"

"They'll find out that I'm..."

"That you're...?"

"Nuts!" he almost shouted the word. "Mad! I'm going off my rocker and it's getting worse. I can't do anything without... it's beginning to affect my work, and I can't stand it anymore."

Megan set down the rake and shoved aside the inane Zen garden. It wasn't helping. She rewound and listened again to his outburst. She felt again what she had felt in the session – a strong sense that Dr Smith was a man balanced precariously on a knife-edge, one small push away from falling into uncontained panic.

She heard her voice respond with calm, slow, comforting words, falling back on good old Rogerian empathic reflecting to contain Art's emotions. With another client, she might have amplified the feelings, encouraged the release and the relief of a catharsis, but not with him.

"You're afraid of what you're thinking. You're feeling out of control and you're worried about what's happening to you."

"Yes, I am. Very worried."

She could hear the slight relief in his voice, the rising panic temporarily checked by the unusual validation of feeling understood.

"Will you keep it confidential – that you're seeing me? You won't tell anyone what I tell you? You won't greet me in public?"

As she listened to this section of the recording, where she again tried to set Art's mind at rest about confidentiality,

Megan's eye was caught by the potted cyclamen on her desk. Its deep red flowers were marred by a few brown and desiccated leaves. Had she not watered the plant enough – or perhaps too much? Unsure as to whether it was diseased or perfectly healthy, she extracted a pair of scissors from her desk drawer and began snipping off the dead leaves. They crumbled in her hands. From there, she wandered about her office, the recorder tucked under one arm and headphones in her ears, pruning and clipping all of her neglected office plants. They were in a pitiful state. She could only hope that she had greener thumbs with her clients than with her plants.

When the recording arrived at the place she especially wanted to listen to, she went back to her seat at the desk and picked up a pen. She stared at the last notation she had made in the session notes:

Anxiety (Obsessive-Compulsive Disorder)? Or ?Personality Disorder?!

She sat still, focused intently now, trying to assess whether she was listening to anxious obsessional fantasising, or real and destructive intent.

"Art, what are you worried will happen? Are you scared something will happen to you, or is it that you're worried you'll *do* something?"

"How did you know that?" his response came rapidly, urgently.

"I'm a therapist, Art, it's my business to know this stuff. What are you worried you might do?"

His answer came in a gabbled rush.

"I'm scared I'll do something bad – threaten someone, or ride them over, or hurt them. I have access to drugs, you know, some of them can be toxic. Maybe I'll do something very bad. The thought keeps coming into my head that I'll hurt someone. What if I can't control it? The images that flash across my mind, the things I imagine doing – they're really bad. And are they just imaginings, or are they really memories? What if I've already done something? Have I done anything to you?" he interrupted himself.

"No, Art, you haven't harmed me."

"But what if I have? It's like a voice whispering to me. My throat closes and it feels like there's a vice around my chest and I can't breathe. And I know that something bad is going to happen to me to my family. Or I'll do something, something terrible, unless I, unless…"

"Unless you what?"

"Unless I make things even… And check that I haven't hurt anyone. Have I hurt you? Listen to me!" his voice was rough with self-disgust. "I know I've asked you that already and I know I haven't hurt you. And I *know* you just told me that yourself. I know it's insane to think this way, but I still worry." There was a groan, and the hard thump of his hand against his head.

"Don't do that, Art. You definitely have not hurt me." There was a pause, then Megan heard herself ask what she had to, but was reluctant to because she knew it would only increase his distress. "In your checking, have you found out that you've hurt anyone else?"

"No, at least, I don't think so. But what if I didn't actually check – what if I only thought I did? Or what if I didn't check properly and need to do it again? And again?"

She could hear, even over the recording, that his agitation was rising.

"Arthur, Art! Focus on me, Art. What did you mean about needing to make things even?"

"Huh? Oh. They must be even, the same on the left and the right. And even numbers."

"What must?"

She heard the long silence on the tape, remembered how he had tapped on the arms of the chair with his hands and looked at her, as if evaluating whether he could trust her with his truths. Eventually he replied – softly, sounding embarrassed.

"Shoelaces, toothbrush strokes, steps … lift buttons." He had smiled bleakly at her when he said the last words. "I'll do something bad, unless I go back and check, unless I go back and do it right. Evenly. Twice."

She reached over, clicked the stop button and let out a slow breath. Listening to the session again had confirmed what she had thought at the time. On the bottom of the session notes she wrote:

Diagnosis: Obsessive-Compulsive Anxiety Disorder

(obsessions: symmetry, order, harming others; compulsions: symmetrical behaviours, e.g. tapping, counting; plus checking)

Next session: education on disorder, discuss meds, set treatment plan.

She underlined her diagnosis. He was harmless. He caused pain only to himself and posed no real threat to others. She was not wrong – she was sure of it.

There was a knock at the door and Patience came in.

"I'm going now. Are you still working?"

"Just reviewing some cases before I knock off," said Megan, kneading a knot in the back of her neck. "Cheers, Patience, have a good evening."

Patience rolled her eyes. "Thulani's mother and sister are coming up from Newcastle to visit. I don't need to throw the bones to know it's not going to be a good evening. Better thing *you* have a good evening. Women in your condition need lots of rest."

"What do you mean – women in my condition?" Megan had not yet told Patience about the pregnancy. But Patience just smiled knowingly and went off with a little wave of her fingers.

25

Naughty

Setting aside Arthur Smith's file, Megan mentally reviewed the rest of the day's appointments. The termination session with Zanzi Nyoka – who was mostly recovered from her trauma – had gone well, and although her session with Tony Thomas has been emotionally demanding and thought-provoking, Megan felt they had made real progress. She realised that she was beginning to look forward to Tony's appointments, perhaps more than was appropriate. He was a challenging and stimulating client, and she found she enjoyed his intelligence and the verbal sparring that characterised their sessions.

Again, he had arrived five minutes late for the appointment. She wondered if he was generally careless with time, or if, like some of her clients, he deliberately arrived late so as to avoid any chance of bumping into the previous client.

"Sorry I'm late. I was mucking about with images of the Mona Lisa in my studio, and I lost track of the time."

Megan had intended, today, to begin with a thorough history-taking, beginning with the family as it had existed before he was even born, but somehow they had instead wound up talking about the cause and effect of conditional acceptance in parents. Once more, he surprised her with his unorthodox views.

"Do you really think, Megan, that conditional acceptance is a bad thing?" he asked, a grin creasing his attractive face.

"Don't you?"

"No."

"Are we talking about the same thing?" Megan had said. "I'm talking about the type of relationship between a parent and a child where the parent sets conditions – standards of achievement or behaviour or appearance – that must be met by the child if it is to receive love, acceptance and approval. A relationship where the parent says, directly or indirectly, 'I love you when you get straight A's, when you're obedient. I find you unacceptable when you fail, or when you're unpopular, or fat.' Is that what you understand by the concept, Tony?"

"Pretty much," he nodded.

"And you don't think that it's dysfunctional or unhealthy to set conditions like that for a child?"

"I think it's impossible not to."

"Tell me more about that."

"Unconditional acceptance – that's the line you psychologists pedal, isn't it. But we're kidding ourselves if we think we can accept another person on the planet – let alone annoying little nippers – without wanting to change them in some way so that it's easier and more comfortable for ourselves. Why should we accept or love someone who messes our house, steals from us, and embarrasses us in public? How *can* we approve of that? It's the same for you, really."

"For me?" said Megan, surprised.

"Yes. How can you unconditionally accept a patient whose behaviour appals and repulses you?"

"You don't think we can disapprove of the behaviour while still loving and accepting the individual?" she countered, trying to keep the discussion off herself and her profession.

"I think that's specious nonsense, idealistic psychobabble claptrap!" He reached out a long arm and brushed at the air, as though sweeping away cobwebs, but his gentle smile took the sting out of the words.

"Really?" said Megan, taken aback by the vehemence of his argument and wondering if he really believed what he was saying or if he was merely trying to play devil's advocate again.

"You tell me how it's possible to separate the person from his actions. Wasn't it you who was telling me just the other day that we are what we repeatedly do?"

He'd got her there, she thought, backed her nicely into a tight philosophical corner of her own making. It was high time she got the discussion off generalities of abstract theory and delved into the real world of lived, personal experience. Weren't they supposed to be exploring his childhood today, anyway?

"You have no children," she stated.

"No," he said, running a hand through his hair and looking surprised at the turn in the conversation.

"Then you must be talking from the experience of being a child."

"Must everything stem from one's childhood?"

This time, Megan merely smiled at the attempt to deflect her back into a debate on psychological theory.

"Did your parents accept you unconditionally?"

"Hardly," he snorted. "But who could blame them? I was a naughty kid – I probably deserved most of what they sent my way."

Victims often blamed themselves. The adults in their lives usually told them that it was their fault and they believed it, too young to know better. Paradoxically, it also gave them some sense of control in a situation in which they were largely powerless. If you behaved badly, you could tell yourself that your mother or father rejected you for what you did, rather than for who you suspected you were at your core – unworthy, unlovable, contemptible.

"It sounds like you were told you were naughty and that you deserved what you got. Does the adult-you still think that? That the things you did were unacceptable?"

"Oh yes – well, don't we all think that about ourselves?" He smiled ruefully.

"We're talking about *you*, Tony," she chided gently, then asked, "What did you do?"

"What do you mean?"

"What did you do that was so bad, that was unacceptable?"

"Stuff. Naughty things."

"Like what?"

"I'd make a mess in my room or the bathroom, once I made a fire behind the garden shed. I regularly stole from my mother's purse."

"That's significant. Stealing from a parent is often the child's attempt to even the score when he feels short-changed on the parent's time, attention and love. He steals from her because he wants something more from her, but doesn't know how to get it."

Tony was no longer smiling, he looked thoughtful. Perhaps she had hit a nerve.

"How did your parents respond when you did those things?"

"The usual way – shouting at me. 'We brought you into this world and we can take you out again!' – you know the sort of thing. And hidings, leaving me in a cold bath when I messed the bathroom. Once, my father banged my arm in the car door."

"On purpose?" Megan asked, inwardly flinching in horror. Outwardly she maintained her neutral game face, determined not to shut down his confidences by displaying shock or judgement.

"He slammed the door on it three times – bang-bang-bang," Tony gesticulated, "so I hardly think it was accidental. I remember him. I must have been about nine years old."

"Tony," she spoke gently, but it needed to be said, "it sounds like abuse."

"Does it? It wasn't always the physical stuff I found hardest. My parents when I was –" He stopped himself – perhaps it was getting difficult for him to continue. He was dry-eyed, and speaking in a completely calm voice, but those emotions had to be sneaking up on him.

"When I was twelve, my parents drove me to the rubbish dump. It was the one down in the dip in Bez Valley – I can still see it in my mind's eye, still smell it. It's the kind of smell that sticks on you, you know? It gets into your hair and your clothes. Anyway, they said I was rubbish, so I belonged on the rubbish dump. They dragged me out of the car – I was screaming, hanging onto the seat belts, the door handle – and they put me inside a skip. Then they drove off. Left me there. All I could think was … what if they never came back?" His eyes were out of focus now, staring off into the distant, still vivid, memory. One of his hands was rubbing unconsciously along his long leg.

"I guess they probably just drove around the block, but it felt like I was in there forever, among the bags of stinking rot." He shuddered. "One of the workers at the dump peered over the top of the skip and laughed at me. He had only two teeth left in his head, both of them here," he tapped one side of his face. "I was so scared, I would have wet my pants, but I was too scared to make more of a mess – what if they did come back? Good thing I didn't, because they did return, asked me if I'd learned my lesson, if I'd be a good, neat, clean boy from then on."

"Tony, you're describing all kinds of abuse. That kind of pain – the rejection and abandonment, the message that unless you were perfect, you were worthless – that would definitely have left you with feelings of deep fear and rage. And you wouldn't have been able to express your anger for fear of incurring more abuse. The damage would just have lain there, banked in your subconscious, collecting interest."

"They weren't all bad – I don't want to give you the wrong impression. There were good times, too, laughs and fun. It got easier as I got older, learned how the world worked. My parents – when I was older – we got on better. They left me to my own devices a lot of the time."

"Was that because you were different – had perhaps learned to fake well? Or do you think that they found it easier to cope with an older child?"

"Maybe that."

"Quite a turnaround – from beating you and abandoning you at rubbish dumps, to letting you get on with your own thing," she commented.

"It's like they were a completely different set of parents," he said, with a weak attempt at a smile. "And here I am, sitting before you today. I survived." He clasped his hands in the air in mock celebration of the grand feat.

"*Surviving* shouldn't be the best we can say of our lives, Tony. We should be raised in conditions in which we can thrive."

"Could've, would've, should've," he said dismissively. "But are any of us really, when it comes down to it?"

Megan saw the question for what it was – an attempt to back off the personal and retreat to the impersonal safety of the theoretical and rhetorical. She thought, though, that he had probably had enough for one day and allowed him to draw her back into a discussion of best child-rearing practices. It was good practice, anyway, to ensure that clients were anchored in the cognitive realm, and had their protective defences back in place before returning them to the world.

Next time she would explore with Tony what impact his childhood experiences had left on him, and discuss the options of using trauma techniques or hypnosis to help him in healing from them and building a better self-concept than the one he had presumably been left with.

Megan was glad she had had a gap after the intense emotions of the session with Tony and the next appointment. It had given her a chance to catch her breath, have a cup of raspberry tea (good for strengthening uterine muscles, according to the books) and return some calls. One of these had been to Mike and he had suddenly sounded so sweet, had asked so tenderly how she was doing (as close as he had yet come to asking her how the pregnancy was going), that a sharp pang of missing him had pulsed through her, misting her eyes and causing her throat to ache.

The last session of the day had been with Alta Cronjé. It was heartening to see how much better she was doing. Alta's relationship with Johan had improved, sex was mostly back on track and she was full of plans for the future. She was more determined than ever to press ahead with charges against Dr Trotteur. Megan had given her a very summarised account of her visits to Stacey Cole and the Reddys. Alta was saddened for the women and their families, but also understandably disappointed because of the implications for the case against Trotteur.

"One dead and one who can't testify – that's not much help to us. It's still just my word against his. We've got no proof, no witnesses."

"I know," Megan conceded, "but I'm making a plan to get more information."

"What?" asked Alta, her eyes gleaming in anticipation.

"Ask me no questions and I'll tell you no lies," said Megan, only half-kidding.

Alta rubbed her hands together excitedly. "*Lekkerrrr!*" she said, with a laugh.

26

Locked out

Two things were clear to Megan: one, she needed more information and two, she was not going to get it by politely asking Trotteur to hand it over.

Surely, in amongst all his cases, there were other patients who had been badly treated? If she could just lay her hands on his records and contact his patients, then she knew she would be able to amass more evidence, enough to sway a jury of his peers at the Board.

She knew *what* she wanted. The *how* of going about getting it was the tricky part. She looked down at the spidery mind map of ideas on the paper in front of her and experienced a moment of surreal disbelief. A brainstorm of ideas for stealing confidential information – that was what it amounted to. It hardly seemed possible that she was contemplating it. She, who never so much as parked in a handicapped bay or cheated on her tax return, was now spending her Friday evening in her office, considering various ways of breaking and entering a medical colleague's consulting rooms.

She looked at the options she had mapped out and evaluated each in turn, tapping her front teeth with the end of a pencil.

Steal keys from Trotteur's receptionist/nurse

She discarded this idea almost immediately as impractical. She supposed he must have a receptionist, but Megan had no idea who the woman was, where she kept the office keys, or even if she had a set at all – Trotteur might well do his own opening and closing.

Bamboozle a night cleaner

Tempting. This seemed like a workable option at first thought. Every night, an army of navy-clad cleaners swept through the clinic's office suites, emptying bins, dusting, polishing and vacuuming. She had seen them at it on the odd occasion when she had worked very late.

How hard could it be to don a white coat, clip her hospital ID onto it and walk confidently into Trotteur's office as if it was her own? But the more carefully she thought about it, the more potential problems she could envision with this plan. What if the cleaner checked her ID, compared it to the name on the door and rumbled her that way? What if there was a policy that cleaners were not to admit anyone into the offices without a security officer being present? Where had this idea sprung from – had she read it in some hospital memo? What if, somehow, she got the poor cleaner into trouble? She scratched a cross through the idea.

Force door open with crowbar

The simplicity of this plan appealed immediately. It could be done easily and quickly and no one else need be involved. At least, she *thought* she would be able to do it herself. The main problem was that breaking the door open would leave evidence that the office had been entered. There was nothing of great value to steal in the suites – the reason why the sum total of each office's security amounted to a single lock on the sliding door – so burglary would seem an unlikely explanation for the break-in, especially when nothing would be taken. Trotteur would surely begin to wonder why his was the only office broken into and what the motive might have been. She had no wish to put him on his guard.

She had to get into his office in a way that left no traces. She sighed and pushed back from the desk. Breaking into places always looked so easy in the movies – a simple matter of sliding a credit card between door and frame, or a twist of a hairpin. She doubted it would work so smoothly in real life.

But why not try?

On a sudden impulse, she extracted her medical aid membership card from her wallet and rooted about in her desk drawer for a hairpin. Armed with these felonious tools, she went into the empty corridor outside her rooms and slid the glass door closed, glad that Patience was not there to witness her attempts at lock-picking.

All the offices had the same metal-framed sliding glass doors with similar locks. If she could open her door without a key, she would be able to open Trotteur's. It took mere seconds to discover that there was no way a credit card could open this door – the door slid at least a centimetre into the frame when it closed, leaving no room for a card to slide between lock and frame.

Looking left and right to check that she was still alone, she stuck the hairpin into the keyhole. Now what? She wiggled it about hopefully in a random way, realising as she did so that she had no clue as to the inner structure or workings of locks. Just as she was about to give up on the whole absurd process – she was a shrink for crying out loud, not a cat burglar – the pin hooked into the lock. She pressed her ear against the door as she had seen countless criminals do on TV, although she had a vague idea that listening for the tumble of locks was for safe-cracking, not lock-picking. Carefully, she twisted the pin, straining her ears to hear some click which might signal success.

She heard and felt nothing, so she turned the hairpin more. Looking down at her hands, she saw that she had merely been twisting the thin metal over itself, so that the protruding part resembled a corkscrew.

"I give up," she muttered to herself in irritation. She yanked the twisted hairpin out of the lock at the same moment as she realised that the door was locked and her keys were in her handbag on the desk in her office.

"Dammit!"

She kicked the obstinate door and cursed again before setting off in the direction of the hospital's main security office. Half an hour later, she was back at her desk crossing out the crowbar and lock-picking options and noting, for the record, that there would also be no way to beg, borrow or steal a set of keys from the guards in the security office. They had seemed polite and patient but, sadly, not stupid – verifying her identity carefully before escorting her back to her rooms and opening the door with a key extracted from a safe in their own office.

Bribe the building manager

She drew a line through this idea immediately. There was no way it was likely to work. The manager would be more likely to report her to the hospital authorities than aid and abet her efforts.

Which left only one more idea on the list.

27
After hours

The white-coated figure waited outside the main entrance to the Acacia unit, eyes scanning the car park, then coming to settle on a tall man who stood, cradling his bleeding arm, outside the adjacent Emergency unit. He wore an orange tank top over black jeans and, at first glance, it seemed that the spray of dark red spots might be a pattern on the stretched fabric. He was enormous, his head too small for the thick neck which triangled down to the steroid-pumped muscles bulging in his arms and shoulders.

A woman, eyes wild and lipstick smeared, limped out of the unit on six-inch heels. She walked up to the man, slapped what she could reach of his face and screeched, "I'll kill you, Benni, you bastard! If he dies, I'll kill you!"

She beat her small fists against his chest. The man bowed his head, held his injured arm out to the side, away from the woman. A steady tick of blood dripped into a small puddle beside his Caterpillar-booted feet.

"I'll kill you, Benni, I swear I'll kill you."

She was sobbing the words now, her arms flailing uselessly against the wall of his chest. He pulled her closer with his massive arm, held her tight against him, brushed his lips with infinite gentleness against the top of her head.

"Are you the doctor?" a voice cut in.

A man, short, dishevelled-looking and carrying a battered tan briefcase, walked towards the clinic's entrance, sparing no more than a second's glance for the couple bathed in the red glow of the Emergency unit's light.

"That's me. Are you Joe?"

"Uh-huh. So, which way?"

"Follow me."

They moved through the silently sliding automatic doors.

"Thank you for coming out so late at night."

"No problems. Part of the job, hey," said Joe, looking around and giving an appreciative whistle at the plush and gleaming interior of the clinic.

The foyer was quiet this late, stripped of the hubbub of the daily hustle. A single intake clerk dozed at admissions, his head resting on the back of the chair, his arms folded across his chest. A cleaner's head bounced rhythmically as he buffed the floor with a rotary floor polisher, the headphones plugged into his ears leading a red vein to some device deep in a pocket. The coffee shop was closed. A few desperate souls, their faces tight with worry, pale with exhaustion, clung to plastic cups of coffee from the vending machine. An orderly pushed a wheelchair across the foyer to park it alongside the row which already waited, empty and expectant, for the next day's burdens.

They took the stairs, Joe Cohen explaining he never rode in lifts if he could avoid it.

"Only last year I was stuck in one for three hours. Three hours between floors there in the Carlton Centre. Funny, hey – me stuck and not able to get out?"

The corridor was dimly lit after the fluorescent brightness of the stairwell. They walked past the darkened rooms on either side until they stood outside the right office.

"This is it."

Joe looked at the door, cocking his head like a parrot eyeing a treat. He set his briefcase on the tiles, crouched down on his haunches and peered at the lock.

"So – can you do it?"

"This? No problems." His voice sounded scornful. "Piece of old tackie."

Joe opened his briefcase. Inside was a shamble of tools, keys, a small drill and a few screwdrivers. He picked up a thin metal implement, shorter than a pen, with a bent, pointed hook, and another with an end which looked like it had been beaten flat, then bent into a curved wiggle.

With small, delicate fingers, he inserted first one pick and then the other into the lock. He had just begun to manoeuvre them when he said, "There's it," and pulled them out again. He pushed the door open along its tracks.

"That was quick."

"Ja, these locks are a joke, man. You actually pay me for my travel time more than my work time. And speaking of…" He looked up expectantly, tossing the tools back into the case and closing it with a twist of wire.

"Sure. You said R850?"

"Ja, sorry for that. After-hours fee." He folded the cash, stashed it in a pocket of his jeans and said, "Don't lock yourself out again," then strolled off to the stairs at the end of the corridor.

"Don't worry – I'll never do it again," she said.

28

Taken in

It had been much easier than she expected. She had simply called an all-hours locksmith, told him she was a doctor who had locked herself out of her office and that she urgently needed to get in. She had concocted a cock-and-bull story about the security office being closed until Monday, unless she wanted to call out the manager on his weekend off, but the locksmith had asked nothing more than the address and where to meet her, warned her of nothing more than his extortionate call-out fee.

Megan waited until the stairwell door swung shut behind Joe before she slipped into Dr Trotteur's rooms, sliding the door closed behind her. It locked automatically. She fished about in her handbag until her hands touched the thin metal tube they sought. Pulling out the penlight torch, she switched it on and swept the beam briefly around the office to get a general idea of the layout.

She glimpsed the usual high-ledged reception counter, a waiting area with chairs along walls hung with certificates on one side, tasteful-looking framed black and white photographs on another, and a portrait at the rear. She adjusted the torch to its lowest setting and trained the beam on the floor, stepping around to the back of the counter where the receptionist usually sat. A typist's chair faced the computer monitor which sat, with mouse and keyboard, on the desk, flanked by neat rows of lever-arch files, index books and an internal phone directory. A few notices and typed lists in plastic sleeves were taped to the inside wall of the counter and a small wooden frame held a snapshot of a grey-haired woman with a baby and a toddler perched on her lap.

Megan sat in the chair, and nudged the mouse on the off-chance that the PC was merely in standby mode, but the screen remained dead. She flashed the light under the desk to find the computer's main box and pressed the power button. In less than a minute, it had booted up. On the screen was the familiar Microsoft sign-in box. A name was already set as default in the username field: Beth Finch.

"Hello, Beth," said Megan softly to the woman in the photograph. "Now what would your password be?" Maybe she would get lucky. Perhaps Beth, like many older folk, would be unenthusiastic about technology, unsophisticated about security.

Megan tried the system default *1 2 3 4*, then *1 2 3 4 5* without luck. She thought about the woman's name for a moment, and tried *Elizabeth, Elizabeth Finch, Beth, Beth Finch*, then tried again, with and without spaces, with and without capital letters – all without success.

She thought for a moment, drumming her fingers impatiently on the desk. Then she grabbed the small photo frame and flipped it over, bending back the tiny metal catches to release the backing and extract the photograph.

Yes! On the back of the photograph was written: "Rachel and Jared, Dec 2009".

Deleting her last try in the password field, Megan entered every permutation and combination of the names she could think of. Each time, the machine merely beeped obstinately and displayed the error message.

She checked her watch. She had been in the office for almost fifteen minutes and was no closer to accessing the records she had come for. Perhaps a more low-tech approach was called for. She shone the light behind her where she had noticed two metal filing cabinets. A quick tug at the drawers confirmed that the cabinets were locked. She rummaged in Beth Finch's drawers, found pens, paper clips, a banana, a tube of hand cream and some aspirin, but no keys to the cabinets and no handy aide-memoire of passwords. She looked in and under the pen holder, behind the files, felt under the counter. Nothing.

An idea penetrated her racing thoughts. She sat again, placed her hands on the keyboard and cleared both sign-on fields. Into the Username field, she typed an *A*. Immediately, the field auto-filled with *ANTHONY TROTTEUR*. The password field remained empty. Again, Megan went through the process of trying combinations of his name, again she struck out.

It occurred to her that there might be some clue in his office – on his desk or shelves, or the filing cabinet keys might be in one of his drawers. Perhaps Beth was as efficient as Patience, and a stack of patient files might be waiting on his desk. A few records would be better than leaving empty-handed. The door to his office was ajar. She walked into the room.

For a moment, she was tempted to switch on the lights, but realised immediately that while the lights to this inner office might not be visible from the corridor, they would be visible to anyone – a patrolling security guard perhaps – in the car park. Unlikely as it was that anyone would be staring up at this office at midnight on a Friday, she decided not to take the chance.

The sweep of the thin beam of light revealed an office far more luxurious than her own. A thick Persian carpet covered most of the floor, two comfortable armchairs faced an enormous dark, wooden desk behind which was a tall-backed, black leather chair as big as a throne. Windows ran the length of one wall, low bookshelves the other. On the wall above these, box frames held a collection of what looked like antique medical instruments.

She swung the torch beam over the desk again. The light flashed and reflected off something resting on top of some papers in the centre of the desk. It was a perfect half-globe of what looked like glass, about the size of half a cricket ball. She stepped closer, reached out a hand, picked up the glittering object and shone the light onto it.

With an involuntary shudder and a cry of revulsion, she dropped it at once. It landed on the desk with a soft thunk.

Her heart kicked deep inside her chest, her stomach heaved into her throat. Her mind refused to believe what her eyes had registered. Preserved for eternity inside the dense glass was, unmistakably, some kind of small ovoid organ, cream-coloured with tiny red veins marbling its slightly lumpy surface. Attached to it, running over one side of its surface was a slender fleshy-pink curve of some kind of tube or ligament.

Ovary. Fallopian tube. Some rational corner of her brain supplied the labels, but the rest of her mind was spinning. A shiver rippled over her scalp. Her head was turning, pulling her eyes away from the macabre thing on the desk to stare back over her shoulder at what she had seen, but not fully taken in when she first entered Trotteur's rooms. Dazed, she walked back to the reception room, raised the tiny torch – now so heavy in her hand – shone it on the walls and looked again.

Black and white prints – photographic prints – of people-less landscapes were arranged, perfectly straight and at absolutely even intervals along one wall. The bottom-right corner of each print was signed with a date and the intials ATT.

"Photography... I do mostly landscapes..."

Her feet walked her to the back of the room where a coloured print of a portrait hung on the wall, the gestalt of it instantly recognisable by the low, wide neckline, the folded hands, the long, dark hair. But the muted greens and browns of the background were now behind a face strangely unfamiliar, perfectly symmetrical, the features of one side copied and flipped over to make the other. The smile was uniform, lacking even a semblance of mystery, the hands were oddly placed.

"I was mucking about with images of the Mona Lisa..."

She swung the beam to the wall with the framed certificates, knowing what she would see. The degrees were conferred on the inductee Anthony Thomas Trotteur. *Anthony Thomas* Trotteur.

"Please, call me Tony..."

Blood pounded behind her ears. She switched off the light.

29
Rattled

For a full minute, Megan just sat, her breath coming in gasps, as she absorbed the blow that had set her reeling. This butcher who had hacked into and out of woman after woman and called it *improvement*, this misogynistic monster who had tortured vulnerable women's minds with his whispers, who had maimed their bodies and devastated their futures, this man was *her client* – charming, urbane, intelligent, *attractive* Tony Thomas.

She felt sickened, and livid with herself. Just what kind of a psychologist was she not to have suspected something? She was supposed to be an expert and yet had been so easily fooled by his façade of normality. And why had he come to see her anyway? My God, he had sat in her room, told her jokes, debated free will and determinism with her, told her heart-wrenching stories of his parents. Was any of it true?

Anger vied with shock. And won. She would get what she had come for and make sure he got what he deserved. She headed back to Beth Finch's computer and held her trembling hands poised over the keyboard.

Think! Think about what you've been told. You know things about this man, she told herself. Think about what he's told you. She tried another succession of words as potential passwords: *perfect, cut, extra, just right,* even – in desperation – *Ihatewomen* and *I hate women*. Each tap of the enter key was answered by the beep of the error message.

Think about what he told his patients – Alta and Stacey and Nirvana – the women he "improved". Then a thrill of premonition tingled through her. She knew what it had to be. Carefully she typed: *Drknowsbest*. It did not work. Perhaps abbreviations were not perfect enough. Holding her breath, she typed *Doctorknowsbest* and hit enter.

Got you, you bastard! The logon screen vanished and the main screen materialised before her eyes, the creepily symmetrical Mona Lisa as its wallpaper.

Working quickly, she examined the icons on the desktop, then accessed MS Word. Scanning the document directory and opening some likely-looking files, she saw that there were some letters – none personal, a few reports and typed lists of diagnoses- and treatment-codes. She pulled a memory stick from a pocket, inserted it into the flash drive and copied this file onto it. Then she clicked on a document labelled *clientrecords_master.doc*.

Bingo! It was a list of clients, together with their contact details (telephonic, postal and e-mail) and the date of last visit. Checking the file properties, she saw that it had last been updated on the first of February. She copied the file to the flash disk, exited the program and then opened up the billing system – MedBillings, the same software that she, along with most of the practitioners in the clinic, used.

It would take a while and a whack of memory to copy all the patient statements across. What she needed to do was extract the records of those patients who had had surgery performed on them by Trotteur. She knew it was possible to sort the records according to their ICD-10's, the diagnostic and treatment codes which, annoyingly, had to appear on every patient statement. She herself had run extracts on her own records based on psychological diagnoses from time to time. Off the top of her head, she could have quoted the codes for depression, anxiety, victim of crime, stressful life events and a dozen other conditions, but she had no idea what the codes were for gynaecology and obstetrics.

She scanned the desk again. Surely the efficient Ms Finch… There! In the dull glow of the screen, Megan could see a plastic sleeve stuck on the inside of the counter. Inside was a list of codes and their explanations. These must be the codes most commonly used in the practice which Beth Finch had typed for easy reference and quick billing so that she did not have to wade through the full list each time she gave a client a statement.

Megan checked the list and then ran a procedure to sort the records using the codes for gynaecological procedures: cryosurgery; pelvic laparoscopy; cervical and uterine biopsies; endometrial ablation; tubal ligations; vulvectomy and vulval excisions. She chucked in anything that ended in –ectomy, on the basis that it must be the removal of something in the way a hysterectomy was the removal of the uterus. She copied the records, then searched using the codes for obstetric procedures: delivery, caesarean section, episiotomy, dilatation and curettage. Once she had extracted these records from the rest, she copied them across to the memory stick. She was just ejecting the device when she heard voices.

Damn! If it was the cleaners, she would be discovered. Quickly she pressed the power switch for the monitor so that the light from the screen would not be seen from the corridor, and ducked behind the counter. The door rattled. The bright beam of a powerful torch flashed through the office then disappeared. Carefully she peered around the side of the counter and was just in time to see a pair of security guards walking past, already shining their torches into the next offices along the corridor.

Megan sagged with relief against the chair. It was obviously just a routine security patrol – something else she had not factored into her plans for this night-time recce. It was time to go. At any minute, the cleaners might well appear. She pulled out the memory stick, powered the computer down, pushed the chair back under the desk and made sure everything looked just as it had before she had arrived.

She walked back in Trotteur's office. A quick glance told her that only the vile paperweight was out of place. Every part of her being was repelled by the idea of touching it again, but she forced herself to pick it up and place it back in the exact centre of the pile of papers on the desk. As she did so, the letterhead of the top paper caught her eye.

It was a letter – of commendation and thanks, no less – from the Chief Superintendent of Johannesburg Central Hospital. He wanted to express his sincere gratitude and appreciation to Dr Trotteur for volunteering his services at the Obstetrics and Gynaecology units. It was the civic-minded generosity of private practitioners such as the esteemed Dr Trotteur that helped cash-strapped government facilities supplement their limited resources to the greater benefit of the community at large.

Acid rose in her throat at the irony, at the vast gap between the polished, benevolent face Trotteur presented to the public – the same face he had presented to her – and the unspeakable malevolence of what he was probably doing to the never-ending stream of vulnerable patients at the overwhelmed facility. He had to be stopped.

She replaced the letter and the paperweight, checked again that she had left behind no trace of her visit and left, pulling the door closed and locked behind her.

30

Trapped

"'Moxie' – is that even a word?" asked Megan, staring sceptically at the Scrabble board which lay on the carpet between them.

"I'm wounded," said Wade. "Of course it's a word – I found it on my internet dictionary."

"The most reliable of sources."

"It means verve or vigour, or pep. As in, 'It seems to me, Megan, that you have lost much of your moxie'."

"Yeah, well..."

"How's it going, sweetness? Spill the beans. And that's a triple letter on the X and a double word score, so that makes it 48 for me." He wrote the score on the pad of paper alongside the board.

Megan sipped at her cup of raspberry tea and looked at Wade who was lying on his stomach on the other side of the board. She picked out five letter tiles from her rack and, using the E of MOXIE, arranged the word ABSENT. It seemed appropriate.

"Did you want the spilled beans on the AWOL boyfriend, the unplanned pregnancy, the situation at work or the dysfunctional family?"

Wade snorted. "That *was* some dinner party."

"If I tell you that's been the highlight of my last month, would that give you a clue as to why my moxie's been minimised? Uh-uh, no, Oedipus!" said Megan, pushing the dog away from the plate of shortbread towards which he had been inching stealthily.

"That bad? You haven't had a great start to the year,' said

Wade. He snapped a finger of shortbread in two, popped one half into his mouth and tossed the other to Oedipus, who snatched it from the air and swallowed it in a single gulp.

"Wade – he's fat enough as it is."

"Meh," said Wade, gently blowing crumbs off the board and arranging pale tiles to form the word ROMANCE. "So, how *is* it going?" he asked, tapping a finger on the word and adding, "Fifteen for me – not my best."

"Nor mine. If I had the letters, I'd make MORIBUND. If you allowed slang, I could make *KAK*. But since you're a purist, I'll have to make do with BAD."

"Six points. Impressive."

It's more than I've been scoring with Mike," said Megan, tallying the points and noting with disgust that Wade was already 97 points ahead.

"He's still in Cape Town?"

"Yep. It's as far away as he can get from the baby without setting sail for Antarctica."

"Weak," said Wade.

"It is, isn't it? And cowardly and immature and plain bloody pathetic!"

"No, dear, I mean that's my word – WEAK. Twenty-two points. But of course," he said quickly, seeing her glare, "he's weak, too. And plain and pathetic and everything else you said... Are you going to end it?"

"Oh, I don't know. I keep hoping this is just a passing panic, that he'll come to his senses and come back home – to both of us." She touched her still unrounded abdomen.

"Do you *want* him back?" Wade asked mildly.

"I know, I know what you're going to say. He's a good-time Charlie who'll be great as long as things are going well and going his way, but he'll duck as soon as there's a drama. That is what you're thinking, isn't it?"

"It's obviously what you're thinking. Project much?"

Megan threw a piece of shortbread at him. Oedipus caught it mid-air.

"And the baby?"

"It's going well, I suppose. I don't really feel pregnant, though. It's a bit weird. I don't feel very special, or connected or like a new life is miraculously growing inside me, or anything."

"Still your turn, sweets. You think maybe you're scared to bond with it – the baby, I mean? That your life is so hectic and your relationship with Mike too uncertain to really accept what's happening?"

"Wade, you know you've been hanging around a shrink too much when you start speaking like one." She stared hopelessly from her rack of useless letters to the board, then reached for the bag of tiles and slid hers into it.

"I give up. Your turn." She shook the bag and was fishing out new letters when Oedipus gave a sudden bark and ran across the board, sending tiles skittering in all directions.

They groaned at the mess, but the dog was already at the window, sniffing and pawing at one of the curtains. Megan saw that a small gecko was clinging to the fabric just out of Oedipus's reach.

"No, Oedipus! Down! Sit!" she shouted.

She tore the top sheet of paper off the scoring pad and headed over to where Oedipus was leaping and whining in excitement. She folded the paper in half lengthwise and tried to ease it under the small reptile. It was tricky because the creature's claws were entangled in the fabric, but Megan was reluctant to prise it loose with her fingers in case she damaged it. It looked so fragile: the tiny bones were visible ridges under the wrinkled skin and she could see the rapid, panicked pulse on the sides of its throat. She carefully manoeuvred the paper between the gecko and the curtain, and then gently pulled back.

"There you go, little one," she said.

Suddenly free, the gecko made a mad scramble across the paper and slid off the edge. In one rapid movement, Oedipus pounced, snapped it up in his jaws and chewed with apparent relish.

"Eeuww," said Wade.

"Idiot dog!" Megan screamed, and promptly burst into tears.

"Megan, honey, what is it?" said Wade. He took her hand and lead her back to the carpet, where they sat, leaning up against the couch. Oedipus tried to lie alongside Megan, but she shoved him away.

"Here." Wade handed her a serviette and pulled her head onto his shoulder. "Tell me what's the matter. You're not crying for the lizard, are you?"

"No, I'm not crying for the freaking lizard! My life's a mess. And I've gotten myself into such trouble. I don't know what to do," Megan said, blowing her nose, but unable to stop the tears from coming.

"Tell me," he urged.

"I can't. I'm not supposed to – it's confidential."

"You don't have to tell me the names. And you know I'll never tell a soul. What's happened?"

"I've fucked up – that's what's happened. There's no other word for it. And I don't know what to do to get out of it. I'm trapped." Megan blotted at her eyes. Wade rubbed a comforting hand along her arm.

"You remember I told you about that client I had – still have – that was maybe hurt by a doctor at the hospital?"

"I remember."

Well, it turns out that it *did* happen. And not just to her. To other women, too. He butchers his patients, Wade, in dreadful ways. He leaves them mutilated and sterile and damaged in every kind of way."

"But why hasn't he been stopped? Haven't they complained or reported him?"

"They have. At least, some have. But it's hard to report because it's so private and intimate and embarrassing. And it's difficult to prove that he did it negligently, let alone intentionally. It's just their word against his and he's a respected member of the medical fraternity and they're 'traumatised hysterical women'. Two women got as far as bringing cases against him at the Board, but one died in a car accident before the hearing and he paid off the other – and she's still a bloody wreck, I've seen her. Every day he's operating on more women – I found out he even volunteers at Jo'burg Central. God knows what he's doing to those poor women."

"But surely you can get more women to speak up – ask his patients."

"I thought of that, too, and I am going to contact them – I think – but Wade, the way I got his records, his *confidential* patient records, was by breaking into his office, going into his computer and stealing them." This brought on a fresh round of sobs.

"You did what?" said Wade. His hand had stopped its rubbing.

"I know, I know. But how else was I supposed to get the information?"

"You, Mega-Uptight-Wright, broke into a doctor's office, hacked his computer and stole his records?" Megan could hear the smile in Wade's voice. He sounded both amused and impressed.

"It's not funny!" she said, pushing herself off his shoulder and wiping her eyes with the crumpled serviette.

"No," he said, immediately wiping the grin off his face.

"And you haven't even heard the worst part."

"It gets worse?"

"Yes. He … he's my patient, Wade."

"What?" Wade's face was a mask of blank incomprehension.

"When I was snooping in his office, I found … stuff. I discovered who he really is. And who he is, is one of my existing patients. He's been using his middle name as a surname, so I didn't realise. But I must be the worst, the most freaking incompetent, useless excuse for a psych ever not to have noticed that there was something seriously wrong with this man. *Anger issues!*" She made a sound of disgust. "He must have heard that I was sniffing about and came to check me out. And he's been toying with me! And it was a very clever move, because whatever he tells me in sessions is confidential. I'm ethically bound not to tell anyone."

"But he hasn't told you about hurting the women, has he?"

"No, not yet. But even if he had, I couldn't tell, do you see, couldn't testify against him because he's a patient. I'm not even sure I can now testify *for* my other patient, the woman who's been mutilated and traumatised, when she brings her case against him – because he's now also a client and it's a complete ethical conflict." Megan began picking up the Scrabble pieces, stacking them into little towers in her hands.

"So I either have to let her down, abandon my support for her case, or I have to testify against another client, which is a breach of ethics and confidentiality – even *if* they were to allow my testimony. I'm pretty sure he could argue that as he's my client and so is she, it's a complete conflict of interest and dual roles for me to testify."

"But you can stop seeing him and then he wouldn't be a client anymore. Problem solved, surely," said Wade, taking the stack of tiles from her and dropping them into the bag.

"No," said Megan. "My duty of confidentiality doesn't end when the therapy does, I'd still be bound as tightly as I am now. Besides, I'm not even sure I *can* terminate therapy with him."

"Why not? You can't possibly carry on seeing him, knowing what you know. He's dangerous, Megan."

"I know that. But you can't just stop seeing clients because you don't like what they tell you, or despise who and what they are. You have to go through a whole process – several more sessions – of closing off issues, building them up and then referring them to someone else. And who the hell would I refer him to? How could I send him to a colleague if I suspect he's still dangerous? And," she said, picking up a tile and tracing a finger over the letter, "what reason would I give him for terminating? I can't tell him that I'm actually already seeing a patient of his and have now found myself in a dual-role conflict – that compromises her confidentiality. He might well put two and two together and figure out who she is. It would put her in danger. And, anyway, you're not allowed to refuse to see a patient, even for good reason, if they say they're in crisis and need to continue treatment with you. That's clearly stated in the Code, and Wade, this bastard has read the regulations, I'm sure of it. He'd like nothing better than to report *me*, to bring a case against me and so discredit anything I may have to say in the future.

"And if I'm investigated for an ethical breach – not to mention the breaking and entering and info-theft – and get a verdict against me, I can get suspended or even permanently erased from the register. This is my job, Wade, the only way I know how to make a living. He's got me well and truly stuck, and I bet he knows it. I bet he's getting his rocks off on it!" She scooped up a handful of tiles and stuffed them into the little bag.

"Isn't there any way you could report him?"

"No one's going to take an anonymous letter or phone call seriously, if that's what you're thinking. Certainly not the Board – they have very set procedures for complaints – and not the hospital, who won't even want to hear about a case where they might be partly liable to future civil claims."

"The police?"

"You want me to make an anonymous tip-off about bad surgery to the SAPS? Are you kidding me?"

"There must be limits to the confidentiality thing, Megan, exceptions?" said Wade. He was beginning to sound as desperate as she felt.

"There are a few exceptions, but nothing that helps me in this situation." Megan picked up more tiles and dropped them, one by one, into the bag. "You can disclose confidential information if the client seriously intends committing suicide – fat chance with this narcissist – or if he intends clear harm to someone else."

"Well, there you are!"

"No, there I aren't. It has to be specific – you have to know who the intended victim is, what the perpetrator's definite plan is – how, when, where – so that you can alert that person, and the authorities, if necessary. It's not enough that you think he's hurt women in the past and your gut instinct and intuition tells you he'll do it again – sometime, to some unknown someone. And he is way, way too clever to tell me those sorts of details.

"No, the only way I could disclose info against him is if I'm compelled by law – subpoenaed or something, and even that's not a clear black and white situation. How do you get someone to subpoena you when you're not allowed to tell them who your client is or that there's something they ought to know about him? And if you do, if you have testified against a client and it's been smeared across every newspaper, radio, TV and social website (and it would be in this case, the gruesome details are just too salacious to ignore), how much do you think other existing or potential future clients will ever trust you? It's a bloody disaster."

Hiccupping into silence, Megan tipped the last of the letter tiles into the bag and yanked the drawstring closed. Wade stared at her with a horrified expression on his handsome face.

"I don't know what to say, Megan. It sounds like the most insane profession in the world. Like the inmates have written the code of conduct."

Megan just nodded. She felt exhausted, had no more energy – even for tears.

"So what do you think you'll do?"

"I'll have to see him. Have to," she shrugged. "I'll try to get him to spill details of what he's already done, just in case I am subpoenaed one day. And I'll try to trick or manipulate him into letting slip any plans he might have. And maybe, just maybe, I can try to fix him: do or say something that will make a difference, get him to stop. That's supposed to be the point of therapy, isn't it? To heal, to help, to fix?"

"Do you think you can fix this person?" Wade folded the board and placed it back in the box.

Megan shook her head slowly. "No, I don't. For one thing, he's got to be pretty disturbed and this is not my area of expertise. For another, I can't even confront him with what I know without breaking my other client's identity and confidentiality. I can't even reveal that I know *his* true identity. And I just don't know how I'm going to sit in that office, alone with him, and pretend to be all understanding and empathic and unconditionally accepting... Ugh," she said, remembering her debate with 'Tony Thomas' on that exact subject. How he must have laughed at her ridiculous idealism and naiveté.

"Just the thought of it makes me feel physically sick."

"Anything I can do?"

"Another hug would be really good," she said.

31

Confrontation

Megan looked at the man sitting across from her, noticed how he dodged questions, answered only indirectly, gave nothing away. She felt some sympathy for him; more, she felt empathy. She, too, would have liked to avoid and delay and sink into dreamy denial. Most of all, she would have liked to have run far away, to be lying on a beach somewhere, or safely strapped into an airbus headed for outer Mongolia, rather than sitting here, watching this man duck and dive her questions, and reject her interpretations.

But there would be no more escape for him than for her. "Wherever you go, that's where you are." Someone wise had once said it, the Buddha maybe, or perhaps Confucius. Megan knew it to be true. It was time to challenge and confront.

"Arthur … Art," she said, interrupting a complicated tapping ritual involving both his hands, the arms of the chair and the laces of his shined black shoes.

"You're here, presumably, to confront your problems, to deal with them, and that's not going to happen while you're avoiding the vital questions. So starting here and starting now, we're going to get to grips with this. And we're beginning with what you've most heavily avoided."

Art Smith looked up. There was anxiety in his gaze, but something more, too – the look of a small boy considering what would happen if he just decided to yank up the bedclothes and check precisely what lurked beneath his bed.

"I'm talking about your work, Art. What is it that you actually do? What were you doing in that ward?" She leaned forward a little in her chair, staring at him intently.

"I was seeing a patient." He fretfully rubbed at a temple with one hand, then duplicated the gesture identically on the other side.

"You said you weren't an OB-GYN."

She wanted to grab those hands, make him sit on them or something – anything to still their continual fluttering, tapping and picking. How could she ever have considered him potentially dangerous? He was clearly riddled with fear, rigid with anxiety, and suffering wretchedly.

"I'm not. I was seeing a patient who'd been operated on. Her cervix was… I'm… I'm a … an oncologist."

Megan slumped back. "An oncologist?"

"It's a cancer specialist."

"I know what an oncologist is, Art. What I don't understand is why you've been hiding it. Why you say it like you're confessing to being a serial killer."

"But that's what it feels like – like I'm a killer. They come and see me and then they die. Old and young, male and female, rich and … well, I don't see the poor – not here – but the rich and the not so rich. And all of them busy rotting alive on the inside!" He paused, seemed to consider what he had said for a moment, then continued, "And some on the outside – the melanomas."

Then Art Smith began to talk. Out it poured, all the toxic pain and horror that had been poisoning his heart and mind and soul. It was like she had lanced some purulent psychic boil. Once he began speaking, he seemed unable to stop describing his daily work: a grim merry-go-round of death and disease, of blackened lungs and corrupted bowels and cannibalistic blood. The wasted old gentleman riddled with metastases, the children whose brains hosted tumours like parasites, the women who would never bear children. The few who snatched remission – you could never say cure – against the odds; the many who signed up for treatment which left them ill, impaired, wearing wigs and padded bras and colostomy bags; those who died no matter what you did. And the families who remained – the shocked wives and husbands and children – grieving their lives around the gaping hole left by death. Worst of all – the parents – railing at God, the world, the doctors, themselves, at the sheer bloody unfairness of it all.

Megan let it wash over her, tried to let it not stick on her and failed. It felt like he was transmitting his personal and professional demons directly into her. Did they lose potency en route? That was the theory. "It's like passing a hot potato," one supervisor had told her years back, "they pass it to you in therapy, you pass it on in supervision, and so on. It gets cooler as it passes from self to self." It didn't feel that way now. She could see the line of the dead and soon-to-be-dead in her mind's eye as he described them: a never-ending queue of misery and defeat leavened with cruel hope. She preferred the words of her one-time therapy lecturer: "If they can live it, you can hear it." That, at least, was honest.

So she sat and heard about Art Smith's feelings of complete powerlessness against the monster called cancer, his fear that nothing he did made any difference. She helped him connect the dots between his increasing sense of helplessness at work and his futile attempts to control what could be controlled – the number of steps, the evenness of shoelaces, the straightness of cushions – in a vain attempt to gain some slim sense of mastery in his world and to distract from the voracious leviathan at the centre of his life which was beyond taming, beyond conquering.

At the end of the hour, she felt crushed, as if the cushions of cartilage between her vertebrae had been squeezed flat by the weight of Art's pain. Conversely, he left looking a little lighter; he even forgot to tap the door frame on his way out. Perhaps they had exchanged energies. She had no idea, as she sat, pressed into the stuffing of her couch, where she would find the energy to move, or the will to see the rest of the day's clients, especially Trotteur, who loomed like her own personal black cancer in the remains of the day.

By the time his appointment began, she still felt completely unprepared for what she would have to do, who she would have to pretend to be.

"So, where were we? Or should it be you asking that?" said the man she had known as Tony Thomas.

He sat in front of her, his lips twisted in amusement. How could she have thought that smile self-deprecating? It was not: it was arrogant and condescending. His charm was less than skin-deep, a mere trick of camouflage for the beast within. She was silenced, paralysed by the magnitude of what she knew about him. Playing for time to pull herself together, Megan opened his file and looked down at the top paper inside.

"Um, we spoke last time about conditional acceptance, and about your parents."

"Ah yes, which ones?" he said.

"There were more than one set of parents?"

One minute into the session and already he had her on the back foot. She was sure she had sketched a genogram in the first session, she always did. She rifled back through the notes with hands made clumsy by nervousness. The file slipped to the floor, the loose papers slid out and spread into a fan. In a moment, he was kneeling on the floor, gathering them up. She was sure that he was trying to read them as he placed them in a tidy pile and handed them to her. She took the papers from him, careful not to touch his hand.

"Are you okay, Megan? You seem a little flustered." He looked concerned, but she was no longer sure that anything about this man was genuine. The way the irises of his eyes, dark as aged port today, floated above his lower lids no longer intrigued her: now they merely looked creepy.

"Here it is," said Megan, looking down at the first session's notes: mother, father (both deceased), Tony – an only child, unmarried, no children of his own. It was as simple a genogram as you could get.

"I only have the one set of parents listed. What have I missed?"

"Oh, there were many parents, many homes – in addition to 'The Home'," he said, sketching quotation marks in the air around the phrase.

"The home?"

"Yes, I was a home-boy, removed from the custody of my parents at the ripe old age of four, and brought to a child welfare house with a housemother. No housefather: too much opportunity for hanky-panky with the on-site fledglings – a bunch of other little boy and girl rejects." It was the first time she had heard bitterness in his voice.

"You were abandoned there?"

"Oh yes, I was abandoned many times. If we were to *reframe* my childhood – that is what you call it, isn't it, your profession's brand of spin-doctoring (you see how I have done my reading like a good patient, Megan) – then we could say that I am an *expert* in the processes of abandonment and rejection." He rubbed at his chin where the faint silver line of a scar was just visible.

"How many foster parents did you have?"

This was information-seeking, not therapy. She would have to be careful, throw in the odd reflection or interpretation so he did not get suspicious.

"I stopped counting after five. It gets too fatiguing, you see: the desire, the hope, the determined, desperate faith struggling to exist in the face of real, lived experience. The hope that this time will be different, this time they'll want you. Then the honeymoon period when you're all they ever wanted, trying so hard to be what they want, trying to be *perfect*. The love, the affection, the acceptance, the mothering – *bliss!*"

His face wore an ecstatic smile. As she watched, it was wiped away by a grim expression which set his face in hard lines.

"And then the creeping disappointment with you as the reality of your imperfection sets in, the realisation that you're not a doll to play with, not malleable, not – somehow – quite right. And then, inevitably, the return-to-sender. And those were the good ones. The ones who wanted to keep you as a toy for their own pleasure – those were the truly bent ones, Megan, the ones you *wanted* to be taken away from.

"And all the while your file grows thicker with the reports on your imperfections: the little theft here, the experiment with the cat there, the unpredictable temper, the inability to keep friends, complaints that you're too moody, too strange, once even "too intelligent"! All the deficiencies and defects that make it impossible for you to be adopted or kept or loved."

Megan had no idea what to say. Compassion and empathy for the child he had been, warred with disgust and horror at the man he had become. Her therapist-self felt moved to help, her logical-self told her to stay detached, and to think carefully before she said anything.

At university, during her Master's degree, Megan and her nine fellow interns had been assigned an unsettling and difficult exercise which had challenged their preconceptions. Each intern had been asked to identify their own personal nightmare of a client: the type of person who would make their flesh crawl, their negative judgements rise, their empathy dissolve – the kind of person they would have to refer because they simply could not imagine working with him or her.

The nature of the invented "clients" had been revealing: an unrepentant paedophile (Megan's choice); a campus rapist (suggested by a young female intern); an ANC cabinet minister who beat his wife (the product of an older, white, male intern's fear); a lesbian couple contemplating adoption (a black, Christian male had suggested that one). As always, the imagined revealed the denied. At the time, Megan had wondered if the exercise was just one big projective test concocted by a nosey lecturer.

Each of them then had to volunteer to play one of the hypothetical clients, so that every intern got the opportunity to role-play a therapy session with the very client whom they could not ever envision counselling. Being the client was surprisingly easy; one person's bogeyman behind the door, it turned out, was another's dressing gown on the hook. Megan had had no problem in playing the lesbian who would be mother of the year, but she had been amazed that the men in the group were unfazed at the idea of playing the role of rapists. Perhaps it was not so surprising when she remembered that most standard personality tests could not pick up a statistically significant difference between rapists and "normal" men.

No one had much wanted to play the paedophile, but one young intern had eventually stepped up, sat in the chair opposite Megan and told her "his story". He described how he had himself been abused as a child, explained his deep need to belong in a world where he was a despised misfit, confessed his longing for a non-threatening kind of love. To her amazement, and a little to her horror, Megan had felt a growing understanding and empathy. He really was just like any other client: wounded and suffering, floundering about and using harmful ways of trying to ease or disguise the pain. She had found herself to be absolutely capable of counselling the unacceptable client.

The exercise had stood her in good stead in the years since. Amid the majority of truly good and likeable clients who instantly evoked her compassion and admiration, she still had to listen to the thankfully few clients who expressed vile feelings, confessed revolting or unspeakably stupid acts, expounded their indefensible ideologies and risible thoughts. And always, every single time, she had been able to connect to that deep inner swell of empathy which lifted her above petty judgements and into understanding.

She could allow that empathy now, even for this man. She could sympathise, understand, maybe even help. Or she could try to get more information out of him, attempt to entrap and thwart him – these, too, were impulses into which she could tap. She just was not sure that she could do both at once: be both his counsellor and his enemy, his therapist and his opponent. How do you do therapy with a man when your goal is no longer to aid, but to deceive and to trick him into his own downfall? Nothing she had ever learned, in theory or in practice, had prepared her for this.

32
Double agenda

Megan gave herself an inner shake and forced herself to focus on the repellent, and pathetic, man in front of her.

"So many rejections, so many abandonments," she said at last.

"Eventually we found a good fit, though – that's what they call it, 'fit'. As if they were trying on jeans, rather than children. Well, I suppose the whole process was a lot like child-shopping. Eventually, I was placed with a pair of older parents who left me alone much of the time and didn't want to know too much about what I was up to. Those are the parents in your little picture, Megan," he pointed at her notes. "A good fit: no pets, no other children, not too many expectations – those were requirements listed in my file by then."

"How old were you then?"

"I must have been twelve, because I remember my thirteenth birthday was with them. They gave me a microscope set as a present, and I got given a pack of modelling clay by my "uncle" Brian – he was a dodgy one, too."

"What do you mean?" Megan interrupted.

"It was terracotta clay, the sort that you could model and then leave out to dry so that it got hard. It felt so good between my fingers – soft and pliable and malleable. I could turn it into anything, anything! I could make it just how I wanted." His long fingers moved with the tactile memory of moulding, and he smiled at Megan. "I can still smell it, the clay," he said.

"Your uncle?" she prompted. "The dodgy one. What did he –"

"He's not the important part of what I'm trying to tell you, Megan!" he snapped. His face contorted briefly into a grimace and Megan watched, fascinated, as it rearranged itself into the usual benign expression within seconds.

"I'm trying to tell you about the modelling I did with the clay. Please pay attention. I began with making little figures of animals – cows and ducks and snakes, you know, that sort of thing. But soon I moved onto making human figurines. I was good, too."

"You were an artistic boy?"

"Anything but Artistic!" – again the momentary sneer – "No, I was *exact*. Precise and meticulous. And my little figures were models of accuracy. I read up on the ratios of the body and made sure my little people complied. Did you know, Megan, that the length of the inner arm between the wrist and the inner bend of the elbow is the same as the length of the foot, for example? No? Well, I did. So I made little mommies and little daddies and little kiddies and babies, and my picture-perfect families were in great demand, I can tell you."

"You finally had the perfect family."

He ignored this interpretation and continued animatedly, "I started selling them on the playground, and soon everybody wanted some. Well, the girls and their mothers, mostly. There was this craze at the time – printers' trays – do you remember them? People hung them on their walls and put all sorts of knick-knacks and miniature mementos in the little compartments. Well, everyone wanted my miniature people for their trays. They were excellently done, very detailed. They were even anatomically correct – under their clothing. What a shock the mothers would have got if they'd pulled down the little pants!'

Megan swallowed. "Did the boys want any?" she asked.

"Some did – they wanted little soldiers mostly. But not for show, they wanted them to play with. War games, cops and robbers, rubbish like that. They always wound up snapping heads and arms off. It made me angry."

"You didn't like their games? You didn't play with them?"

"Megan, if you're trying to assess whether I was socially integrated, there's no need to pry so subtly – just ask."

"Okay, then – did you have friends or were you a bit of a loner?"

"I was alone – not a 'loner', mark you – by choice. I've always been discriminating."

"Tony, what do you think you missed out on by not being part of a group of friends your own age?"

"Nothing, nothing at all. Those children were idiots, cretins – and I mean that word in the technical, psychological sense. They were far below me intellectually, and ignorant as pigs. When they weren't squealing on the playground, then they were clustered around the arcade games in the corner cafés. Space Invaders! Pacman!" he almost spat the words out, so deep was his contempt.

"Puerile idiocy. War and shoot-'em-up games which didn't even look real."

"You would have preferred that the violence was more realistic?" She needed to steer him to the subject of violence – violence and women.

"Naturally. Though the goals of the games – destruction and devastation – would still have been contemptible. It is so easy, Megan, to destroy and mar and damage. It is much harder to improve, to enhance and, ultimately, to perfect." He paused, looked down at his slender hands and seemed to be thinking for a few moments. "These days, of course, they have excellent computer games."

"You play computer games?"

"That surprises you, does it? It shouldn't. I've told you I like to make things functional and perfect. I started with the SIMS games when they came out, but there's such a range now. You can craft your own avatars, build a virtual second life with your own perfect people in lives of your own creation, under your own control."

"You like control, perfection."

"They are the only goals really worth pursuing!" He leaned forward and looked so animated that for a moment, Megan thought he would stand up, but then he settled himself back into the couch.

"I still have them, you know, the perfect ones – the ones that I made right."

"You've lost me."

"The figurines, the clay figures! I only ever sold the imperfect ones, the ones with flaws. The faultless ones I kept for myself – I still have them. And do you know the really funny thing? Those morons never even noticed that the ones they bought were inferior, substandard failures. They never even looked closely, just accepted the second-rate. Most people are like that." He shook his head in contemptuous disbelief.

"Do you think maybe they preferred them that way?"

"What do you mean?"

"Well, it's the oddities and the idiosyncrasies that separate great art from machine-made, mass-produced tat. We love, and therefore we value – or maybe it's the other way around: we value and therefore we love – the imperfection of a hand-carved mask, the deliberate fault in the hand-knotted Persian that makes it unique," she took a quick breath, "the mysterious beauty of the Mona Lisa's crooked smile."

"In my office I have a rather special copy of the Mona Lisa, Megan, which is truly beautiful – quite an improvement, really." This time his smile was unmistakably sly, almost as if he knew.

"An improved Mona Lisa?"

"Oh, yes. You'll have to come see it sometime, Megan."

Did he suspect that she already had?

"What's it like, Tony, valuing perfection so highly, believing that you were rejected because of your imperfections, and yet having to live in a world filled with the imperfect, the unfixable?"

He said nothing for several moments, merely rubbed at his chin and his mouth. Eventually, he said, 'One does what one can."

"How?" Would he take the bait?

"In one's little corner of the world, with the tools at one's disposal, one does what one can to make things a little more perfect." He said it in a way that made her realise she would get nothing further from him in what remained of the session.

33

Asking questions

Patience came into the office. She was wearing a caftan of dazzling purple and cerise, and carrying a cup of tea which she set down on Megan's desk. She eyed Megan intently.

"No more clients until 2 pm. Now it's time for tea."

"Is this rooibos?" asked Megan, pointing to the pale amber liquid.

"Yebo," said Patience.

"I don't drink rooibos."

"Expecting mothers must not have so much caffeine," said Patience. Ignoring Megan's 'tsk' of exasperation, she continued, "When is your next check-up with Dr Weinberg?"

"What do you mean?" Megan avoided meeting Patience's sharp gaze.

"I mean you must go see him again. Get him to check you out. To me, you don't look pregnant."

"I never told you I was!"

"Mn-mn-mn! If I knew only what I was told, then I would know less than a virgin on her wedding night. I'll make the appointment for you," she said and sailed magisterially out of the office.

Megan got up and closed the door behind Patience, hoping she would get the hint, then returned her attention to her computer and to the new cellphone lying on her desk. On the PC screen was the anonymous Gmail account which she had just set up for "Medical Research Services International", its inbox pristinely empty apart from the welcome messages from Google.

She had compiled a mailer, starting with an introductory spiel about MRSI having been commissioned to conduct a research project on women's experience of gynaecological surgery and subsequent psychological outcomes. Two thousand women around the country, it stated, had been randomly chosen from hospital records to participate in the survey. Their anonymity was guaranteed and they would be contributing to the development of women's health services by taking a few minutes to complete the questionnaire which followed below.

Here Megan had drafted questions asking if the participant had received gynaecological or obstetric surgery in the last year, and if so whether she had been satisfied with her experience. Did she feel any of the procedures had been unnecessary? Was she satisfied that she had given informed consent for every procedure? Had she had any negative, frightening or traumatic experiences in hospital? At the end of the questionnaire, Megan had included an open section for any comments that the participant might want to add, then, in bold capital letters – highlighted for good measure – had typed the instruction: PLEASE RETURN COMPLETED E-MAIL QUESTIONNAIRE TO SENDER'S E-MAIL ADDRESS BY USING THE 'REPLY' FEATURE. UNDER NO CIRCUMSTANCES SHOULD THE QUESTIONNAIRE BE SENT TO YOUR DOCTOR.

Then she had sent the mailer to every patient with an e-mail address on the lists she had copied from Trotteur's records. It had taken her the better part of a morning in which she had only two clients, but at least it felt as if she was doing something.

The new cellphone was a pay-as-you-go cheapie, possessing only the most basic functionality under its bling pink and silver casing. She checked the voicemail which she had set up with a message, recorded in her calmest and most encouraging voice, urging the caller to leave their name and contact details. "You have … no … new messages," the dulcet toned voice said. Megan was disappointed but not too surprised. It was only a day since she had put up the notice.

"Attention female patients: Have you been badly treated by your doctor? If you have been operated on without good reason, or had surgery done without your permission, or if you have been traumatised and left with pain, then please call me. I want to help you." At the bottom of the page, she had made a fringe of vertical cuts, and had written the new cellphone number sideways on each strip of paper. Back in her varsity days, they had used notices like this to advertise vac jobs, second-hand textbooks for sale, and invitations to raves. Now she was hoping that one or more of the women waiting in the chaos of disorganisation and desperation that was the OB-GYN unit at Johannesburg Central Government Hospital would read the notice, tear off a slip, and call her with more information that she could add to the thin dossier of evidence against Trotteur.

Talking to the nurses, trying to get something out of them, had proved the difficulty of her mission. They were no more interested in listening to her explanation and request than they were in listening to the pleas and cries of their patients.

At an intellectual level, Megan knew that the health workers at Jo'burg Central Hospital were burned out, leached of any impulses to compassion, any vestiges of the professionalism of their vocation, by a healthcare system which left them overwhelmed by the challenges, by the sheer bloody impossibility of providing a competent service to the needy millions, while thwarted at every turn by the impediments of bureaucracy, underfunding, corruption, inferior equipment and inadequate staffing.

She knew the apathy, callousness and cruelty were both products of and protections against the helplessness of the untenable, yet unchanging, working conditions. She knew that to walk these corridors, littered with bloodied sheets, to pass trolleys and cribs carrying the overflow of patients from overcrowded wards, to climb the six flights of stairs to the unit because the lifts were continually out of order, would sap the will and crush the spirit of anyone.

She knew – in theory she even understood – yet still she had been shocked at their attitude. Ahead of her, in the long queue at the nurses' station, had been a man still in his blue overalls, evidently hastily scrambled from his work to be with the woman, obviously in labour, who now leaned heavily on his arm. When he begged for her to be admitted, helped, given a bed, the three nurses sitting and chatting behind the counter had at first ignored him. Then one of the three, a male nurse, had said to him, "Can't you see we're very busy here? In addition, we are hungry and need to have our lunch. Where's our Kentucky, brother? When we are hungry, we can't deliver babies."

The man had gently lowered the woman to the floor where she sat panting, leaning against the pale green wall, then he had disappeared down the corridor, presumably in search of the deep-fried bribe.

Megan had been about to take her turn when she heard a groan from behind her. She turned and saw a girl, shockingly young and clutching a swollen abdomen, next in the line. Megan stepped back and allowed the girl to go first.

"Please," said the girl to the nurses who were studiously avoiding eye contact, "the baby is coming and it's too soon. And the pain-" She gasped as another contraction hunched her body over her belly. A whimper escaped between her clenched teeth.

"These girls," said one of the nurses to the others, rolling her eyes in contempt as she spoke. "These girls who can't keep their legs together. They come here and gasp and moan at us." She turned hard eyes to the girl and said, "You panted and screamed enough when you were making this baby. Now you must shut up. Here you are no one special. Go and sit."

"But my baby is coming and it's too soon, it won't live. You must stop the labour."

"Let it come. One less baby in this world is not such a bad thing. Go and sit." She shouted and motioned at the row of waiting patients and partners and squirming babies on one of the benches, and they shuffled up to make a small gap.

"And don't make my bench or my floor dirty with your mess. When you feel it coming, you must go sit on the toilet."

By the time Megan stepped up, she knew her quest was futile. At her enquiries about Dr Trotteur – how they found him as a doctor, whether they had any complaints – they had merely turned blank stares at her.

"What are you doing here? You think because you are white you can come ask questions and cause trouble?" said the male nurse.

"No! I just–"

"Just nothing! Go away. We don't work for you, *Madam*." They all laughed. Megan felt her face flame.

"No, I don't think you work for anyone. You don't work at all." She turned and walked away from the desk, stepping carefully between patients sitting on the dirty floor.

Out of sight of the nurses, she took the fringed notice from her bag and stuck it to an old, cork noticeboard on which were pinned cautions about AIDS, exhortations to abstain from sex and, incongruously, a large glossy poster of white, sandy beaches and palm trees, advertising a travel package to Mauritius departing in 1997. There were not enough drawing pins to hold the existing notices in place – some of them hung askew from a single pin – so Megan rummaged in her handbag and extracted a paperclip from the crumbs and fluff in the bottom of the lining. She bent it open, then used it to pin her appeal to the noticeboard.

A few of the women waiting on a broken bench opposite the board watched her with dull eyes, but nobody seemed interested enough to get up and read the notice. She was just leaving what was beginning to seem to her like one of Dante's seven rings of hell, when she heard a soft voice call, "Sisi." A small, thin, birdlike nurse stood in one of the corridors leading off her own, beckoning with a crooked finger. Megan walked towards her, curiosity surging.

"This way," whispered the nurse.

She clutched Megan's upper arm with a surprisingly firm grasp and steered her down the corridor. Bundles of soiled bedding and surgical scrubs were piled up against walls painted in the pale green of cheap primer. Megan was horrified. Perhaps her face showed what she was feeling, because the nurse continued a bit defensively, "The company that does the laundry has stopped. They say the hospital hasn't paid the bill."

She pulled Megan into an alcove off the corridor. Just then the lights went out, leaving the corridor dimly illumined by the weak light that fought its way through the grimy windows which looked out onto the inner walls of the three other faces of this tower block.

"Power failure Probably never paid that bill either."

"Are there generators?"

"Only for some of the operating theatres and ICUs, not for here. My name is Pumla."

"I'm Megan." They shook hands.

The nurse paused, checked the corridor and then spoke softly and quickly, "I heard you – asking the others about Dr Trotteur."

"Yes. Do you know him?"

"We all know him." Pumla's face was pinched with anxiety. Megan waited, holding the silence.

"He hurts the patients," Pumla said eventually.

"Hurts them how?" Megan asked.

Pumla did not reply.

"Please," said Megan. "He has hurt a woman I'm trying to help. I've found out that he has hurt many other women, done terrible things to them. I'm sure he must have done it here, too, to these poor women. We want to report him, to stop him, but we need witnesses."

"I can't testify, I won't be a witness," said Pumla quickly, looking alarmed. "But I will tell you this: he excises before he has results. Okay, in this place it can take weeks to get biopsy results, so he says he is playing it safe. He says they – the patients – might not return, might not have the opportunity for another operation. And that is maybe true, because there is a backlog for surgery, but still – the other doctors don't do it."

"What does he cut?"

"Their genitals. He removes the vulva, tightens the vagina, he does hysterectomies – too many. He does sterilisations but when you check the charts, there is no consent from the patients. And ... sometimes, when he delivers babies, he ... he uses the forceps very hard – I think he must damage the babies, one was bleeding from the ear afterwards. He never uses the suction cup, for the head, you know?"

Megan nodded.

"Sometimes he says anaesthetic is not needed and the women suffer. And twice, twice I have seen him pull the baby out. Once it was breech and he pulled it by the feet – and he put his foot against the woman like this," she braced her leg high against the wall and simulated yanking back forcefully, "and pulled – hard! That baby's hips were dislocated, and it is very hard on the mothers." She stepped out of the alcove for a moment, looked left and right, then stepped back to Megan.

"Don't any of the women complain – the patients, I mean?"

"What do they know? They are poor and ignorant, they believe what the doctor tells them. Besides, you have seen how it is here: no one will listen, even if she complains."

"Please, please won't you consider testifying?" pleaded Megan, but the nurse shook her head adamantly.

"No. He will get me fired. I have children to feed, a large family to support. I am the only breadwinner in my house. I cannot be unemployed."

"I understand," said Megan, and she did, but still, she was bitterly disappointed. "Here is my card. Please, call me if you think of anything else or if you change your mind."

"I won't change my mind. But I hope you catch him," said Pumla. She grasped Megan's hand tightly for a moment and whispered, "I will pray for you." Then she turned and walked rapidly away down the dimly lit corridor.

34

Breeding

"Last time we spoke about how you enjoyed making perfect figurine families."

"We did."

"Intact little families. Unlike your own... Perfect little families with perfect little children who weren't rejected or abandoned."

Tony rubbed at his chin, but did not respond. Well, she was no longer here to do therapy anyway, thought Megan, and changed tack.

"I wondered if you've ever wished you could perfect real people?"

"It's tempting, but hardly possible."

"Meaning?"

"I never told you, did I, what I do for a living?" said Tony with a slow smile.

This was something she was not supposed to know. Was he testing her, or simply getting ready to tell her?

"You said you're a photographer."

"I am a photographer – I like to create images. But what I do for a living is medicine."

"You're a doctor?" She tried to inject her voice with surprise.

"I am indeed."

"But, why did you never tell me?"

"I had to know I could trust you, Megan, that I could rely on your confidentiality, your ethics. Now that I know I can, I can tell you everything."

"Everything?" This might be the moment when he finally began to talk about what he had done.

"There's so much to learn about me, Megan. 'I contain multitudes'."

"Walt Whitman."

"Very good, I'm impressed. Do you know the full quote?"

"Isn't it something like: 'Do I contradict myself? Very well then, I contradict myself. I contain multitudes'."

"'I am large. I contain multitudes'," he corrected, "from his 'Song of Myself'."

"Are you large? Tell me about your multitudes. The song of you."

He paused for a long moment, looking at the afternoon light streaming through her window, playing off the glass paperweight on the desk. "There's so much to learn about me, Megan," he repeated. "For example, don't you want to know where I work?" *Was* he fishing to see what she knew?

"Yes – of course."

"Here, Megan. I work right here at Acacia."

"Goodness! It's amazing that we've never bumped into each other or cross-referred. I didn't even know that there was a Dr Thomas working here." Two could play this game.

"Ah … time for another confession." Megan raised an interrogatory eyebrow.

"I only told you part of my name."

"What?" Megan tried to force as much astonishment into her voice as she could.

"My name *is* Tony Thomas." He reached into a pocket and extracted a business card case. "But my full name is–"

Megan took the card he handed her and read the name aloud as though she had never heard it before. "Anthony Thomas Trotter?" She deliberately mispronounced his surname as she thought most people would on first saying it.

"Not trotter!" His nostrils flared slightly and she saw his hand clench on the arm of the sofa. "That's a pig's name. It's Trotteur. It's from the old French word *trotier*, meaning a messenger."

"And are you? A messenger?"

"Nominative determinism, now? I thought you believed in free will."

Megan ignored this. Looking up from the note she had just made, she said, "We need to get your personal details form updated when you leave. Tell me, was there a reason why you didn't use your real name?"

"My *full* name," he corrected.

"Your full name. A reason why you didn't want me to know who you actually are?"

"Think I'm paranoid, do you? You know what the bumper sticker says: just because you're paranoid doesn't mean they aren't out to get you!" He laughed uproariously.

"Why would they be out to get you – have you done something wrong?"

"That was a joke, Megan. I think they must have cut your sense of humour gland out of you when they trained you. Did it used to be here?" He tapped his own left cheekbone, while staring at the dent on hers. "Is that what caused the depression in your cheek?"

She waited, but he said nothing further, just looked at her with that infuriating faint smile twisting his lips. She read his card again.

"So, you're an obstetrician-gynaecologist. That surpises me. I would have thought plastic surgery would be the chosen field for someone who values perfection as much as you do."

"You are so perceptive, Megan. But one can maximise the odds of the perfect offspring being born by taken the best care of the brood mare, you know. Make sure that mothers have only the babies they want and will keep and take proper care of."

Brood mare! His misogyny was staggering.

"Though I did actually start specialising in plastic surgery – I had a full scholarship for academic excellence and underprivileged origins (the poor little foster child thing was useful for something, you see) – so I could afford to specialise. But I found plastic surgery limiting. I could only improve appearance, seldom function. And plastic surgery only changes the surface appearance, you know, it doesn't go deep inside, where I longed to be."

"You longed to work inside people? Do surgery?"

"It upset me, I admit, that a perfect face, or a face capable of being made perfect, could sit atop someone imperfect on the inside. Dirty and rotten. So, no, ultimately I decided against plastic surgery. Besides, so many people were so ugly and deformed that they would never be flawless anyway. Many were damaged by their genes, their incubation and births. There are some people, Megan," he looked at her intently, as if he really wanted her to understand this, "who simply ought not to breed."

"Tony, do you really seriously believe what you're saying?"

"Quite. There is enough ugliness in the world. We should be eliminating it, not adding to it."

"But to prevent people from 'breeding', as you call it, on the basis of something as superficial as appearance!"

"Oh, you're wrong there, Megan. It's not superficial at all. Oddities of appearance are often the outward benign congenital anomalies which are correlated with serious, deeper pathology. The same genetic mutations, or teratogens or abnormal development processes which lead to deformities of appearance also cause deformities of development and function. Witness the hooded eyes and webbed fingers of the Mongol, the flattened lip of the foetal alcohol syndrome baby, the haemangiomas and furrowed tongues of the schizophrenic, the sandal-gap toes, facial asymmetry and increased distance between the eye sockets of the autistic." There was an almost zealous glitter in his dark eyes and he spoke rapidly and passionately.

"You think these people should not be born," said Megan trying, and failing, to keep the revulsion out of her voice.

"What is their purpose? What do such sub-normals contribute to the improvement of form and function in this world – answer me that."

"You speak, Tony, like a disciple of eugenics. The logical extension of your beliefs are programmes of racial hygiene and ethnic cleansing, the horrors of Nazism."

"They knew a thing or two, those men. They spoke the truths that we in this politically correct age are too cowardly to voice."

Megan was speechless, she felt her face must reveal the disgust she was feeling.

"Oh, I've shocked you again." He gave a small giggle. "But this time I'm only kidding – trying to rattle your cage. I've been playing devil's advocate because you know how I like a good debate, Megan. I don't really believe all that perfect specimen nonsense, you know." He waved a dismissive hand. She must have looked dubious, because he continued, "I don't! I'm a doctor for God's sake. I have the stethoscope and Hippocratic Oath to prove it. Honestly – would I work at helping and healing if I really thought that way?"

"No, that's true. Your work wouldn't be that of helping and healing. It would be something very different indeed."

The look he flashed at her was alert, perhaps even suspicious. She would show her hand if she asked again if he had ever tried making real people perfect. She saw, now, that they would dance about the truth interminably, that she would never get any real facts out of him while his guard was up. Perhaps if his guard was down, though…

"I have an idea, Tony, something I want to suggest to you. For our next session."

"Oh, yes?"

"We've explored, a little, how your early experiences of being abandoned, abused and rejected might be the root of your issues."

"My *issues*?"

"Your anger and your unrealistic expectations, Tony. That *is* why you came to see me, isn't it?"

"Oh yes, of course. Why else?"

"I've often dealt with clients who have rage: old and deep-seated. And I find that the conventional approach of "talk therapy" is of limited benefit. It brings about understanding and insight in the rational mind, of course, but no real release or change – because the heart and the mind are not one. The conscious mind trundles along nicely in therapy, but the subconscious holds onto its primal fear and rage. Talk therapy doesn't touch the core," Megan touched her solar plexus with a hand, "the primitive emotions, the damaged inner child."

"What are you proposing?"

"How would you feel about a session of hypnosis?" She had hardly finished the sentence before he started laughing derisively.

"Hear me out," she said. "We could use it as a way to reclaim, re-parent and heal that abandoned, wounded inner child, that rejected little boy inside who thinks perfection is a precondition for love and acceptance, that poor little home-boy." She noticed that he was rubbing his chin again, his fingers feeling along the almost invisible silver line.

"Or, if you prefer, we could use the trance state to do some work with rage-containment and safe, controlled release of pain for the wounded part of you who is angry at himself for being contemptibly less than perfect, and enraged with the imperfect, rejecting world?"

He paused for a moment and seemed to be studying her carefully, assessing something.

"Which?" he said. "The hurt child or the angry man?"

"Either. Both," she shrugged. "We can see what your subconscious wants us to do, and go along with that."

"It's an interesting idea, Megan, I can't say it doesn't intrigue me a little. But," he shook his head, "it won't work. You'd never be able to hypnotise me. *I* wouldn't go into a trance. That only works on those with a weak will and inferior mind-power."

"You're probably right," said Megan.

She thought carefully about her next words, tailoring her usual double-bind to fit his views on "sub-normals" and "mind-power".

"Although the only folks who tend to struggle to achieve trance are those who have rather dull imaginations or lower, concrete intelligence. They're too limited: they can't achieve the necessary levels of abstract thought, can't work with the symbolism of the subconscious mind. And those with attention deficit problems, of course – they can't sit still or concentrate long enough to succeed in attaining the alpha brainwave state." She leaned forward slightly towards him and gave a conspiratorial smile.

"But at the very least you'd have a wonderfully relaxing session in which you learned the process of progressive relaxation. That, in itself, is a great technique that you can use to reduce stress and manage anger in your day-to-day life."

He looked at her for a long moment, the dark, floating irises of his eyes unreadable. "I suppose it might be revealing. Okay then, let's do it!"

35

Yea and nay

It had been a really long and a really bad day – possibly the worst of her life, thought Megan as she flung her handbag aside, kicked off her shoes, put the tall glass of wine on her bedside table and flopped onto the bed. Oedipus immediately leapt up beside her and licked her face until she buried it in the pillow. He turned his attentions to her feet, licking squelchily between her toes with his warm tongue; it felt both revolting and oddly comforting.

The day had started well with two relatively easy sessions with long-term clients. When she checked the new cellphone, she was delighted to find a text message from Pumla Phahlane. She had reconsidered and would be willing to submit a statement about what she had witnessed of Trotteur's brutal and abusive practices at Johannesburg Central Hospital. There was more good news waiting in her Gmail inbox: a returned questionnaire to the fake survey intimating complaints about the doctor. Then, mid-morning, an elated Alta Cronjé had arrived for her appointment. She was smiling broadly and in her hand she waved a piece of paper like a medal of triumph.

She had hardly taken her seat in the consulting room before she was telling Megan all about it. It was a letter from the Health Professions Council – a response to the complaint that she, with Megan's help, had written and sent to the Medical Board. It confirmed that they had received her letter, had logged the complaint and would be scheduling a hearing to deal with the matter.

"They say that they'll 'treat the matter as expeditiously as possible, given the extremely serious nature of the allegations'!" said Alta, reading aloud from the letter. "They'll notify me and 'the accused' – *lekker* ring to it, hey? – 'the *accuuused*' as soon as they've set a date."

"That's such good news, Alta. How are you feeling?"

"Great! It's finally happening, you know? It's coming to an end and then all this will be over and I can just rest and be peaceful. It's going to feel so good to stop him, too. To make sure he gets what he deserves. Bu-ut," she drew out the word, and the smile widened still further, "that's not all my good news."

"There's more?'

"Ja – can you guess? No? I'm pushing *poep*!"

"You're–?"

"I'm preggers! Preggers! Me and Johan are so happy – he's over the moon."

"Congratulations! May I give you a hug?"

"*Ja*, of course," said Alta and they embraced in a tight squeeze. There seemed to be a lot of unsaid things in the hug, and both had bright eyes when they sat back down.

Megan had wanted to tell Alta that she, too, was pregnant, but the sharing of that kind of personal news and the fact that she would be away from the practice for several months had to be communicated to clients very carefully. Some took affront and felt abandoned, others seized on the opportunity to divert therapy from their own difficult issues and focused instead on the therapist, some began to resist deep work in anticipation of the day when she would not be there to see them. For all these reasons, she was planning to tell clients only much later, perhaps around the five- or six-month mark when hiding the pregnancy would become difficult anyway.

Alta's delight and Megan's joy for her made what happened later in the morning that much more unreal and painful.

Megan had gone for her scheduled appointment with Dr Weinberg, but looking around at the burgeoning bodies of the other women in the waiting room, she still did not feel like she belonged. When Weinberg asked how she was, Megan replied honestly.

"I feel fine – I don't even feel nauseous anymore. But I also don't feel pregnant."

"Would you like me to show you?" Weinberg asked, smiling in the knowing and gentle way of those whose daily work involved miracles invisible to the naked eye.

"Yes! Please."

She had gone through the ritual undressing in the examination room and then Weinberg, accompanied by his ever-smiling nurse, had entered, dimmed the light to reduce the glare on the ultrasound screen and started the scan.

"It will need to be an internal ultrasound, I'm afraid," said Weinberg, slipping a condom over a phallic-shaped probe and knotting it so that it wouldn't slip off. "An external ultrasound this early wouldn't give a very good picture. Now just relax – there you are, in just a moment you'll see the little foetus and the tiny heart beating away, and then you'll be convinced that it's real."

Dr Weinberg had wiggled the probe this way and that, fiddled with the controls on the machine and its monitor, and subsided into ominous quiet. Behind him, also staring at the screen, the nurse cleared her throat but said nothing. She was no longer smiling.

What's wrong? Where's the heartbeat? Why aren't you saying anything? Megan wanted to shout her terror at him, but she did not want to hear his response, his confirmation of what she already knew – something must be very wrong.

Weinberg had sent her to the radiology department for a scan, explaining that their machines were more sensitive and powerful than his. Clutching the referral note, she had wandered down into the bowels of Acacia Clinic to the busy radiology department, filled out the ubiquitous forms and been given a glass along with a large jug filled with water.

"Drink it all, fast as you can without making yourself sick. Do not go to the loo – we need a full bladder to get the best image," the assistant behind the counter said. Megan focused on the way the woman's plucked, arched eyebrows moved as she spoke; it helped her not to think. Then she took the only available seat in the waiting area, between a man coughing relentlessly and a grey-faced teenage boy clutching a wrist which was bent at an odd angle, and tried not to think about what was happening. She drank glass after glass of water while she stared at a sign which said, "NB!!!! If you are pregnant, please inform the radiologist and/or technician!"

Her bladder was close to bursting when her name was eventually called. Again the darkened room, again the probe – doubly uncomfortable now because of her full bladder, again nothing pulsing in the image on the screen. The radiographer said nothing, except, as she left the room, "I'm sorry. I'll do your report straight away and you can take it back to Dr Weinberg."

"It's a molar pregnancy, I'm afraid – or a blighted ovum, in old language," Weinberg had said, his face grave and his voice grim. It was not a viable pregnancy, he explained, it would not have gone much longer without a spontaneous abortion occurring – that was what he called it, "a spontaneous abortion". It had just fooled her body into thinking she was pregnant so that hCG hormones were secreted and she had experienced some of the symptoms.

"It's important that we evacuate the uterus completely. Any uncontrolled growth is not desirable and we don't want to take a risk of a hydatidiform tumour developing. We need to do it as soon as possible. That means tomorrow, I'm afraid, otherwise my next surgery is next Wednesday and that's leaving it longer than I would like."

The words washed over Megan: *blighted, not viable, fooled, evacuate, tumour. Tomorrow*. She felt dazed, numb with shock. Her puzzled brain seemed to be working very slowly – at complete odds with her racing heart. All she could take in was that she was not pregnant – maybe never had been properly – and that she had to have surgery.

"My nurse, Gwen, will give you all the information you need," Dr Weinberg said, handing her over to his nurse. "Mrs Wright needs a D&C, let's do it first thing tomorrow. You'll need to move Mrs Cele down the list. Tell Mrs Wright when and where to report tomorrow, please, then call down to confirm the theatre is booked and get her name onto the surgery board."

Only one word of this penetrated the dull fog which enveloped Megan. "I'm not Mrs," she said to the nurse. It seemed important to get this right.

"I understand. Is there someone I can call to come fetch you, now?"

"What? No, no, I … I have to go back to my office and get organised. I need to cancel my clients for tomorrow. They won't be able to come now."

"I suggest you cancel them for a good week. Give yourself time to recover, dear, physically and emotionally you're going to take bit of a bruising. Here is the information you'll need. Don't forget to get someone to collect you afterwards – tomorrow, I mean. You won't be in a fit state to drive yourself home."

Back at her office, dry-eyed but trembling, she had told Patience everything. It was only when the woman wordlessly hugged her tightly against her massive bosom that Megan felt the tears and the wracking sobs come.

Patience would organise the practice, cancel all the clients for the next ten days, but there were calls which Megan needed to make herself. She went to the bathroom, fixed her make-up, and debated whom to call first. She needed to tell Mike – she could not let herself think how he would respond – and Wade, and her family. Her family! She could not face her mother and Cayley, would not be able to get through the single therapy session that remained that day, due to start in half an hour's time, if she had to speak to them. She would call Wade, tell him no sympathy was permitted yet – it would only send her off again, and there would be time enough for tea and tears afterwards. After tomorrow. She would ask him to call her family, tell them not to call her until tonight.

She must get through this last session – she just had to. She had prepared so carefully for it, scripted almost every word of the hypnosis induction she intended using on Trotteur. Bugger reparenting the inner child. If she was going to be away for a while, it was even more important, somehow, that she try to stop him from hurting more women. She had no idea if it would work, but she wanted to try. She needed to feel effective at something.

She did a quick visualisation exercise on herself. She imagined packing the fact of the blighted pregnancy, and all the grief and fear that went with it, into an old-fashioned trunk, which she locked closed and then stowed on a shelf labelled "Later". She focused on clearing her mind, then reoriented herself to the present and opened her eyes.

She steeled her expression to show only friendliness before asking Patience to send Trotteur into the office. Once he had greeted her and sat down, she pulled out the small footstool she kept for the purpose and slid it under his feet, then she began.

36

Monster

"There you are, that will help you be more comfortable and relaxed."

She was already beginning to seed her talk with words that would prepare Trotteur for trance. She would repeat them as often as she could without arousing his suspicion.

"How about you pop one of those cushions behind your head so your neck can *relax*. That's right – all *comfortable* now?" She put the slightest stress on the words so that the emphasis would be discernible only to the subconscious mind.

He smirked and said, "Is this when you dangle a pendulum in front of my eyes?"

"Oh no, I've never been *comfortable* with that method. It's not so *ease*-y, you know." This time, she spoke the words she wanted him to register subconsciously just a little more slowly. "Perhaps, though, you might allow yourself to stare at a spot on the ceiling … that's right."

"Now, Tony, I'm not at all sure that you'll be able to *relax fully and go into trance*." Already, she was beginning with the subliminal suggestions. "As you told me last time, you don't think anyone would be able to make you *go into trance*. And so you may allow yourself to *relax now and go into a deep trance* or perhaps you will prevent yourself from *relax*ing and just sinking into a *comfortable* state. Whatever is best – that's what you'll decide."

She guided him through the fixed-eye induction which she normally used, and at the usual point, his eyes closed. This was no guarantee that he was in trance, though, he might be faking or just relaxing. She then went through several deepeners, the last of which walked him down an imagined flight of stairs with suggestions to relax more deeply on each step.

"… and now step down to seven, deeper and deeper, more and more relaxed … soon you may find that your breathing slows right down. As you breathe in, deeply," she timed the words so that they matched his own inhaled breath, "think about breathing in *rest* and calm and *relax*ation. And allow that to spread through your body and mind. And as you exhale," again, she matched the words to his action, "think about breathing out stress and letting go of all worry and all distractions … down to six … more and more and more relaxed, all the way down…"

Her voice was slow and hypnotically ponderous now – the sort of voice which would surely make a conscious Trotteur laugh in ridicule, but he merely breathed deeply. His face looked blank and relaxed. "Five … and if any distracting sounds or thoughts come into your mind, just notice them, don't engage with them, just let them pass through and drift off and away, just *drift off and away*."

Megan took her time with the induction, using repetition and soothing imagery to install what she hoped was the deepest possible trance. She studied him carefully. It *looked* like he was in trance. He was slumped deeply in the couch cushions and he sat perfectly still, breathing slowly and deeply, the long fingers of his hands limp in his lap. Body paralysis was one of the markers of hypnosis – nobody sat that still when actually awake – but, still, he might be faking to see what she was up to.

She did not dare test his depth of trance as she usually did with clients – by telling them that they were so deeply relaxed that they couldn't open their eyes and then asking them to check whether they could. She was afraid such a direct method might alert his conscious mind, make him mindful of the fact that he was in trance (if indeed he was), and that he would then take it as a challenge to wake himself up. For the same reason, she would not be able to use direct methods or express suggestions that he stop harming women.

He might be in trance, but he was not unconscious or

asleep, and his conscious mind would hear any suggestion that blatant and would start resisting, or waking him up. Moreover, if he caught on to what she was doing, he would immediately know that she had been doing more serious investigating and that she now knew all about him, was possibly amassing evidence against him. That was something she did not want him to know until the Board hearing. She would need to be as subtle and imperceptible as she could to plant her suggestions.

"So as you relax and just enjoy this sensation of feeling so calm and so *deeply relaxed*, I would like to tell you a story: a story about a hero who slayed the Anger Monster. Would it be okay for me to tell you the story? You can just answer 'yes' or 'no'."

For a few moments Trotteur said nothing. Megan's mind raced. She wondered if he was thinking it through, looking for the catch, or if he was trying to work out how he would respond if he truly was in trance. Or, was this in fact the typical delayed response of true deep trance?

"Yes." The word was spoken softly, with the bare minimum of lip movement. His voice sounded as if it was coming from a long way away. It certainly looked like trance.

"Well, this story starts with a forest – a deep ancient forest – dark with the shade of old trees," Megan began, using the sing-song, slightly monotonous voice of hypnosis, placing an emphasis of tone or timing or volume on the words she wanted to implant at a subliminal level. "I wonder if you could see the forest in your mind's eye. And when you can see this ancient, primal, dark place, please let one of the fingers on your right hand lift and lower so that I know."

Again there was a pause, then with an almost imperceptible twitch, the index finger on his right hand rose a few millimetres and then a few more, in small spasmodic movements. Megan was convinced. Trotteur, she was sure, was in a deep trance.

"Okay, that's excellent, now just relax and sleep deeply and perhaps you might find yourself moving into that forest as I tell you this story..."

In Freudian and Jungian symbolism, the forest was often a metaphor for the primal feminine; it was something, Megan thought, to do with pubic hairs being like trees and the shade representing the unknowable and slightly sinister mysteries of womanhood as perceived by the old analysts. Normally, Megan did not set much store by such psychoanalytic symbols and meanings, but today she was willing to try anything and everything. Besides, it was pretty certain that his hatred of women was related at least in part to the abandonment and rejection by his mother and subsequent mother figures. Why was it that it was always the mothers who were blamed? The distracting thought twitched at her thoughts, but she forced it to "drift off and away"; this induction needed to work at many levels and she needed to keep her concentration.

It seemed fitting to return Trotteur, symbolically, to the core mother, in the form of the unconscious archetype of the crone. The symbolism would not stop there. Trotteur used a knife of sorts – his scalpel – violently to cut and mutilate women. A Freudian would say this represented a sexual violation of the women, a symbolic rape: the knife being the phallic symbol which penetrated their genitals. Megan also planned to tap into Arthurian legend – she thought Trotteur would fancy himself as king – and she could use the associations of trees in gardens, of forbidden fruit. Layers upon layers *within* layers of messages – enough to confuse and bypass conscious controls and unconscious defences, the commands hidden inside permissive and tentative language, the suggestions designed to register only in the subconscious mind. She looked down at the carefully prepared and meticulously worded hypnotic script she had written and continued.

"Now, Tony, perhaps you can just *relax* and *listen to me* as I tell you about our hero, a powerful, intelligent man, who penetrates the thicket of forest, going deeper and deeper on his important quest. There is a monster, you see, which threatens him and his village. An angry monster which breathes fire when crossed or threatened. The whole community is at risk of being destroyed by the angry monster's actions, but especially the women, who have such tender skin that they are more easily burnt, and the monster seems to prefer breathing his fire on them."

Had that been a tiny twitch at the corner of Trotteur's mouth? Go slowly, deeply and *very* carefully; this time the instruction was to herself. Just then, the universe sent her a gift, the helicopter ambulance flew over the hospital and landed on the helipad beyond the car park. The noise was considerable, but Trotteur did not stir a muscle. There was no way that he was not in trance. It was time to get to the heart of her script.

"So the hero walked along a path laid down years and years and years ago. A path which lead into the heart of the forest, to the deepest place inside, and there he found a witch. Some in the village said she was a wise woman, and a healer, and many came to talk to her when their hearts were burdened."

If Trotteur was not in as deep a trance as she hoped, then he ought to take this bait and feel more reassured that he could see through her metaphor. He would think that Megan had concocted a story in which she, the wise and healing therapist, was represented in the form of the witch who would send him to slay his own monstrous anger. He would think that it was one of those anger reduction techniques that she had said could be done in hypnosis, and he would be right. At one level, this was exactly what she was doing. Heaven knew the man could do with a reduction in his rage, but her real message would be more craftily and subtly implanted.

"The hero asked the witch, 'How must I slay this monster of anger that threatens all? I am but a man, yet the monster is fierce and hot and may destroy me.' The witch replied, 'There is a way, but *you must listen to me* very, very carefully. *You must do as I say* down to the last instruction; if you don't *obey me*, then you will be destroyed by the monster.' The hero took up the challenge. 'I will do it,' he said. And the witch said: 'At the end of the forest, just before where the world ends or begins...'" Megan inserted one of the confusing nonsense phrases that muddled the conscious mind, and engaged it in trying to figure out what was meant, leaving the subconscious mind more free to listen to the subliminal suggestion which she was now about to embed, by emphasising only certain words in her script.

"… 'there is a tree that the patient women, one after another, have planted to harvest its fruit which they love. Stuck in the base of that tree, which is called the patient tree – after the patient women who planted and tend it – in the place where new life begins, is a blade, a sword of great power. You must pull that sword out, do you hear me? *You must pull out the blade from the patient women's* tree, and *never put it back, never put the blade back into* the fruit or the tree of *a patient* woman. When you have slain the monster, *you must* bring the blade back and *lay the blade down safely* next to the tree,' the witch told him. 'I understand,' said the hero. 'I hope so,' said the witch. 'It is important that you remember this instruction in the deepest parts of you so that even when you have forgotten, which you will, *you will remember* this order: *you can pull the blade out but you cannot put it in,* or something terrible will happen to you. *If you try to cut* the tree or the fruit of *a patient* woman, then you will find you cannot or *something terrible will happen*. When we wound others, we wound ourselves – it is the eternal way,' the witch told him and she spoke the truth. Then she told him to take the magic sword and find the anger monster and slay it."

Tony lay immobile against the cushions, but the second hand of the clock on the wall behind him moved relentlessly on. She needed to move more quickly.

"So just stay deeply relaxed, Tony, deeper and deeper with each breath that you inhale … and exhale … as you focus on that hero who walked deeper into the forest, right to the edge of the trees. And there, just before the place where the world ended and the nothing began, he saw the tree. It did not look like anything special to him, but he was not there to see the tree: he was here to claim the blade of majesty and power. He saw the sword stuck deeply into the base of the tree, where all life comes from. He grabbed it and pulled it out. It came out smoothly and easily. It was smaller and plainer than he had imagined, hardly bigger than his hand, with a steel handle and a wickedly sharp blade." Megan was trying to conjure the image of a scalpel, without mentioning the name of the thing.

"He looked up at the tree. It was not beautiful enough, the branches were not perfectly symmetrical, the arrangement of flowers did not please his eye, parts of the trunk were too thick, or scarred by knotholes or disease. He thought he could improve that tree, prune it into better shape, he thought he knew best. So he picked up the blade to make a cut, was about to plunge it into the tree, when the words of the wise old crone came back to him. He remembered what she had told him: *You cannot cut the patient* tree because of the magic power in the blade. She explained it to him when she said, '*If you try to cut a patient* woman's tree or fruit, *something terrible will happen* to you.' So he remembered the words – it's very important to *remember those words* – and pulled back the blade. He ran quickly from the forest to the outskirts of the town where the anger monster was.

"And perhaps you can allow yourself to see it, Tony, just see that monster – so full of anger and rage, so old, it has been there for a long, long time. Can you tell me what it looks like?"

"… stitches … s'in Piggy…"

"It has stitches, well, well. And piggy, hmmm?" She had no idea what he meant and no time to explore it further.

"Well that is interesting, but stitches or no, something needs to happen to this monster to save the hero, and for the hero to save others in the village. What needs to happen, Tony?" It was rubbish, of course: primal rage could not be cured in a session by slaying a mythical symbolic monster. But it might help a little, and it would reassure Trotteur by giving him a clear memory of what they had done in the session. She would do her best to ensure it was all he remembered from the trance.

"… Must kill it."

"Yes, the anger monster needs to be destroyed. So the hero can now slay the monster with his magic blade and perhaps you join in. Maybe you may even find that you become the hero, *you are the hero* in this story, Tony."

It was important to make the connection for the subconscious and better to do it in this part of the story, where it would arouse less suspicion from a watchful conscious mind.

"Allow yourself to puncture the monster. Let the rage leak out like air from a balloon, and let it drift away into the air, until the monster falls – empty and limp and floppy – down to the ground; and you feel so good, so satisfied, you have triumphed in this quest."

She almost smiled at the imagery of turning the erect libidinal urge of the knife into an orgasm of violence against rage itself, and returning Trotteur to a post-priapic stage of replete satisfaction.

"And, Tony, you can remember this part of the story in the front of your mind, very well, clear as a bell as the bell knells in the village." More of the mind-distracting nonsense phrases. "The people are cheering, the anger is gone and you are feeling so proud and so good and it is time to return the knife to the dark forest where it belongs. So sleep, deeply. Keep going deeper as you just *relax* as you go *deeper and deeper* into the forest, walking the path you know well, back to the tree of the women. It's time to *put the blade down safely*, that's what the witch said he must do, or something terrible would happen, *put the blade down safely next to the patient* women's tree.

"So the hero walked," Megan was using 'you' and 'he' interchangeably now, deepening the association in Trotteur's subconscious mind, hoping that it would hear the instructions to the hero as orders to itself. "… walking slowly, feeling relaxed and relieved that the anger was gone, to the edge of the forest. And when he got to the women's tree, he began to *put the blade down safely* next to the tree. But then he saw one of the fruits of the tree. It looked so ripe and juicy and moist, he was so tempted to cut into its sweet flesh, to stick the knife in and carve it open and let the ruby red juices flow. So he picked up that beautiful gleaming knife, felt it in his hand, stronger than it looked, filled with power. He got excited at its power, at his power."

Megan snuck a glance at Trotteur's lap. Sure enough, she could see an erection straining against his trousers. Sick pervert! A part of her own mind registered that she seemed to have abandoned the ideal of non-judgemental, unconditional acceptance completely. She hoped it was just for this man.

"So he took that knife and made to cut into that delicious, tempting, imperfect flesh, but as he did so, *Tony*," – she called to his subconscious with the use of his name, signalling it to pay close attention to what followed – "something terrible happened. Let me tell you what happened."

Then Megan implanted the subliminal suggestion she had devised, and reinforced it with imagery and repetition. She finished by reiterating: "The tree and the fruit of the tree of the *patient women must not and cannot be hurt or cut* according to the magic of this place and the witch. Then, when he saw what he had done, he came to his senses and he *remember*-ed what the witch said he must do with the knife: that he must *put the blade down safely* beside the women's tree. And he did this, and all was well. And he left the forest. He had slain the anger monster, put down the sword and could now lead a peaceful and happy life, free from anger. He felt no need to return to the witch – he had no more need of her ear or her advice."

Megan hoped his subconscious would heed this suggestion, too, and that he would stay the hell away from her in future.

"Now there are parts of this story, about slaying the monster of anger that you can remember clearly in the top and front of your mind, but you can allow the other parts to sink deeply, so deeply into yourself that you can't consciously remember them and that's okay because your subconscious mind will remember them for you without any effort, so you can just let them sink down deeply now. And the subconscious will remember what the conscious mind has already forgotten."

Then Megan proceeded onto the reawakening and reorientation phase, first bringing him up to a lighter level of trance, encouraging him to begin to be aware of where he was and the sounds he could hear, and suggesting to him that it felt like he had been at this level of trance all the while. She made deliberately clear and direct suggestions that he would in future feel much less angry, and then she returned him to full wakefulness.

Trotteur stretched his long frame and yawned. "I must say I feel very relaxed," he said.

"That was the goal," she said and smiled at him. "I'll be on leave for the week or so, but–"

"Oh, are you going away?"

"… but Patience is already booking for after that, if you want to make another appointment on your way out. Else you can call when you feel you need an ear or some more advice." Which would be never, if the suggestion which she was now reminding his subconscious of, had taken effect.

"I do feel very good – like I've slain that anger monster," he winked at her, "but I don't think I was in trance, Megan, I can remember *everything*."

Megan's mouth went dry. The wink and his words could mean he had seen through it all. Or they might mean that he could only remember what he could remember – which felt to him like everything, but wasn't. There was no time to probe further: Trotteur was already moving out of the office. She squeezed in one last seeding.

"That's how it works, Tony. When you're in trance, you're not unconscious, and afterwards, you're not amnesic. You will remember what you need to remember."

He had left, waving three fingers in greeting, and she had sat, staring for long minutes into the ethereal heart of her dandelion paperweight, as though herself in trance.

Even now, hours later and lying on her bed, tickling Oedipus softly behind the ears, she had no idea whether it had worked. On balance, she thought probably not. It had been a long shot – post-hypnotic suggestions were notoriously unreliable, especially if they went against the grain of what the subject truly and deeply wanted to do. It normally took many sessions, direct and indirect suggestions, to plant complex command suggestions. Usually, when clients wanted to change long-held patterns of behaviour – smoking or overeating or panic reactions – she recorded hypnotic inductions for them and sent them home with the instruction to listen daily for at least fourteen days.

So she was doubtful about the possibility that one session of indirect and subliminal suggestions would alter Trotteur's behaviour. She may well have achieved nothing. Still, she had tried – done her best to stay his hand for the period before he had his hearing and while she was out of action – and she felt better for the effort. If she was honest with herself, perhaps this session had been more about herself than him. It had met her desire to feel she was doing something, and her need to distract herself from the grief which threatened to overwhelm her. Moreover, in the hypnosis session, she had done almost all the talking – which meant she did not have to listen to him, all the while faking empathy and hiding her revulsion.

Her cellphone rang from inside her handbag. More from habit than a wish to talk to anyone, she fished it out and looked at the caller display. It was Mike, finally returning the message she had left on his voicemail that morning, a message which had begged him to call back urgently.

So, there was still one more thing to do before this longest of bad days' work was done. She took a large gulp of wine, and answered the call.

37

Plotting

Something will have to be done. Something will have to be done, he thinks as he takes the entry logbook from the guard at the gatehouse. He ordinarily amuses himself by giving patently false names as a protest against the time-wasting uselessness of this "security" ritual. Since he started therapy, he has been working his way through the emotions. It pleases him that entry logs in office blocks and hospitals and gated communities have documented their visits from Mr RU Happy, Mr I.M. Sad, Mr B Cross. Who should he be today? Not Mr Happy. No, certainly not that. Perhaps Mr Disappointed, though that seems too mild a word for what he is feeling now.

Mr Calm and Relaxed: that is who he had been after the session with Megan – at least that part of the session had worked for him. He had really felt rather good as he made his way to the Gehenna that was Johannesburg Central Hospital's gynaecology and maternity unit – until the moment he had seen the notice. It stood out, new and virgin white against the old posters and yellowing notices on the board, the two slips which had been torn off like missing teeth in a uneven, mocking smile.

As he read it, a wave of ire washed away the lingering relaxed contentment. He ripped the notice off the board and crumpled it in his fist, looking around suspiciously at the staff and patients in the unit. Could this possibly be about him? He spun on his heel and stalked back to his car which was parked in the litter-strewn dark bowels of the hospital. There he sat for a moment, trying to calm himself. He loosened his collar which was a noose around his throat, and opened a window, but the rage rose through him and flowed hot into his hands. They clenched into fists and hammered again and again and again against the steering wheel. A short woman in too-tight shoes walking past the row of parked cars looked at him with a raised eyebrow. *Useless cretinous bitch*, he thought.

Then he screamed it out the window, "Useless cretinous bitch!"

It calmed him a little to see her jump with fright and start trotting in the direction of the lifts. He unfolded the paper, smoothing it flat with hands that were not entirely steady. He took out his phone, fiddled with the settings so that his number would be blocked, and dialled the number printed on the tear-off slips. The solicitous voice which invited him to leave his details gave no name, but immediately he recognised its tone and cadence. That voice, which this very afternoon had lulled him into relaxing and into listening to stories, now fanned the fury which was burning inside.

What did she know about him? Who had she been asking? What had she been saying? He needed to shut her up, so that no more treacherous little words could trickle out of that luscious mouth. He must stop the oozing and the seeping.

It had taken him the whole drive over to this wretched yuppie squatter camp to calm himself, to make the connection between the notice at the hospital and the reply to a survey on "the patient's experience of gynaecological services" which had been copied to his e-mail address by Miss Acron, one of his more beautiful and satisfied clients.

His hand is steady now as he waves it in spurious greeting to the guard who lifts the boom, and steers his car along the rows of nearly identical cluster houses, all built to some idiot's idea of a Tuscan village, all bizarrely out of place in the heart of the African Highveld. "Little boxes, little boxes, little boxes made of ticky-tacky, and they all look just the same". The refrain plays in his head.

He is certainly disappointed. She has gone down in his estimation, despite her fine eyes and burnished hair. Even as a therapist, he has no more respect for her. "Slay the anger monster" indeed! Did she really think he was stupid enough to fall for such puerile drivel? She is no better than some charlatan performer in a second-rate theatre. And he is no planted patsy in the audience, paid to play along with her silly games. Games that she has been trying to play inside his head while all the while she is plotting against him. How dare she?

What he needs to do is arrange a little something to get Miss Wright's focus back where it belongs – off of his affairs and squarely back on her own tawdry little life. In his experience, there is nothing like a personal crisis to help one prioritise, to bring home what really matters in life. But he will have to find out more about the interfering Miss Wright, more than the bare bones of information he has gleaned from the clinic's staff directory and the telephone book. What does she love, what would she hate to lose?

He drives slowly past a unit with a neglected front garden behind a palisade fence. The kikuyu lawn which comprises most of the front garden is looking parched in this late summer heat. A fat golden retriever is energetically digging up one of the few flowering shrubs. Perhaps it is digging for an old buried bone. These obsessions with things long buried...

Its size declares that the dog is greedy. Really, life could be quite serendipitous on occasion – tossing you the very opportunities you needed, like a hunk of meat to a hungry dog.

It is clear now what needs to be done. He leaves the complex and heads back for the clinic, whistling the tune from "Little Boxes". He must check his operating list for tomorrow because he wants to plan the day – he has some shopping to do before he returns here.

38

Soft as a breath

Megan looked down at the small pills cupped in her hand.

"Two? Are you sure?"

"Doctor's orders," said the nurse cheerfully, handing Megan a plastic cup of water. "Swallow this one and pop the other one under your tongue and just let it dissolve there. I know it's a difficult day for you, dear, but we'll try to get it over with as quick as we can. Now take your premeds."

Megan did as she was directed and lay back against the uncomfortable pillows of her bed. She was in what Wade had called the "nay" ward, along with three other women. Their faces, bare of make-up and jewellery, looked pale and vulnerable. One of the women, in the bed adjacent to hers, was asleep. The other two each had a man – husbands or partners – sitting beside them, talking softly and holding their hands. Megan stared down at her own hands – rings off, nails bare of polish, a white plastic bracelet labelled with her details fastened around one wrist. Mike had said he would catch the first plane out of Cape Town that morning, but he was not here yet. She had told her family and Wade to stay away until after the operation, thinking she would not be able to face them, but now she felt very alone.

The nurse came back a little while later, with two orderlies in tow. They lowered the backrest so that she lay horizontally on the wheeled bed and set off out of the ward down the corridor which led to the operating theatres. Megan stared up at the lights passing overhead, but this immediately brought Alta Cronjé's experience to mind and so she looked quickly down at the hospital gown she was wearing instead. The swift movement made her feel dizzy. She wondered if the premeds were kicking in.

The hospital gown was patterned with little bluebirds that reminded her of the Twitter bird. "What's happening?" the Twitter bird asked in its perpetual blue-framed box. What's happening is this, she should tweet now, I'm rolling along, rolling along with bluebirds on my boobs. No, she couldn't tweet that, couldn't tweet now – how absurd. The medicine must be making her loopy. And drowsy: her eyes wanted to close just as if she herself was going into a trance. She had to explain something to the orderly walking at her head.

"I'm not going into trance," the word came out *tance.* "I'm going to the theatre, but not for a play. For an operation. S'going to dilate and curett– … curat– … cure me. Doc Weinberg, not Doc Khumalo. S'a doctor, not a soccer player."

She was battling to speak, her tongue felt thick in her mouth and her head felt heavy and muddled. It was hard to focus her eyes, even on the little bluebirds, so she closed her eyes and floated for a bit.

Her eyes opened as she was lifted up and transferred to the operating table. She could see the blurry form of a green garbed man connecting her to various monitors which beeped and glowed as he switched them on. *So I'm alive then?* She wanted to joke, but what came out sounded like, "Live'en…"

"Oh, hello, Mrs Wright, you're awake? I'm Dr Matthee, your anaesthetist. I'm just getting you hooked up, so when the doctor comes we can send you straight to la-la land." A woman in scrubs with a green mask appeared at his side and handed him a folder which he consulted before continuing, "I see from your chart that you've never had any adverse responses to anaesthetic before – is that right?"

What she wanted to say was that she felt cold and wanted a nice duvet to cover her, but she did not try to respond: it seemed like too much effort to try to say the words. Her tongue seemed to be a long way away from her brain.

"Excellent, here he is now. We can begin. The doc will be down at the action end of things, and I'll be sitting behind you here, at the pretty end," said the anaesthetist, rubbing her cheeks with his warm hands. It felt nice. She allowed her eyes to close again.

"Oh – are you doing this surgery? I thought she was Weinberg's patient?"

"He had some minor emergency – a domestic crisis with a pet, I think, so when they asked for a substitute, I volunteered to help out. She's all mine, now. Aren't you, Megan?"

Megan's eyes opened wide. She stared up into the dark sherry-coloured eyes above the green mask which covered his mouth. She opened her mouth wide to scream, but only a muted gargle came out. She struggled to lift herself, but her body was heavy and leaden and would not obey her brain's commands. With all her might she tried to force out the words of protest as loudly and clearly as she could.

"No. Not him. Not my doc'r!"

"That's right," he said in a voice intended to reassure others even while it terrified her. "I'm not your usual doctor. But Dr Weinberg couldn't make it and so you'll be in my hands today. But there's no need to worry, I'll do a perfect job, I promise. You'll be as good as new – better actually!" He laughed. "Doctor knows best."

"He can't!" She had to make the nurse and anaesthetist understand, she had to stop this. "He's m'patient!"

"Oh dear, we are a little muddled from the premed, aren't we? You're *my* patient, Megan. Now be calm like a good girl while Dr Matthee sends you to sleep. Sister, you're blocking my light standing over there. Please move to the other side and give me some room over here... A bit further back, please... Thank you."

Megan tried to scream, but she could no longer find her lips on her face. His voice spoke again, from close by to where she screamed and sobbed inside the immobile lump that was her silent, unresponsive body.

"You can go ahead, Martin."

"Her BP seems a bit high, I'll have to keep a close eye on it here."

"Perfect. Sister, see if you can be of any assistance to Dr Matthee. I really have no need of your help."

Megan felt a faint touch at her right ear. Raising her impossibly heavy eyelids a fraction, she saw that he had pulled down his mask and was leaning over to her ear.

"Now I do like to send my ladies to sleep with a little message, Megan, and now it's time for *you* to listen to *my* words."

"Okay, Mrs Wright," came the loud voice from behind her, "you seem quite out of it already, but I'm going to count you down anyway, okay? I'll count backwards from 100 and you see how far you can go before you fall asleep."

She tried to focus her mind on the loud voice which was counting, tried desperately to shut out the dark whisper.

"One hundred ... ninety-nine..."

His whisper, right into her ear, was as soft as a breath, yet she heard it as clearly as if he had shouted it.

"... ninety-eight ... ninety-seven."

"I'm going to rip out your womb, Megan, because it's as rotten and useless as the rest of you."

"... ninety–".

39

Battle of words

The first thing she saw was a small, golden pyramid.

Megan blinked her eyes. Sitting on top of the cabinet beside the bed where she lay curled on her side was a triangular plastic box of stacked golden chocolate balls. There was a large tag attached, with something printed on it. She blinked again and focused her gaze on the writing. "Chocolate cures everything and is cheaper than therapy," it said.

"Hello, sweets. Are you back?"

Wade sat beside her bed, holding one of her hands in both of his. She could see she was in a small hospital room, private, from the looks of it.

"Oh Megs, I'm so, so sorry." Cayley was there, too. She leaned over Megan and scooped her up into a tight, bony hug. "It's so horrible for you."

Megan's eyes were hot with tears. There was an aching pain deep inside, but another, more urgent awareness intruded. Her heart was racing. She could feel it thudding in her chest. Something was wrong.

"What's wrong? What happened?"

"Don't you remember, sweets?" said Wade, his brows contracted over his hazel eyes.

"You lost the baby, Megs, I'm sorry. They had to do a D&C," said Cayley, now arranging the cushions more comfortably behind Megan's head and running a cool hand down her cheek.

"I know that," said Megan, pushing herself up onto her elbows. The haze was clearing from her thoughts now. "But what did he do? To me – what did he do to me?"

She pushed the bedclothes down and felt her belly, sliding her hands over it as if she could tell the damage wrought on the inside by running her hands over the outside.

"What did he do to me?" she pleaded, looking from one to the other of them.

"Are you feeling okay, Megs? Should I call a nurse?"

"Wade – stop talking. Get the chart out of there," Megan pointed to the wire basket at the foot of the bed, "and tell me what was done to me. Cayley, you need to take a look under the blankets and tell me what you see."

Cayley looked at her blankly for a few moments, and then said, "You want me to check out your vajayjay?"

"Just do it, dammit!"

Wade and Cayley exchanged a glance, but then Wade moved to get her chart and Cayley poked her head under the sheet.

"What can you see?" Megan demanded of them both.

"I'm no doctor," Wade began, "but from what I can figure out, they did something called a D&C, and your BP and temperature are fine."

"Cayley?"

Cayley pulled her head out. "Megs, really! You're wearing undies. Ugly ones. And a pad. What else am I supposed to be looking for?"

"Please, Cayley, I need to know that nothing was … cut."

"Okaayy," said Cayley slowly.

She disappeared below the sheet again. Megan reached her hands below the sheet and pulled her panties down. Wade turned his back on them both and furiously studied the medical chart.

"Okay," came Cayley's voice from under the sheet. "Today's vajayjay report: all seems normal in appearance on the outside. I have no information on the inside Satisfied?"

Megan was not reassured. "Wade, what else? Does the chart say anything else?"

Wade turned a few pages. "Honest, sweets, it's in code. I can't–"

"Give it here," said Megan, snatching the chart from his hold. She was trying to decipher the notes and figures when a nurse, with the doleful eyes and drooping lids of an old basset hound, came in the room.

"How are you feeling, Mrs Wright?"

"It's Miss. Miss Wright!" Megan snapped. Then she took a breath and tried to ask what she needed to know in a calmer voice.

"Please, can you just please tell me exactly what happened in the surgery with me?"

"It was a bit of a strange one," said the nurse, attaching a blood pressure cuff to Megan's arm.

"Why, what happened?"

"Well, first of all, Dr Weinberg was supposed to be operating, but he couldn't come. They say his dog was poisoned! Can you believe it? Then he was scared maybe someone wanted to break in to his house, and he didn't want to leave his wife and–"

"So Dr Trotteur operated?" Megan interrupted.

The blood pressure cuff inflated, signalled a reading to the monitor and then deflated again.

"He was supposed to, was all gloved up and he started, but then next thing he was bleeding all over the table and the floor. But not into you," the nurse assured Megan as she removed the cuff.

"*What*?"

"He cut himself. His hand must have slipped or something, but he cut his other arm. Quite badly, too, he needed many stitches. Then, of course, he couldn't do you, so they had to wait until Dr Maseko finished the surgery he was busy on, then he came and did your D&C."

"Is that all he did?"

"Yes – that's all you were scheduled for. It was just a bit of a delay, but everything went fine. Dr Maseko is perfectly competent, you know." She said the last part a bit fiercely.

"And I've still got my ... there was no hysterectomy or any other excisions?"

"No, why should there be?"

Cayley and the nurse were staring at her as if she was behaving very strangely, but Wade's concerned gaze told her he understood.

"How are you feeling," asked the nurse. "Any pain?"

"I'm fine," said Megan, exhaling a deep breath and feeling her shoulders slump in relief. "I'm fine." It was true, she was. Her plan had worked. It had come down to his words against hers, and hers had held. "But I'm very sore, I'll take something for the pain."

The nurse looked confused, but counted a couple of red and green capsules into a medicine cup and placed it on the bedside table.

"You'll be able to leave this afternoon – we just need Dr Maseko to check and release you." She made a note on the chart, dropped it into the wire basket at the base of the bed, and walked out of the room.

"Want to tell me what that was all about?" asked Cayley.

"Later," said Megan, nodding her chin in the direction of the doorway. Moira Wright was just coming in, stowing a cellphone away in her large, leather handbag.

Oh my dearest, my pretty little girl, how are you?" she leaned over to kiss Megan and enveloped her in a cloud of cloying, spicy perfume.

"Okay, I guess."

"My poor baby. Is there anything I can get you?"

Megan winced at the word "baby", shook her head.

"It's terrible for a mother to see her child suffering. You never stop being a mother, you know, even when your babies are all grown up."

Her mother meant well, Megan knew, even if her words only salted the wound.

"Mo-om," said Cayley.

"Would you like to come home when you're released? I can pop you back in your old bed, in your old bedroom, feed you up and take good care of you?"

"No." God, no. "Thanks."

"Well, at least it's all over now, Megan, it's all behind you and you can just move on with your life again." Mrs Wright patted her daughter's shoulder.

"Mom!" said Cayley.

"What?" asked Mrs Wright, her voice already beginning to sound injured. "I'm sure Megan agrees with me, don't you dear?"

"You think this is a good thing? That it's all worked out for the best? That my baby is dead."

"Well, really! I wouldn't put it quite that way, dear."

"How would you put it?"

There was a loud retching noise from behind Mrs Wright.

"I feel sick, I'm going to puke!" said Cayley.

"What's the matter, baby?" asked Mrs Wright, transferring her attention from Megan to Cayley.

"That salad I had in the canteen. It's making me feel sick. I need to vomit. Where's the bathroom? Mom, help me," said Cayley, gagging conspicuously.

"Oh, dear. If it's not one, it's the other. Come with me baby, quick, I'll help you find one. But please don't be sick, Cayley, not now. Not yet."

Mrs Wright took Cayley, who was doubled-over and making choking noises, and hustled her out of the room. At the door, Cayley turned her head and, behind her mother's back, winked at Megan and blew her a kiss, before hauling her mother away. The room was suddenly silent and still.

"Are you okay, Megs?"

"No. Not really," said Megan, and she began to weep. Wade held her gently, handing her tissues but saying nothing, while she bubbled over with the mixture of loss and grief, fear and relief, emptiness and guilt. A pile of crumpled tissues later, as she was shuddering into silence, there was a new voice from the door.

"Uhm, I'm here." Mike stood just inside the room, looking uncomfortable. He held a cellphone in one hand and a bunch of cellophane-wrapped Proteas in the other. Airport kiosk flowers.

"Mike!"

"Better late than never, I suppose," said Wade.

"What's that supposed to mean?" asked Mike, giving Wade a sour look.

"I'll see you later, Megs. Press the button if you need help," said Wade, and walked out.

"Wanker," muttered Mike.

He put the flowers on top of the bed alongside Megan. She stared at them. They looked a little battered, the ends of the petals were beginning to brown and fold over into dry, sharp points. Mike walked over to the window and peered out. Then he sat down in the chair beside the bed with a long sigh, as if he had spent an exhausting day on his feet, and ran a hand through his blonde hair. It was getting long, it needed a cut. Mike puffed out his cheeks with a breath, looked around the room and put his cellphone down on the cabinet beside the bed. Buying time. Eventually he looked directly at Megan.

"Well?"

"Excuse me?"

"I mean, what happened?"

"When?"

"Huh?"

"What happened when? What exactly do you want to know? What happened when I was pregnant? What happened when I had a scan and they found no heartbeat? What happened when I went home alone last night and came in alone this morning to have the remains cut out of me? What happened in the op. or after? You'll have to be a bit more specific, Mike, you've missed so much."

"*Ag*, come on Meggy, don't be like that."

"Like what?"

"All pissed off at me. It's not my fault you miscarried. I didn't do anything."

"Except run away when you found out I was pregnant – and stay away when I decided to keep it. Except for not being there for me the only time I've ever really needed you."

"Meggy…"

"Don't Meggy me!"

"Okay, then, Megan. Happy now? Look, I'm sorry it happened, sorry you had to go through this, this *kak*," he said, the words at odds with the obvious relief in his baby blue eyes. "But maybe, in a little while, you'll … you know … see that it's for the best that it's … gone."

"It was *not* for the best. And it's not gone, it's dead!" Megan snatched the pyramid of chocolates and threw it at his head. He deflected it with a raised arm. There was a crack and golden balls rolled in every direction across the floor. "I wanted that baby, you complete and utter moron. I. Wanted. It. And I needed you – here, with me. But you – Mr Goodtime Charlie – just headed for the hills." Megan could feel self-pity rising inside, constricting her chest and closing her throat. "You probably even found someone there to comfort you."

It was a shot in the dark. Later, she could not even be sure what had made her say it, but the dull flush which coloured his face and the quick flick of his glance to the cellphone told her she was right.

"Ahh," it was a short cry, an expulsion of breath and pain. "You did, didn't you?"

"Look, you've got to understand, Meggy. It meant nothing, she's no one–"

"That's supposed to make it better, is it? That you cheated on me, not for some grand love, but for a no one who means nothing to you?"

"It was just… I just felt so alone, you know. You were all focused on the pregnancy and I–"

"You're saying it's my fault for neglecting you?" The self-pity was gone now, replaced by anger and contempt. "Do you know, Mike, that until now, until this very moment, I never comprehended the full extent of your narcissism?"

"There you go, therapising again! Can't you speak plain English?"

"Fair enough. Here it is in plain English: you're a selfish pig! Now bugger off – we're finished."

Mike's face was red, his features thick with anger and resentiment. Megan was amazed that she had ever found him attractive.

"I need to get my stuff from your place."

"Any time. Just call ahead so I can make sure I'm not home. And don't forget to leave your key." She shouted the last words at him as he stalked out of the room.

"Bastard," said Megan.

It came out quietly; she thought her rage might be spent. But then she saw his cellphone on the cabinet beside her. She seized it, got out of the bed and walked gingerly to the door, her breath hissing through the pain. She stuck her head out into the corridor and yelled, "And you can take your bloody cellphone with you!" She hurled the phone after him. At the sound of her voice, he had turned to face her and now his hands scrabbled to catch the phone, but it slipped through his fingers and hit the floor hard.

It was not very mature, Megan knew, not very evolved, but it *was* very satisfying to see him on his hands and knees, groping about on the floor, picking up the bits and pieces of shattered metal and plastic.

40
Stuck pig

The bitch! The dirty, stinking, filthy bitch!

He stares at the row of neat black stitches which wind down and across his left forearm, creeping through the flesh like some many-legged insect. Reminding him of that other time, that other place.

She has done this to him, he knows it. She has done something or said something in that wretched session of hypnosis and it has contaminated him, infected his mind and subverted his will. When he lifted that scalpel, its blade glinting in the bright light of the overhead lamp, when he brought it down to her tender, rounded flesh – just to make the smallest, satisfying nick (the real cutting and slicing would come later, after his hands had reached inside the core of her), the blade refused to move closer. No, that was wrong. His hand refused to move closer. It stuttered and shook. Baffled, he grabbed his right hand with his left, steadied it, and made to move the blade into her flesh. And then, unbelievably, his own hand turned on him.

It burned like a flame and bled like a stuck pig ... no, not that, never that. It bled like a ... like a river.

He had stood like a simpleton, burning and bleeding and staring bewildered at the gaping wound, until Martin Matthee ordered the nurse to lead him away. To be stitched. To be scarred.

He had cut his own arm. No, that too was wrong. She had done it. She had done it just as much as if she had been holding the scalpel – she, who had turned his own hand against him with her vile, treacherous words. She had stitched him up. You could never trust a woman, liars and lie-ers, they were all the same, said one thing while really their words were doing something else to you. He would like to cut out her tongue. He would like to cut out all of their tongues!

What else has she done to him? How much does she know? Who else knows? Who has she told, and who has told her? Ah, yes. That is the real question, the mother lode. A part of his mind registers the bitter irony of the term. His mothers – the first and all the others – had been empty of any value. Empty rotten whores and holes, the lot of them. Just as she was – an o-thing, wasn't that what Hamlet called them?

And one – at least one – of the o-things has been tittle-taling and tattling. So which little she-dog has been yapping away to Megan Wright? Which other dirty, stinking girl will he have to silence before he finishes his "unfinished business' with Miss Fucking-Wrong and terminates his therapy permanently?

41
Little boxes

Megan stared at the two brown cardboard boxes in front of her – one big and one small – but both, as it turned out, too large for purpose. Oedipus sniffed at both of them and then flung himself down on the carpet with a deep sigh.

Megan had collected all of Mike's belongings from the town house and dumped them unceremoniously into the larger of the two boxes: his toothbrush and comb, a few CDs (Eminem and Radiohead, mostly), a copy of SA Rugby Magazine from the top of the toilet cistern, some underwear and a few shirts from the wardrobe in the bedroom, and from under the bed, a dust-covered green vuvuzela dating back to the World Cup. There were so few of his things in the town house that they barely filled half the box. Perhaps that, right there, should have been a clue, Megan thought, that Mike had never been committed to her, to them.

She looked up from where she sat on the floor and scanned her bookshelf, then extracted two volumes from her collection and tossed them into the box. *The Peter Pan Syndrome: Men Who Have Never Grown Up* and *Why is it Always About You? The Seven Deadly Sins of Narcissism*: those should provide him with more edifying reading than a magazine about rugby. After a moment she took down a book for herself: *Emotional Vampires: Dealing with People Who Drain You Dry*. Healer, heal thyself.

Without Mike's stuff, little as it was, the rooms somehow looked even more bare and empty. Perhaps for the first time, she was seeing – really seeing clearly – the space in which she lived: blank walls, windows hung with ill-fitting, hand-me-down curtains from her mother, a couple of dead and moribund pot plants, an absence of personal touches. She realised that the stark bareness had been disguised for her until now, draped in hopes and dreams and furnished with the fantasy of what she and Mike might have been. She had been in a kind of limbo, renting this anonymous place, not committing to as much as a change of wall paint while she waited to see how the relationship would go – whether they would move in together, perhaps even buy a place together. She had had been so busy doing the nothing of watching and waiting that she had never really set down roots and created a nest for herself.

She hoisted the box onto one hip and walked to the front door. Oedipus lifted his head hopefully, but sighed and let it drop again when she walked past the rack where his lead hung. Megan walked outside and placed the box squarely in the middle of the front path. Perhaps it would rain soon. She went back inside, locked the door behind her and shot the deadbolt for good measure. Then she approached the other, smaller box and allowed herself to dwell on that other emptiness – the void inside.

She had never truly felt pregnant, never fully attached to more than the idea of having a baby, let alone forged a personal bond with the life that had grown inside. So why did she feel so empty, so hollow? The baby felt more real now, in its absence, than it ever had been in its presence. Inside the second box was the sum total of her purchases for the new baby: two books on pregnancy. It was as if she had been researching some intellectual enterprise. Where were the Babygros and booties that every broody mother starts collecting? Where were the Winnie-the-Pooh wallpaper borders, the tiny teddy bears, the lace bibs? She had invested as little into the pregnancy as she had into the town house.

A superstitious thought intruded. Maybe she had jinxed the pregnancy with her lack of attention and connection. Perhaps it was precisely because she had never really bonded with the little soul inside her that it never took hold, that it shrivelled up and withered away. Blighted: that was the word Weinberg had used, maybe she had blighted it with her doubts and uncertainties and ambivalence.

She told herself to stop being stupid. Fully one third of first pregnancies end in miscarriage. She wondered how she knew this fact. Perhaps she had read it in one of the pregnancy books, certainly Weinberg had never told her. They didn't tell you the potentially awful news while they were examining you and congratulating you – they didn't tell you until it had already happened.

She needed to make some changes in her life, and they would begin here and now. This weekend she would start looking at new properties. She would choose something that pleased purely her – something with lots of light and airy space. She would buy, not rent, and put down roots – literally as well as emotionally. She would plant a garden with sapling trees, and bulbs destined to emerge only in a year's time. She would commit to herself and her home. She would buy paintings and hang them on the walls, clothe her bed in fine Egyptian cotton, stack her shelves with something more than books, stock her cupboards with couscous and cake flour and gelatine – and learn how to cook with them. She would heal herself and feather her nest, and start something new.

This place would be easy to leave, she thought, as she wandered restlessly from room to impersonal room, Oedipus trailing in her wake. In fact, she needed to get out of it soon or she would go nuts. Everyone had advised her to take a few days off after the miscarriage and operation, to rest and recuperate. But one day at home had been enough to convince her that she needed to be back at work, needed the challenges of clients to distract her from her grief and self-absorption. She picked up the phone and dialled.

"Patience? Hi, it's me. How are you?"

"How are *you*? Are you all right? Can I help you?"

"I'm okay, but I need to come back to work."

She waited for Patience to say it was too soon, that she should rest some more, take it easy. But Patience said nothing and Megan felt a moment's intense gratitude and love for the woman who knew her so well.

"So will you call all the clients we had to cancel, and reinstate their appointments? Starting from tomorrow. Just don't call Tony Thomas."

"Not yet or not at all?"

"Not at all. Not ever."

42

Doubts

Having been so determined to be back at work, she was irritated to discover the next day that she wished she were back at home instead. It was so difficult to focus, to screen out all the thoughts about the pregnancy, and the break-up with Mike, and the case against Trotteur, that she did not think she was being of much help to her clients. All of her attention and energy seemed to have been used up in her first appointment, which was with Alta Cronjé.

Alta confirmed that she was doing well, though she seemed a little low in energy to Megan. She said she was keen to get going with her idea to learn more about being a counsellor, and reported that her husband, Johan, said he felt like he had the "old Alta" back again. The pregnancy was progressing well, the doctor had told her it was a boy and Johan was thrilled. Her daughter, Marlien, could hardly wait to become a big sister.

Alta's big news was about the hearing at the Health Professions Council. She had been notified that it was scheduled for two weeks' time and if Trotteur had not already been notified of the fact and summoned to appear, he soon would be. Megan wondered if he were in the hospital at this moment, or whether he, too, had taken leave following his injury. Wherever he was, she intended to stay well clear of him.

"I thought, you know, that when this happened, when the time came when I could face him eye to eye and take him down, that I would feel great and … like … excited," said Alta, sighing deeply.

"And you don't?"

"Not really, hey. It's a bit of an anti-climax. Mostly I feel tired – *siek* and *sat* and *gatvol* for the whole thing. I just wish it was all over, that I could rest and relax."

"You want to get on with your life."

"It's enough now, you know? It's gone on for long enough. Too long, actually. I can't handle it if it drags on for ever."

The rest of the day seemed, to Megan, to comprise a series of noes to a succession of clients.

"No, Yvonne, even though your husband is in the terminal stages of cancer and is draining the life and love out of you and the children with his bitterness and self-pity, you may not put a pillow over his head and smother him."

"No, Stephen, I do not think that going ahead and having an affair with your daughter's tennis coach will re-energise and enrich your marriage."

"No, Zahira, I don't think that because your teenage son has some porn magazines under his bed that he's a pervert who should be sent to Boys' Town."

"No, Maria, however sorry he may say he is, I don't think that he'll never hit you again. In fact, if you do go back, I can pretty much guarantee you that he will hit you again, with worse to follow."

Megan had been on the receiving end of a no, too – from Pumla Phahlane.

"No, I've changed my mind, I can't testify against him."

"Pumla, please, we really need you."

"I'm sorry, I can't help you."

"Why? Has something happened?"

"I just… I'm afraid. He… I just can't do it anymore, I'm sorry for you. But please don't contact me again," she had said, her voice tight with fear, and the line had gone dead.

Now Megan sat with the self-confessed infidel, who was rambling on about his marriage and his back problems and his craving to visit the masseuse again, and Megan was battling to present even a semblance of attention. What was wrong with people? Were they all deranged? Or just terminally stupid? And what was she doing here when she could be at home, curled up under the duvet in bed eating ice-cream, and thinking of nothing? Why had she–

Her thoughts were interrupted by loud banging and shouting coming from the reception room. Then her office door crashed open and an enormous man, red-faced and broad-shouldered, stormed in. Henk leapt over the back of the couch and hid behind it.

"It's your fault! All your fault!" The man pointed a finger at Megan. His face was glazed with tears and his hands, his whole body was trembling. He picked up a stack of books from the table and hurled them at the shelves behind her desk.

"Crap, it's all crap! That's what I think of it – what I think of you. You were supposed to help her, get her better and now look what's happened!"

"Sir, please," said Megan, "What is the matter?" She could see Patience behind him, speaking softly but furiously into a telephone. She had probably already pressed the panic button.

"She's dead, isn't she? She's dead, that's what's the matter! And my little son. And what must I do now – tell me that. What am I supposed to tell Marlien?"

"Marlien?" said Megan, thinking quickly. "Are you Johan Cronjé? What's wrong? Are you talking about Alta?"

At the sound of the name, the man's arms fell limply to his sides and his head swung wretchedly from side to side.

"My Alta, my *Alta'jie*. She's dead. She killed herself."

"What! What are you talking about? I just saw her – this morning – and she was fine."

"She couldn't have been fine. She's killed herself – here in the underground parking... She never came home, I came to find her and she was there, in the car, dead and all pale and ... she must have done it straight after her session with you this morning. What did you say to her? What?!"

"Nothing! I ... nothing that would... Are you sure?"

Johan Cronjé shuddered, gripped by a paroxysm of wracking sobs. Before she could get herself together or think of a thing to say, three men in security uniforms burst through the door and seized Johan Cronjé by the arms, dragging him backwards out of the office.

"Stop!" shouted Megan. "Stop – that's not necessary. This man's wife has just died. He's upset. Let go of him right now!" When they hesitated, looking uncertain, she said firmly, "I'm fine. He's not dangerous, you don't have to restrain him. Now, let go of him!"

They exchanged a look with each other, then released Johan Cronjé and stepped backwards. Megan took hold of Johan's shoulder, shook him gently and said, "Come, Johan, show me. Take me to her, take me to Alta."

Johan Cronjé wiped his sleeve across his face and stumbled out of the office, followed by Megan and the security guards. They walked down the corridor and made the trip in the lift down to the second level of basement parking in silence. Megan's mind was in a confused whirl. There had to be some mistake, had to be. It could not be Alta.

In the basement they pushed past the small crowd forming outside the lifts and walked past the lines of parked cars. A part of Megan's mind detached from the bewildering maelstrom of emotions inside. She noticed the oil patches and tyre marks on the floor, smelled the exhaust-fumed air, heard the buzzing of a fluorescent strip light flickering overhead.

In the far corner of the garage was a blue Opel Kadet. Parked behind it was a white Golf trimmed with the yellow-and-blue line that indicated a police vehicle, a blue light flashing mutely on its roof. A female police officer was standing beside the open driver's side door of the car. A male officer was unwinding yellow tape from a large reel and cordoning off the area with it.

"Uh-uh. You can't come here, lady," he said, stepping forward to block Megan's path.

"I know her. I'm her psychologist – I saw her for an appointment this morning."

"You were supposed to be helping her and now look, just look!" she heard Johan Cronjé shouting from somewhere behind her. "You were supposed to help her!" The words rang in the basement.

The officer looked at her with keen eyes, then stepped aside to let her pass with a warning not to touch anything, and she made her feet take the final steps to the car. The female officer stepped away from the door and now Megan could look, could see inside.

Alta sat in the driver's seat, her head back against the headrest, her lips and face chalky pale and blank of expression, her eyes mercifully closed. But what drew Megan's horrified gaze was the blood – dark and red and sticky-looking. Alta's right arm hung limply at her side, but her left arm lay palm-up in the lap of what had been a yellow dress. The fabric, now a deep red, was bunched up about her thighs. Along the width of the forearm were two deep, parallel cuts, stretching from one side right across to the other. Trails of blood, now drying into cracked crusts, lead into the red pool which stained her lap and the seat, and spilled into the footwell. Megan retreated from the car, from the sight of her client reduced to this.

"I can't believe it," Megan said to the police officers, to Johan Cronjé. "I just can't believe she did this. What did she use?"

"We found this," said the policewoman, holding up a plastic bag with a scalpel inside. A smear of blood stuck the sides of the plastic bag together.

"A scalpel? Never! She'd never have used that."

"We found it in her hand. She meant to off herself, for sure. She sliced open her leg, too," said the policeman. He gave a low whistle.

"What?"

"Here," he demonstrated a cutting motion against the inside top of his thigh, near the groin.

The detached part of Megan's mind remembered that once, at a medical conference, she had discussed methods of suicide with a forensic pathologist who had stated that never, in her twenty-five years of practising, had she seen a successful suicide attempt by means of cutting the wrists. Most wrist-cutters were making a plea for help. It was difficult and very painful to cut deep enough to sever the artery. Most attempters used their dominant hand to cut their other arm first, then did not have the strength to cut the wrist of their dominant hand, especially when tendons were severed. It took a long time to bleed out from the wrists, and the cutter usually changed their mind and got help in time. There was a popular belief that cutting up the length of the forearm – "up the street, not across the road" – made death more likely, but this was more urban legend than fact. A deep slice across the radial artery would do the trick, but it would be slow. Severing the bigger blood vessel in the leg would bring death more quickly and surely.

"I don't believe it. I *can't* believe it. I saw her this morning and she was fine – a little tired perhaps – but there was nothing to suggest that she might do something like this."

"Nothing? Nothing at all?" asked the policewoman. That was when the doubts began to creep in.

Megan walked to where Johan sat on a kerb, crouched over his knees. When he threw off the hand she tried to rest on his shoulder, she went back up to her office and explained what had happened, in broken sentences, to a shocked Patience. Patience pressed a cup of hot sweet tea on her, but wisely refrained from trying to discuss it. Megan sat at her desk, ignoring the tea and passing the heavy dandelion paperweight from hand to hand as she thought.

She felt shaken to her core. She must have missed something. But Alta had seemed fine, said she was doing well. There had been no sign, no hint of suicidiality. Or had there? She thought back to the flowers which Alta had brought her. People planning suicide often gave tokens of love and appreciation away, as they said their thank-yous and goodbyes. What had Alta said that day, that day that felt like a thousand years ago but was really only weeks ago? Something about expressing thanks and appreciation. It was no good, thought Megan, she could not remember and the exact words would not be in her session notes. She would have recorded the fact of the gift, not what was said about it.

She cast her mind back to the session of this morning, tried to replay exactly what Alta had said. Was there anything that could have hinted at suicidiality? No.

Maybe.

Alta had said she was tired, sick and tired of the whole issue with Trotteur. She wanted it to be over. Oh God, thought Megan, oh God. She had thought that Alta was talking about the scheduled Board hearing, that she was eager to get on with the rest of her life, but that had been her own interpretation of what the client had said. What Alta has *actually* said was that she wanted it all to be over, that she had had enough and could not face it dragging on. Given what she had done afterwards, the words now took on a completely different significance.

Megan had missed it, had not seen the hopeless exhaustion, had not heard the despair in those words. She must truly be an appallingly incompetent therapist. She had completely missed Trotteur's psychopathy when it had sat before her in the charming form of Tony Thomas, and had now failed to see Alta's active suicidiality when it, too, must have been staring her in the face. And Alta had done it at the clinic, right after her therapy session. That must be some kind of message to Megan.

Megan knew she was to blame. She had not saved Alta, not from her trauma, or from herself, and certainly not from Trotteur. It was all over now. Alta was dead and she, Megan, was responsible. Pumla was refusing to testify. There was no case against Trotteur, no evidence and now no witnesses. She hurled the paperweight at the opposite wall. It dented the soft walling and bounced off, hitting the carpet and rolling under the wingback chair.

She had failed.

43

A call

He looks down and finds that his feet are carrying him along the corridors, up stairways and along more corridors, past office after office: gastroenterologists, orthopaedic surgeons, dermatologists and urologists. He is tired, he has had to stay up all night, thinking. His mind is on the call he has just received.

The call propelled him out of his office, charged him with an urge to run. When he heard that Mrs Mdluli was calling from the HPCSA, elation had filled his chest. This was the notification he was waiting for. The hearing had been cancelled due to lack of evidence and witnesses. They were sorry to have troubled him and wished him a good day and would never trouble his precious time with petty grievances again. But that was not what the bitch had said.

What she had actually said was that the Board had been notified that the complainant was now unfortunately late – couldn't they even speak proper English, these people? – but that she had to inform him that the hearing was nevertheless going ahead as there was still a signed affidavit from the complainant. In addition, a witness, Mrs Cronjé's psychologist – who had been treating her for psychological complications following the surgery which Dr Trotteur had performed on her – had come forward and wished to make a submission to the panel hearing the case. Dr Trotteur was please to present himself at the Board's offices in Pretoria at the originally stipulated time and date. The relevant documents and statements would be forwarded to him by day's end so that he could take legal advice, if he so desired.

He thought he had heard a hint of grim satisfaction in her voice. It made an itch rise inside him. At the centre of the anger in the centre of himself, there was an itch which needed to be scratched. Like the itch on his arm.

He needs to see it again.

He pushes back the sleeve of his white coat and stares down at the scarred ugliness. It is repulsive: black stitches knotting his flesh together, the raised red welt already beginning to form a ridged, thickening keloid. As he looks at it, it seems, for the briefest of moments, to move slightly, like the minute, sinuous writhing of a blood-red asp. And it itches so! He rubs, then scratches at it.

"Excuse me."

He looks up, realises he is standing in the middle of one of the corridors, blocking the way while he worries at the weal. A woman is trying to get past him. Aren't they always? She is looking at him oddly. Her eyes flick down to the scar, then back to his face, a mixture of pity and revulsion in her gaze.

"Bitch."

"Excuse me?"

He brushes past her and starts walking again, looking down at his feet. Right and left, right and left. His steps tap out a chant: What to do? What to do? It is a conundrum. He glances to both sides and discovers that he is passing the offices of one Megan Wright, Counselling Psychologist. It is an answer to the question, he knows it. He knows best, after all.

He walks on, right and left, right and left, towards the wards, no longer looking down, but looking up into the faces of the people he passes. There is something suspicious in their expressions, something accusatory in the way they look at him with their dull sheep eyes, that makes the itch stronger. He passes a group of nurses, chatting outside the entrance to the gynae and obstetrics unit. He recognises them, lifts a hand – the whole one – in greeting as he walks by. They nod, seemingly respectful, but when he snaps his head around to look back, he sees that they are clustered in a tight huddle, whispering and looking slyly at him out of their ugly, misshapen faces.

Again he feels the slight shifting of the snake on his arm. It is warning him. He tries to stroke it gently, to soothe it still, but the fury and the hot itch are unsated. He scrapes at it with his nails, sighs at the temporary relief.

He walks on, back to his floor, back to his office. There are two men coming towards him. They are doctors, by their white coats. It is Weinberg and Matthee. They are talking intently to each other. Are their whispers about him?

"Hello there, Gavin," he says. He crams his voice full of friendly nonchalance.

"Oh, hello, Dr Trotteur." Trotter! Again!

"It's Trotteur," he barks. "It's pronounced Tro-teur, not trotter. I'm not a pig!"

Both men stare at him. Their mouths are mute but he can see something behind their eyes – mistrust and doubt and censure.

"I'm not a pig, and I'm not blind, you know – I can see what you're thinking," he spits and hurries on. He needs his office. He needs to sit in his safe chair at his desk, to gaze at the instruments on his wall and fondle the paperweight in the drawer until the cool calmness returns. He blows inside the cuff of his left arm. It is still now, he can send it to sleep.

44
Niggle

Something was tugging at a corner of her mind. Megan wished she could swat it away like a fly, but it would not be ignored. She tried to focus on the leaves of the oak trees which formed a living arch over the narrow road where she walked. The first leaves were just beginning to turn yellow, responding to the hint of coolness in the late afternoon breeze. Autumn would be here soon, taking all of three weeks in this crazy-fast town, and then winter would arrive with the first cold snap. Again she felt the tug; there was something she had forgotten, or something she had not consciously recognised.

Realising that the only way to be rid of the niggle was to allow it to surface into awareness, Megan stopped resisting its intrusion. She gave herself over to the walk, allowed herself to be lulled by the rhythm of step after step as Oedipus trotted ahead, for once undistracted by scents on trees and lamp posts. She allowed her mind to go blank, and immediately, there it was: the scalpel.

Alta's wounds had been made with a scalpel, and this simply made no sense. No matter how hard she tried, Megan could not see Alta somehow acquiring the surgical knife and then slicing herself open with it, not when she had already been so damaged by such a knife. Then again, perhaps using that particular implement had been a message to the world, to Megan: this is what ruined me, now it has killed me. But no, that definitely did not fit. The woman who put up posters to register her disapproval of corrupt cops was not the sort of woman to leave cryptic, ambiguous clues. She would have signed out with a clear and decisive suicide note. And – another memory intruded – she would not have killed herself this way, leaving a bloody mess for her husband or a stranger to discover.

Megan had a vague idea that at Alta's first session, when she had been assessing the client's level of depression, they had discussed suicide. She was sure that Alta had said she would never kill herself because it was wrong in the eyes of God, and also because of what it would do to her husband and daughter. Hadn't Alta also said something about pills and champagne being the way to go? Megan quickened her step, she would have to check her notes in Alta's file, but she felt more and more certain that she was right. Alta would not have done it, and she would never have done it this way.

Alta had been excited about the new plans for her life, delighted by the pregnancy and happy that her relationship with her husband was improving. She had not been tired of life, only of the ongoing issue with Trotteur, and she was hardly likely to have killed herself to avoid the very hearing she had been working to bring about.

Megan felt energised, but not cheered, by her growing conviction that Alta's death had not been suicide. Whether or not Alta had killed herself, it was still Megan's fault. Either way, she should have seen it coming, and prevented it. At least she no longer felt quite so helpless. There were a few calls she needed to make now, and the first of them was to Johan Cronjé.

"Alta did not commit suicide, Johan, I'm sure of it. There'll be a post-mortem – there always is unless the death is clearly from natural causes. I'll find out the name of the forensic pathologist from the police and call them, tell them I suspect foul play. They'll check her over carefully, screen for substances, and hopefully we'll find out what really happened."

"You think...?"

"I think she was murdered, Johan." The image of Alta in the bloodied car flashed before Megan's eyes. She saw again the arm lying palm-up in the lap, the two perfectly neat and symmetrical cuts on the arm.

"And if she was murdered, then I know who did it."

45
Coming undone

When he walks into his rooms, he immediately sees two men sitting in the waiting room. They are not doctors. It strikes him that they do not seem to be with any of the waiting brood mares. He raises an eyebrow at Beth behind the reception counter.

"Oh, Dr Trotteur – there you are! These gentlemen have been waiting for you, they're from the SAPS."

Immediately, the waiting women lift their heads, look from him to the men, who now stand, looking at him with keen interest. Trotteur glowers at Beth Finch. Has she no discretion, no intelligence? She wilts beneath his gaze – he has that power – and continues in a softer, more acceptably respectful voice.

"This is," she consults a piece of paper on the counter, "Sergeant Pieterse and Warrant Officer Mtibe, and they wish to speak to you."

"As you can see," says Trotteur, gesturing to the patients waiting in the room, "I'm very busy and now is not a good time." Sometimes one does need to state the obvious.

"We'll only take a few minutes, sir," says Mtibe and, before Trotteur can cut him off, he adds, "We want to talk to you about the death of one of your patients. Shall we go into your office or would you prefer to talk here?"

The eyes of the waiting patients are now definitely wary and apprehensive as they stare at him. One cow turns to the woman next to her and whispers something. He thinks he hears his name.

Humiliation burns and churns inside. The creature on his arm is awake again, it twists painfully, a fiery cord binding his flesh, but he forces himself not to touch it as he leads the way into the office, closing the door hard behind the two men. He sits down behind his desk and studies the men over his steepled fingers. Sergeant Pieterse is a tall, bulky man in his thirties with buzz-cut brown hair. His cheeks are pocked with the pale craters that bear testament to a fierce clash with adolescent acne vulgaris. Trotteur stares at the disfigurement with distaste before transferring his attention to Warrant Officer Mtibe. What the hell is a Warrant Officer anyway? He is younger – probably not yet thirty – and smaller. He slouches comfortably in his chair and studies Trotteur with lazy eyes.

Trotteur ignores this insolence and addresses himself to Pieterse: "What can I do for you?"

"We need to ask you some questions regarding the suspicious death of one of your patients, a Mrs Alta Cronjé," says Pieterse. He opens a small notebook and tests a yellow ballpoint pen against the paper.

"Suspicious – how?"

"You're not surprised, Doc," says the one with the lazy eyes. "You knew she was dead, then?"

"I ... I heard about it, yes."

"Who told you?"

"Hospital grapevine – I can't remember who precisely."

"Uh-hm," says Mtibe, with a look at Pieterse. Pieterse writes something in his book, while Mtibe rocks back in his chair and gazes around the office. There is something unsettling about the soft, tuneless whistle which comes from his lips. Just who is in charge here?

"Well, sir," says Pieterse, "you may have heard–"

"... on the hospital grapevine..." interjects Mtibe.

"Yes, on the hospital grapevine, that Mrs Cronjé committed suicide, right here in the basement parking at Acacia Clinic. But that is not so."

"She didn't do it here? She did it somewhere else?" asks Trotteur.

Mtibe's chair comes down onto all four legs with a dull thud. "She didn't do it at all," he says.

"I'm afraid I don't understand." Under the desk, Trotteur rubs hard at the burning itch in his arm which will no longer be denied.

"As per regulations, a post-mortem was conducted on Mrs Cronjé's remains," said Pieterse.

"How extraordinary. It seemed like a clear-cut case of suicide. From what I heard."

"On the hospital grapevine," says Mtibe again. A slight smile twists his lips, but there is no humour in it, only menace. Trotteur feels another itch – in the palm of the hand which longs to slap the impudence off the man's face.

"Well, it's standard procedure, because it wasn't a 'natural causes' death. We also initially thought it was suicide, Doc," continues Pieterse, "but the post-mortem kicked up some strange findings." From an inside pocket, he extracts a folded wad of paper and holds it up. "Post-mortem report and affidavit from the forensic pathologist."

"Terrible," says Mtibe, examining a cuticle and nibbling off a filament of skin, "what had been done to that woman. And not just in that garage."

"Do you want to know what they found, Doc? Apart from," Pieterse reads from the report, "pale mucosae ... reduced lividity ... ah, here we are: fatal haemorrhage resulting from penetrating wound on inside of left wrist and forearm dissecting the radial artery and penetrating wound on left inside thigh severing femoral artery."

"I can't see how it concerns me."

"Number one," Pieterse holds up a thick thumb, "according to the toxicology report, Mrs Cronjé had high concentrations of ketamine in her blood and plasma levels. Now, you would know–"

"... being a doctor," interjects Mtibe. His eyes are fixed now on Trotteur.

"Yes, being a doctor you would know that ketamine is a very fast-acting general anaesthetic. The pathologist said it was originally used as a horse-anaesthetic. The report also says that it would have 'stimulated the circulatory system, increasing heart rate and blood pressure', which I think means..."

"She would have bled faster," says Mtibe.

"Bottom line? She was drugged, Doc."

"I'm sure many suicides take something to make their passing easier, to dull the pain."

Mtibe made a disbelieving sound and shook his head at Trotteur. "It was injected, not swallowed. And according to the pathologist, it would have worked extremely quickly, within seconds. If she injected herself with it before she cut herself, she would have passed out immediately and would not have been conscious enough to make those cuts."

"I fail to see what this has to do with me."

"Number two: there's also the question of where she would have laid hands on a powerful drug like ketamine."

"That's a drug only doctors have access to. Doctor," says Mtibe.

"And thirdly," Pieterse holds up three fingers, "there's the matter of where she was injected – in the hairline at the back of her neck, under her hair."

"Almost as if it needed to be hidden," says Mtibe.

"Which doesn't make a lot of sense, nè? If she was offing herself, what's the problem with people finding out she took something first? It might even bring her family some comfort to know she didn't suffer. And it's not an easy place for her to have reached by herself."

"Uh-uh, not easy." Mtibe shakes his head in agreement and bites with small, sharp teeth at the cuticle.

"Plu-us, there's number four: what happened to the syringe? We couldn't find it in the car, it's nowheresville."

"Perhaps she threw it out the window."

"Nah, I don't think so, Doc. Inject herself behind the neck, and then before she passes out open the window, chuck it outside where someone else might step on it, then close the window again? And why would she do that anyway? And then still have time before she passes out to make those nice neat cuts? No ways, Doc."

Trotteur checks his watch impatiently. He has had to transfer it to his right wrist and the movement still feels unnatural.

"Look, this is all very interesting, I'm sure. But I'm a busy man and this has nothing to do with me. I can think of no reason why you should be here, talking to me."

"Can't you?" Mtibe's glittering black eyes blink slowly. They are like the eyes of a crocodile lazing in the shallows, Trotteur realises now, waiting to snap its jaws on its prey. "You can't think of any reason why your life would be easier if Mrs Cronjé were out of the way?"

"We know that she had laid a charge against you at the Medical Board, Doc, that you stood to lose your licence."

"How did you ... who told you that?" The asp is tightening its coils around his arm.

"Where were you on the 19th, between the hours of 9 a.m. and 3 p.m., Dr Trotteur?" asks Mtibe.

"It's pronounced Tro-ture."

"Where were you?" The eyes look hard as flint now, not lazy at all. Trotteur rubs at his arm.

"I was at home. As you can see." It pains him to do so, but he rolls back his sleeve and shows them his scarred arm with its pulsing snake of stitches. "I had an accident and so I cancelled my patients for a few days."

"Now that's very interesting, Doc," says Pieterse.

"Ve-ry in-te-res-ting," repeats Mtibe, sounding out the syllables grimly.

"Because we have the access log from the parking in the basement. It registers the date and time every time someone with an access card enters and leaves. And it shows that you entered the garage at 7.55 a.m. and left it again at 9.23 a.m. on the date in question," says Pieterse, flipping back through his notebook and reading off the times.

"Well, yes, I did actually pop in to catch up on some admin and to collect some files to take home to work on them, I remember now."

"Now he remembers," says Mtibe to Pieterse, who nods. Then he looks back at Trotteur and asks, "Anyone see you, er, catching up and collecting?"

"This discussion is at an end," says Trotteur, standing up. "I've had enough of being treated like a suspect – it's outrageous! I'm not going to answer any further questions without my lawyer being present.

Mtibe shakes his head, saying, "Lawyers."

"That's okay, sir. We'll call later to set up a time to interview you down at the station. We need to get full statements from everyone in this case – the husband, the pathologist, and you."

Trotteur ignores him, stalks to the door and opens it.

"And of course," Pieterse flips through to an earlier page in his notebook with his stubby fingers, "from Mrs Cronjé's psychologist."

Trotteur spins around to face him. He cannot believe his ears. Her. Again! The wave of rage that surges up inside him almost fells him. He puts out a hand to the door frame to steady himself. "Her psychologist?"

"Yes, she's been very helpful in assisting us with our enquiries. It was her who suggested we talk to you," says Pieterse and he brushes past Trotteur into the reception room.

"We like it when members of the public assist us. Makes a nice change," says Mtibe, walking out then turning back to hold out his hand to shake Trotteur's. Trotteur glares at him, and closes the door behind them with a bang.

Trotteur stands behind the door, leaning against it, rubbing furiously at his arm and thinking. How much would she be able to say? Did death end the duty of confidentiality? Would the husband be able to authorise disclosure? He imagines Megan Wright with a dent in both cheeks, her lips stitched closed with knots of stiff black thread. The image makes him smile, relaxes the tension in his shoulders somewhat. There is a knocking from somewhere distant behind him. He ignores it.

Carefully he folds back his sleeve and inspects his arm. The prickling is unbearable. He tugs at the black stitches along the puckered, red welt. One of them is coming undone. It is unravelling, the black ends of the thread stick into the air like the arms of a miniscule drowner, waving for help. As he watches, they wiggle on the crest of a moving red wave. He pulls one of the tiny black arms right out of its socket. Then he wrenches at another until it comes loose. He digs his fingernails right into the flesh and scratches deeply. It feels good, but he can't reach the deeper itch. He stares at the gaping sides of the wound, now oozing blood.

Loose ends need to be tied up. Otherwise things begin to unravel and come apart.

46

Scratching the itch

It had been a spectacular sunset, the dusty Johannesburg sky somehow catching and holding the flames of crimson, coral and cerise which licked at the horizon, but now it was completely dark. From the window of her office, Megan could see the lights of the city radiating out in the night, but none of the stars, which must surely still be somewhere above. The parking lot, bathed in yellow light, was mostly empty now that visiting hours were over. Megan spun her chair back to face her desk and looked down at the cellphone in her hand.

She was both excited and nervous. Another witness who might be prepared to testify would certainly strengthen the case against Trotteur, but she was worried about keeping the woman safe. She could not allow a repeat of what had happened to Alta. Her hand was damp as she keyed the sequence of buttons to bring up the text message so that she could read it again.

I was Mrs Cronjé's nurse in the post-op ward. I have something to tell you about Dr Troture but he must not know I'm talking to you. If you see me you must not greet me because I'm afraid. Can I visit you tonight after my shift ends at 8pm? I know where your office is. I will come there. From Sr Mercy Sibisi

Megan glanced up at the clock on the wall: 7.45 p.m. She remembered joking with Patience about a Sister Mercy, but it would not hurt to double-check. She called the cell number from which the message had been sent. A smooth female voice announced that she had reached the voicemail service of the number, and that "the person you wish to contact is not available. Please call again later." A standard service provider voicemail message. Megan thought for a moment, then she picked up the receiver of the landline, looked up the number of the post-operative ward in the clinic's internal directory, and dialled the extension. It rang for a good half minute before a harassed-sounding voice answered.

"Marula Ward."

"May I please speak to Sister Mercy Sibisi?"

"Hang on." Megan held the line for several minutes, listening to clattering noises and voices in the background. Eventually the same voice came back.

"She's busy changing a dressing. She'll be finished now-now. Do you want to leave a message?"

"No, that's okay, thanks. I'll call again later."

It was coming up for 8 p.m. Megan guessed that Mercy Sibisi would still have some hand-over procedure to the new shift and would need to gather her belongings before making her way from the ward to Megan's office. The nurse probably wouldn't arrive before 8.20 p.m., Megan estimated. She spent the time compiling a list of questions. The office and the corridor beyond were so silent that Megan could hear the ticks of the second hand on the wall clock.

It was just gone 8.15 p.m. when Megan heard the sound of the outer sliding door opening. She got up and headed for the door, and heard the grate and click of the door sliding closed. As she passed the table with the dried-flower arrangement, a sudden impulse made her reach under and switch on the recording device. Over the last months, she had developed a healthy respect for the value of hard evidence. There was a timid knock at her office door.

Megan reached for the handle and was just turning it when the door flew open, knocking into her and sending her stumbling back. She grabbed the wingback and managed to stay on her feet, looking into the red-rimmed, glittering obsidian eyes of the tall man who faced her. His shoulders were heaving and his lips were pulled back in a tight grimace. His hair was unwashed, falling lankly on either side of a face which seemed much thinner. The silver scar on his chin stood out clearly against the ashen pallor of his skin. He was wearing a crumpled blue shirt, with sweat stains under the armpits and a smear of what Megan thought might be blood on the inside of the shirt's left sleeve.

"Anthony Trotteur!" She would not use the title he so little deserved. "Or should I call you Tony?" She spoke the names loudly and clearly, and in the direction of the hidden microphone in the flowers. Perhaps she would be able to get more than one type of evidence tonight. And if he killed her, she thought wildly, at least they would know who to arrest!

"I need a session with you, Megan. Urgently. There are some things on my mind that I need to get off my chest." He spoke through gritted teeth and rubbed fiercely at his arm.

Megan tried to keep her voice calm and steady, tried to speak past the breathiness which filled her throat. "I can no longer be your therapist, Tony, surely you can see that? Given ... given everything that has happened, it would be totally inappropriate."

"Clause 21 of annexure 12 of the Ethical Rules of Conduct for psychologists, in the Health Professions Act 56 of 1974 stipulates that 'a psychologist shall not abandon a client by terminating the professional relationship PREMATURELY OR ABRUPTLY'!" He shouted the last words at her.

Megan worried that he was losing control. She stepped slowly backwards until the desk was between them. While she moved, she held eye contact and spoke, keeping her voice as steady as she could.

"The code also says that a psychologist may not see a client where there is a conflict of interest or a dual relationship, Tony."

"Both of which you already did – at my expense! And more. You're a regular rule-breaker." He wagged a finger at her.

"Look, we obviously need to talk about these matters, Tony, but now–"

"Stop using my name in every sentence like some second-hand car salesman! Where did you learn that repeating the person's name would forge a bond – Psych 101?"

"You're very clever to spot that."

"And now you're trying flattery – just shut up, you cow! You have to see me, have to, have to." He scratched at his arm with the nails of the other hand. He caught her glance, grimaced again, and said, "It's the itch, Megan, it's making me a little crazy. And it's moving again. It's in the rules. You may not refuse treatment to a client in crisis, shrink." He held his arms wide open and Megan saw the bright red stain of fresh blood on the sleeve of his shirt. "And I am most definitely in crisis."

"Given the circumstances, I'm sure allowances would be made. There's also something in the code about not having to see individuals from whom you consider yourself at immediate threat. But–"

"Do you feel threatened by me, Megan? Are you scared?" She could see an eager glint in his eye. He was obviously getting his rocks off at the thought of her fear.

"No," she said firmly. "I'm not scared. But I am in a hurry and I don't have time to see you now. I'm expecting my fiancé, Mike, at any min–"

"No you're not.' His voice was flat and cold. He started walking slowly towards her. "You're expecting Sister Mercy Sibisi."

"How…?"

"I have something to tell you about Dr Troture," he said in a high falsetto voice. "Dr Troture – I thought that was a masterly touch!" He giggled, rubbed his arm against his side, and continued in the high voice, "'but he must not know I'm talking to you'."

He ran his hands over his face, then rubbed his eyes with balled fists. For a moment he looked like a tired little boy, about to cry.

"Have you still not learned to check people's identity, Megan? They say that intelligence is the ability to learn from experience. So what does that say about you?"

He took another step forward and Megan moved around the back of the desk to the other side, keeping its protective bulk between them.

"It was you … who sent the sms?"

"You're not the only one who can use a pay-as-you-go cellphone. But you do have to learn to pay as you go. There's a price to everything, Megan, you have to learn that lesson. Happily, we have plenty of uninterrupted time ahead of us, and a nice, quiet, deserted section of the hospital in which to have our first lesson." He rubbed his hands together, as if in anticipation of a treat. "And," he added, "our last."

Megan snapped her head to the side, as if she had seen something at the window. Involuntarily, his glance followed hers. She bolted suddenly for the door, but he was there ahead of her, turning the key in the lock and dropping it into his trouser pocket.

"Uh-uh," he said, his wild eyes at odds with his indulgent smile. Blood was crusted along the ridges of his nails. "We have some unfinished business to settle, you and I – some scores to even. And you know how I like things to be even." He pointed a finger at the couch behind her. "Please, do sit down."

"Tony, I–"

"I said, SIT DOWN!" He shoved her back so that she fell onto the couch. He paced up and down on the carpet in front of her.

"You know, for a psychologist, you have really bad listening skills."

The scar on his chin stretched and curved as his face twisted between a rictus of anger and a contorted travesty of a smile. His eyes were wide now, the floating irises more unnerving than ever.

"Tony," she began again, desperately deploying all the containment skills in her meagre therapeutic arsenal. "I can see that you're upset."

"*Upset* doesn't begin – doesn't *begin* – to capture what I'm feeling! I itch, Megan, I'm a burning man." He paced back and forth as he spoke, scratching at his arm.

"Angry, I mean. You're really angry with me! You think I've betrayed you. You're feeling abandoned. Another woman who was supposed to nurture you has abandoned you, just like those mothers all that time ago."

"Stop it! Stop talking, you dirty, stinking girl! Stop your words in your hole and swallow them. Talking can't help you now. We're beyond words. Can't you see that?" He turned his face to hers. "I'm very tired, Megan, very, very tired. I haven't been sleeping well. Too many things are troubling me, bubbling…"

He breathed in hard through his nose, the nostrils pinched together. His features were etched with a desperate appeal – for what, Megan wondered desperately. For understanding or acceptance or nurturance? Or for something more malevolent?

"Tony, I'm trying to understand."

"We're. Beyond. Words. 'The rest is silence' – do you know your Hamlet? But before we have that rest, we need to get to the flesh and bones of the matter."

He reached the hand of his uninjured arm into a pocket, and pulled out a hard plastic spectacle case. Keeping his eyes on Megan, he opened the case. Inside, on red velour lining, lay a scalpel. He picked it up and held it for her to see. The light winked off its sharp blade as he turned it in his hands. He sat down in the wingback chair opposite her and placed the scalpel on his right thigh, its tip pointed at her. With head cocked, he stared at the instrument for a moment, then adjusted it minutely so that it lay precisely straight.

"Now, the flesh and bones of this bloody matter are that I received a call today. Two calls, in fact. A call to the ear and a call to the eye. The ear call informed me that the Board is going ahead with its hearing against me, that there is a new witness. That new witness, that interfering busybody of a bitch would be you."

He picked up the scalpel, pointed it at her and then laid it very precisely down again in the same position as before.

"Then there was the other call – a visit from Mr Buzz-Cut and Mr Crocodile-Eyes, in the flesh. It was not a pleasant experience, Megan. I was Mr Humiliated today. They had all sorts of facts and theories and absences and even a little evidence. And guess who the chief instigator, the tittied trouble-maker and agent provocateur is? You."

Again, the ritual with the scalpel.

"And now I am Mr Mega-Pissed-Off! You have wounded me, Megan, inside and out. Outside and in. Just look."

He undid the button on the blood-stained sleeve and pushed it back up his arm. Megan gasped. The weal was vivid red, swollen and inflamed, puckered in places with black stitches, while in other spots the lips of the wound gaped. Fresh red blood was seeping over the rusty crusts and scabs, and a dark flush radiated out across the long forearm.

"You did this." His voice was almost a whisper. "You cut me, to the core. Does it move you, now, Megan? It moves me. It moves on me. There!" He held his arm out to her. "Did you see that? Just then?"

Megan nodded, having no idea what she was agreeing to, but unwilling to anger him with opposition.

"Well, that couldn't go unavenged, could it? An eye for an eye, and an arm for an arm – isn't that what the Good Book says?" He cradled his wounded arm against his chest with his other arm and rocked it slightly from side to side.

"I had to give that tale-telling bitch what she deserved. I had to shut her piehole forever. I wanted to sew her lips shut – yours too – but that would have been bit of a giveaway." He giggled again. "But the cuts had a certain balance, don't you think? A scar for a scar. With interest, of course. And now it's your turn."

47
Scalpel

"Do you mean…?" Megan's voice was a croak. Her mouth was dry and she battled to say the words. "Are you talking about Alta Cronjé?"

"What a disappointment she was. What a stupefying waste of my talent," Trotteur sneered.

"Your talent?"

"She was all lopsided and uneven when she came," he wagged his head from side to side, "and ungrateful when she left. All you bitches are ungrateful. There's no end to your demands – you're never satisfied. Don't know a good thing when you've got it." He frowned down at his arm, then scratched wildly at the wound and tugged at the end of one of the stitches. "Freud would say that's because you don't have a good *thing*, only an o-thing. Would you agree, Megan?"

"What did you do to Alta, Tony?" Say it loud and clear for the microphone.

"I did what was necessary, which was what she deserved." His tone was flat, his face blank of expression. Megan was alarmed at how his emotional state was swinging between extremes.

"Which was?"

"When I got that letter from Miss Efficiency at the board, how I burned, Megan. How dare she? That dirty, stinking…" He blew out a long breath and his features, which had briefly contorted with rage, smoothed themselves out into the bland mask again. "But how very kind they were to tell me the name of my accuser. I hadn't known until then, you see. And with you sticking notices up in hospitals and sending my patients prying, spying e-mails – yes, I know everything, you see! – how was I to know who had been pouring poison into your ears about me? But now I knew. And I knew the sort of person you were, too. You wouldn't let sleeping dogs lie. Bitches! All the sleeping, lying she-dogs who wouldn't stop their yapping. I had to do it for them."

"Them?"

"Yes, them! Pay attention, Megan." His irate eyes were fixed on her.

"Who exactly?"

"The first one took money like the whore she was."

"Stacey Cole."

Trotteur shrugged. "Cole-hole," he said, his voice a sing-song. "Then there was that other one who would not shut up."

"Nirvana Reddy?"

"If you say so – it's not like her name matters. But that one I regret, I very much regret." He sighed deeply, then blew air up and down the length of his injury. "I had to be quick, you see, there was no time for finesse, for my preferred technique. She had to be excised, but there was no time for excisions. *More* excisions, I should say, it's important to be exact, for I had already done some on her sweet, young flesh." He flashed a manic smile at Megan.

"It was you, the hit-and-run!"

"As I say, it is a lasting regret – not the fact of it, but the way of it. So loud and messy and fast – too fast, really, to see the fear or feel the power. I like it to last a little longer." He licked his lips and leered lasciviously at her. "I'm a goer and a stayer, Megan. I hope to have a chance to show you."

He brought his injured arm up close to his face, and crooned to it. "Shhh … and be still."

Then he calmly picked up the scalpel, deftly inserted it into one of the stitches and with a small, upwards flick, cut it open. He laid the scalpel back down on his thigh and then pulled the thread out of the inflamed flesh. "Aaah," he sighed, his eyes rolling in pleasure, "you have no idea how good that feels. Almost as good as cutting her."

"Her, who?"

"Her – any. Does it make a difference?" he said indifferently. "One mound of stinking, rotten flesh is very much like another."

"How did you kill Alta?"

"Simplicity itself. When I knew who she was, I looked up her address in my patient files. I had to pull hers from the archives because, of course, she was no longer a patient of mine. Went to her house early every day and waited outside. Watched, followed, planned. Planning is essential. Well begun is half done." He chanted the last words in a sing-song voice. "And the anticipation is not without its own pleasure. On the third day she arose again and came here. Well, I knew she wasn't coming to visit me, she'd left me, so she must be coming to see *you.*" He picked up the scalpel, pointed it at Megan, wiped it on the material of his trousers and then laid it down again in the precise centre of his right thigh.

"I waited behind her car, until she came back down. Waiting for her to come…" he snickered, "that sounds rude! Waiting for her to come – that was the hardest part, Megan. The ground was so dirty and stinky. But then she came, I leaped up, embraced her like a lover – just in case anyone was watching – and pushed that needle in, deep into the back of the neck." He sighed and smiled at the remembered pleasure. "Such soft flesh there, just below where the hair begins, it's like a woman's inner thigh. Then I placed her in the seat behind the wheel, though I was in the driver's seat all the way, you could say."

Megan winced as she pictured the scene in her mind's eye. His smiles and satisfied sighs sickened her, and she didn't trust his unnatural calm. At any moment he might spin into another rage.

"But then came the moment of uncertainty and revelation, Megan. I wasn't sure, you see, that I would be able to cut her, to slice her up," his right hand dissected the air in front of him, "as she so deserved. And I wasn't sure what poison you had poured into *my* ears. What if I could never cut again?" His eyebrows rose high in a parody of bewilderment. "Of course, I had come prepared, I had a gun in my jacket pocket and was prepared to use it, if necessary. But only with reluctance. Guns are so messy and so instant. The cut's the thing that does it for me: a slice of life! So imagine my delight, Megan, imagine my delirious joy when I discovered that I most certainly could cut her!" Again, the horrible smile.

He leaned back in his chair, but Megan could tell that he was still coiled as tight as a spring. His dark eyes burned with excitement.

"I suspect that you planted some command in my mind that I couldn't cut patients. Perhaps you never imagined I might want to cut outside of the operating theatre? That was a little limited and short-sighted of you, Megan." He might have been lecturing a careless intern. "However, she was no longer my patient: and nothing stopped me when I simply lifted the scalpel and sliced her arm." He mimicked the motion, snatching up the scalpel and slashing at the air twice. "Such beautiful cuts they were: deep, even slices. And then her thigh, so near my original work. And the blood left her and the words never would. So simple and so neat a plan. Though, I see now of course that I was a little too neat: the missing syringe. Like the dog that didn't bark in the night. Ah, well," he hummed a few tuneless notes. He seemed less wild now and had stopped scratching at his arm. "There was at least that fitting and pleasing symmetry, that my contact with her, my beginning and her end, should be bookended by such beautiful cuts, at this place."

He looked up at her. "Nothing to say? Cat got your tongue? That can be arranged – nothing simpler. Please stand up and go stand there," he said, almost pleasantly, indicating the spot in front of her desk. She complied quickly, eager to get further away from him.

"Speak, please. You've always had so much to say, don't stop now." He stood up, moved a pace closer and glared at her. The smile was gone. "I am all ears."

Megan could feel the danger rising. She scanned the surface of the desk for a weapon. It was covered in files and piles of useless paper. The container of pens was out of easy reach, but perhaps if she flung herself backwards …

"I … I …" What could she say? What words could calm this storm?

"Yes, you, you! You are to blame!" His voice rose in pitch, his face twisted again into a grimace of bitter anger. "There is no way around it, no way over it and no way under it," he slid the scalpel into another stitch, cut it, removed it. The wound gaped like a slack mouth and trickled fresh blood. "If you hadn't meddled, it wouldn't have been necessary to silence her. And if you hadn't wounded and scarred me, it wouldn't be necessary to silence you!"

In one swift movement, he sprang at her, the scalpel directed at her face.

48

Clocked

Trotteur rammed Megan backwards and threw himself on top of her. She slid backwards over the desk, sending papers and pens and the telephone flying. Her scream of terror was choked off as Trotteur pinned her down with his body, shoving his left hand up against her throat as he held the scalpel to her face with his right hand. She could feel the point pressing into her cheek. His face loomed above hers, the dark eyes glittering.

"You, too, are not a patient, Megan – your little trick kicked in before I could make you one of mine, so I can slice and dice you any way I like. And you *do* have a couple of holes that need fixing, Megan. I promise you we'll get to them all, in time. But I need to begin with this right here..." She could feel drops of spit as he whispered hoarsely into her face. "This dent, this blemish, this rogue would-be dimple has always bothered me, Megan. It detracts from the ice and the fire. It cannot be allowed to continue."

Megan tried to shout, but it came out as a strangled gargle. Her left leg was trapped under his, she kicked out with her right, but it could find no purchase and flailed uselessly in the air. She bucked and twisted under him, trying to throw him off. Her hands beat and clawed against his body, but he kept his face just out of her reach with his longer arms. The pressure against her throat increased. She couldn't breathe. Black spots began to stipple her vision. Then the edges began to fray into advancing darkness as she gasped for air.

"The only question is whether I should give you another hollow *here*," he pressed the blade against her other cheek, "so that you're nice and even. Or whether we should rather cut this one out?" He returned the scalpel to her dimpled cheek. The blackness was sucking Megan into itself. The choking noises in her throat seemed to be coming from farther away.

"No, I think we definitely need to excise this disfigurement. And what I say goes. You know what they say, Megan: Doctor knows best."

He dug the scalpel into the dimple and began to cut a deep circle. Megan could feel the pressure, then the pain. It felt ice-cold, then blazing hot. Trotteur sucked in a breath of delight and shivered. Megan focused on the burning pain in her cheek. It pulled her out of the encroaching darkness and fired her with rage and returning strength.

There was a fractional loosening of the pressure at her neck as he pulled back slightly to admire his work.

"Not quite perfect," he said, tilting his head from side to side like an artist examining a canvas. "It needs a little more just here." As he brought the scalpel back down and his eyes fixed on the bleeding wound on her face, Megan pulled both her arms inside of his with a quick movement. With her left hand, she batted outwards at the arm holding the scalpel. There was a sharp slice of fire against her upper arm, then she heard the scalpel clatter against the bookshelf behind her. At the same time, she grabbed with her right hand at the injured arm still pressing against her throat, and dug her fingernails into the bloodied mess on his forearm.

Trotteur gave a high-pitched scream of pain. Megan brought her other arm across and clutched at the wound with that, too. She began to tear the edges apart. The hand on her throat loosened its grip as she felt the remaining stitches give way under her ripping grip. Trotteur punched her against the side of her head with his free arm, and then began to wrench at her arms, trying to pull them off his wound. Megan's head swam, once more the black sea of darkness threatened to suck her down, but she clung to the ragged, bloody arm as though to a life preserver, clawing her hands deep into the gash, grabbing and gouging at the flesh.

She gave a violent squeeze with all the force left in her right hand, while her left reached into his pocket and pulled out the key. She brought it across and stabbed it into his arm and twisted. Trotteur howled and lurched back, wrenching his arm free of her hand and the key. He clutched at his arm and Megan seized the moment of distraction to dash for the door, clambering right over the back of the couch and knocking the side table over.

She was within steps of the door when he slammed into her from behind, sending her crashing into the side of the wingback and onto the floor. He forced her onto her back and sat on her hips. This time he put both hands around her throat.

"I. Haven't. Finished!" he screamed at her. "I haven't finished! And now I have no knife so I'll just have to dig it out with my fingers."

He reached out clawed fingers and twisted her head to the side so that the bloodied cheek was uppermost. She felt the pain, but it was as though it was happening to some far-off place in her body, no longer fully part of her. Her eyes were riveted on what she saw lying under the chair: light and hope trapped in solid, square weightiness. She reached out her right hand and closed it around the heavy glass cube. Then she brought it up and held it threateningly in his field of vision and hissed, "Get off me! Get back!"

He looked from her hand to her face and then laughed – a loud merry peal. "You're threatening me with a dandelion? Oh, please," he mocked. "You won't use that. Miss Knows-Right-from-Wrong. You're a fucking psychologist. Help and heal and do no harm and all of that."

He kneeled back on his haunches and laughed harshly.

"*I'm* your patient, Megan, a desperate man asking for help. You *have* to help me. Fuck the women, fuck the retards and the rejects and the defectives!"

"You're the reject, Tony," she whispered hoarsely, cutting a wound of her own. "You could never see that, but you're the defective one, the permanently damaged and inadequate one. Perfectly imperfect – that's what you are, what you've always been. No wonder nobody wanted you."

With a silent scream of rage that contorted his face, he leaned into her. At the same moment, Megan pulled her arm back, then swung the paperweight forward, full-force against the side of his head, smashing a sharp corner into his temple with a jarring blow. There was a single moment when Trotteur looked down at her, surprise rippling across his face. Then he shook his head, and swiped at the air in front of him as if trying to clear a fog. Megan thudded the weight against his head again, and he merely looked stunned as he toppled off her sideways.

Gasping, trying desperately to take a deep breath, she rolled over onto her side and pushed herself up off the floor, onto her knees. Her fingers were locked onto the bloodied paperweight. Trotteur lay twitching on the carpet. A trickle of blood from the side of his head split into two rivulets; one ran down the side of his head and neck and dripped onto the carpet, while the other ran into the outer corner of his left eye, staining it red. His dark eyes were open – they seemed to bore into hers – but he made no movement to wipe away the blood. She stared at him for long moments – perhaps a minute, perhaps several.

"Bastard!" she croaked. "How's it feel, now, *doctor*?"

There was no reply, though she thought she saw hatred glimmering in his eyes. She was about to stand up when he moved.

Without thought, without hesitation, Megan's arm swung back and then flew forward as a silent spasm arched his back and convulsed noiselessly through his body, raising one stiff arm into the air. A corner of the heavy glass cube hit his head behind the ear. The force of the blow reverberated up Megan's arm, and she felt, rather than heard, the splintering of bone beneath her hand.

She collapsed back against the chair, her chest heaving. She was suddenly aware of the pain: her throat burned, her head throbbed, her cheek was on fire. She studied Trotteur carefully. He lay perfectly still. His eyes were closed and there was no movement in his body except for a faint rise and fall of his chest. She looked down at her hands. The fingers of her right hand still grasped the paperweight, now clotted with blood and matted gore. She dropped it and it rolled to the floor with a dull thud. Her hands began to shake, and the tremor spread through her until the whole of her was shivering.

There was something she had to do now, something she must do. She would be able to remember if she could just stop trembling.

She concentrated hard, forced herself to look away from the blood and the glass, to think past the pain. She focused on her knees, the sharp folds of the clean fabric of her trousers. And it came to her: she would have to phone the police. But first she must phone an ambulance. Silly! She was already in a hospital. She just needed to call downstairs. She could hear the phone now, in this profound silence: the continuous beeping tone told her the receiver was off the cradle. Turning her head, she could see that it lay to the side of the desk. It seemed an impossibly long way away.

She looked back at Anthony Thomas Trotteur. She would need to get herself over there and make the call. Time mattered with head injuries. Minutes could mean the difference between life and death.

She looked up at the clock. The long, slender hand counted off the seconds. It snapped to each progressive line and seemed to tremble as it hit the marks. The minute hand was shorter and more rigid, it moved with a steady firmness. Perhaps the seconds collected strength as they coalesced into minutes. Under her constant gaze, the movement of the clock's hands seemed to slow down. Tears slid down her cheeks, burning the cut Trotteur had carved into her face. She pressed her hand to it. And thought.

And waited.

Sitting very still, and as quiet as she would be if unconscious, she waited while she watched the hands of the clock inch forwards.

After a long while, she pulled herself up the side of the wingback and tried to stand. Her legs no longer shook, but her knees seemed to have melted and would not hold her. So she sank back down onto her hands and knees and crawled over to the telephone. And made the call that would summon help.

Then she lay down beside the chair, curled in upon herself and stared at the unmoving legs of Anthony Thomas Trotteur.

49

Locked in

The October air was still, dusty and rich with the heady, sweet perfume of syringa blossoms. They stood in the cool shade beneath the arch of dark branches and emerald leaves, listening to the silence of the veld reverberate in the quiet lull after the man in the grey suit had stopped talking. Tiny blossoms drifted down to add to the fragrant carpet already beneath their feet. A blossom landed on one of the russet curls of hair which lay across Megan's shoulders. She picked up the little flower, noticed the delicate white petals, their undersides striped with the palest lilac, the distinctive black slash of stamen standing out from the centre.

"I always told her it was an invasive weed, but she said weeds were just plants growing in the wrong place. It was her favourite tree. She said it was the smell of spring." Johan Cronjé gestured at the syringa. "I thought she would want her ashes scattered in spring, under a syringa. It's why I waited all these months."

He wiped his eyes with the back of a hand, then lifted the little girl off his waist and gently set her down beside her grandmother, who laid a gnarled hand on the child's brown hair. Marlien Cronjé looked confused. She scrunched at her lacy dress with one hand and clutched at a stuffed rabbit with the other.

"Pappa?"

"*Ek's nou terug*," Johan reassured.

He stepped forward, opened the small wooden box, and scattered the ashes around the base of the trunk. There was no breeze, the ashes fell where they were strewn beneath the fragrant arms of the tree.

Their *dominee* had said the formal prayers. Now family and friends went up, one by one, laying flowers, softly murmuring their own prayers, saying their own goodbyes. Megan walked up to the trunk and hugged it tightly. She could imagine the startled gazes being exchanged behind her, but she thought Alta would understand, and approve. Then she laid down the three fragrant dusky pink roses which she had cut from the enormous rose bush in the beautiful garden of her new house that morning.

"I'm sorry," she whispered to the tree and the flowers and the ashes beneath. "I'm so very sorry."

She walked back to where the others stood. While they took their turns, she breathed deeply of the exotic fragrance and took in the beauty of the farm: the sandstone farmhouse glowing golden in the sun, the long grass just beginning to turn green after the first spring rains, the distant specks of cattle. A dog barked somewhere in the distance.

When the ceremony was over, Johan walked over to speak to Megan. Marlien was back on his hip. She sucked on one of the rabbit's ears and stared curiously up while Megan and Johan spoke the well-worn words that both lied and comforted.

"Would you like to come back to the house for tea or coffee? We've got some cake and *goed*, too."

"And *koeksisters!*" said Marlien with a shy smile.

Megan felt something tug at her core. She kissed her forefinger and touched it to the tip of Marlien's nose. Another, bigger smile appeared.

"Thank you, Johan, but no. I must get going. It's a long drive back to Jo'burg and I have an appointment to keep."

They said goodbye with a brief, tight hug, then Megan walked across the dusty grass to her car, carrying the weight of the pain of the man and the child like a steady ache in her chest.

The road back to the city sliced through dry mielie fields barren of anything at this time of year, but the odd dust devil. The parched earth seemed to be holding its breath for the coming summer thunderstorms, and the ploughing and planting which would follow. There was plenty of time for Megan to think.

She marvelled at the kindness of Johan. He seemed to bear her no grudge. She had been less forgiving to herself. Alta's death was set at least partly against her account. She reminded herself that future women had been spared: a potential saving set against a definite loss

She had survived, emerged the victor, but she had been marked by the events of the year, and of that day five months ago. She touched her cheekbone, felt the dent – deeper, now – and traced the crescent-shaped scar: the outside marks of what had happened. The other scars were internal, invisible, but probably just as permanently disfiguring. She had changed, become less like herself – or less like the self she had once thought she was.

Her beliefs about herself had been profoundly shaken. Once – it seemed a very long time ago now – she had been sure that given a choice about the big things, she would always take what she had once so naively called "the high road". But now she knew different.

She still believed in free will, in choice – perhaps more so now than before – but she was no longer so sanguine or confident about her ability to help others change. Sometimes, they did not want to. Sometimes they were wedded to their pathology – in love with it – and would no more be parted from it than from a lover. That was their choice, and beyond her control.

That night in her office with Trotteur, she had had a moment of total power over another, and like Prometheus stealing fire from the gods, she had grasped it. And she had used it to benefit herself, and to benefit those unknown future women whom she had judged as more deserving than the man who had been her own client. She was not at peace with the choices she had made that night; she did not think they had been right. But she knew, too, that given the chance to relive that moment between her and him, she would choose to do the same again.

She had used her freedom of choice to play God, to reach a verdict, to act as judge and avenger. Now she was on her way to confront the consequences of her decision.

The place she arrived at was very different from the farm she had left two hours earlier. She parked on hot asphalt, not dust; there were plastic plants in linoleumed corridors, rather than trees in the veld; and in the place of the fresh blooming of spring, here there was only a dead sterility. She stopped to ask directions, found the room she was looking for, and entered.

He lay on his back on the high bed, his body immobile. His arms lay on top of the bedspread, the hands pulled up into curled claws of spasticity. On one forearm, a thick red keloid marred the pale whiteness of the flesh. The other arm was punctured by a needle connected to a tube which ran up to an IV bag hanging on the stand next to the bed. Another tube had been fed into one nostril and taped in place on his top lip with white surgical tape. A third tube snaked into the corner of his mouth. His face was lopsided: the right side sagged and drooped, pulling down at the end of the mouth and eye. Two monitors blinked and softly beeped behind the bed.

A nurse bustled into the room and greeted Megan with a nod and a smile.

"Ooh, how nice, you have a visitor today," she said brightly in the direction of the bed. "And how are we today?"

It was clear that she expected no answer from her patient, she did not even make eye contact with him. If she had, if she had stood still and looked very carefully, she would have seen that the dark eyes were staring directly at Megan.

"Are you family of his?" the nurse asked. She did make eye contact with Megan.

"No."

"Do you know, you're only the second visitor he's had since he's been here? No family or friends or anything. Sad, isn't it?"

"Who was the other visitor?"

"His lawyer," the nurse said, flicking a finger at the bottom of the IV bag where clear fluid dripped slowly into the plastic tubing. "He's the one who organised the transfer here for long-term care. They don't have chronic facilities at most of the clinics any more. The lawyer said there were a mother and father still alive."

"Really?"

"Yes. Lived in Durban, I think he said – or was it Bloem? Anyway, neither of them's been here to see him. Not that he would know the difference, would you, Mr Trotter? Poor thing – I really pity him." She leaned over her patient and tilted eye-drops onto the deep brown eyes.

Megan wondered if she had imagined it, or if there had been a flash in those dark eyes.

"Excuse me, luvvie, I just need to move him so as he doesn't get bedsores. Every two hours we rotate him, just like a lamb on a spit."

She laughed loudly at her joke, and used the sheets to manoeuvre her mute and inert patient onto his left side. He now faced a beige metal cabinet. Megan wondered why they bothered putting it next to the bed. Its scratched surface was completely bare, and surely the drawers would be empty. Anthony Trotteur did not need a place to store books, or grapes or get-well cards.

"What's the prognosis?" she asked.

"Ooh, it's never good with these cases, is it? Ninety per cent of these vegetative patients die within the first six months – usually it's pneumonia that gets them. But he's got this far, he might surprise us and go on for a lot longer." She tucked the bedclothes tightly around him to hold him in place. "There we are, I'll be back later to do the bed-bath but I'll leave you alone now and you can have a nice visit. Ooh, you've brought a photo – is that for him?"

Megan nodded.

"It's a kind thought, luvvie, but he won't register it. No lights left on in the top storey, see?" She tapped the side of her head with a finger as she spoke, then left the room.

There were distant bangs and crashes, presumably from trolleys in the corridors, but in the room it was quiet. Megan walked around to the side of the bed, so that she could see his face again. His eyes didn't move. Could they?

"Hello, Tony."

Carefully, she put the framed photo of Alta on the bedside table, directly in his line of vision.

"Here's something to look at, something to think about – if you can think, that is."

She squatted down on her haunches beside the bed and looked at him as she spoke. His dark eyes had lost their old sherry sparkle; they seemed duller, the colour of unpolished dark wood. His skin had an unhealthy sallow pallor and he smelled odd – an unpleasant mix of camphor and geriatric sourness.

"The doctors aren't sure about your condition. 'Persistent vegetative' seems to be the general consensus. But one doctor thinks you might have locked-in syndrome, *coma vigilante.* There was a bleed in your brainstem, plus, of course, the damage to the left temporal area, your speech centres, Broca's area.

"I wonder which you would prefer? To be hopelessly brain-dead, or to be fully awake and aware, but trapped in a paralysed body – unable to communicate, unable to do anything. The endless ache of a pain no one else can see, the torment of an unscratched itch, and completely unable to make anyone else understand – I think that would be a living hell, Tony, like being buried alive."

She reached out and gently moved a strand of hair out of his sagging right eye.

"And totally at the mercy of others – women, mostly."

She stared at him intently, trying to see if there was any flicker of a response.

"If you're locked in, then I'm sorry about that. At least, I think I am. I'm not sorry I'm alive, and I'm not sorry that no other woman will be suffering at your hands. But I do regret that it came to this, and not just for you – for me too. I'm changed, and I don't think I'm the better for it."

The focus of his gaze shifted fractionally. She was sure he was looking at her scar.

"Yes," she said, touching it. "I'll always have that mark to remind me of you... Can you – you who were always so obsessed with how things looked – can you believe me when I say that this," she rubbed at the dented scar, "is the least of the ways in which I'm damaged?"

Somewhere down the corridor, a telephone chirruped. Megan rummaged in her handbag and brought out an enamelled powder compact.

"Do you want to see how *you've* changed, Tony? Here, look."

She opened the compact, blew the traces of translucent powder off the mirror and held it up to his gaze. She was sure he could see it. The dark eyes stared, narrowed and then closed.

"No, it's not pretty. And definitely not perfect. Well," she snapped the compact closed and put it back into her handbag, "I didn't come here to torture you, Tony. Actually, I came to tell you that you were right."

His eyes opened again, the one with the droopy eyelid was slower to move and did not open all the way.

"Do you remember that debate we had about unconditional acceptance? You said it wasn't possible to separate the doer from the deed, and so unconditional acceptance was never really possible. 'Idealistic psychobabble claptrap', I think you called it. I argued with you. I thought I was right, Tony, truly I did. But I was wrong, I see that now. We are what we do, and that's true for me, too. I have to live with that."

She sighed.

"I was wrong about something else, too, Tony. Do you remember what you said about change – that there are two ways to help? You said it was easier to destroy the bad and the unhealthy, than it is to strengthen the good."

She leaned forward so that she was very close to him and looked into the dark, fathomless eyes.

"You were right," she whispered.

Acknowledgements

My sincere thanks to Dr Mariette Hurst, specialist in Forensic Pathology, for her invaluable help with the details of death and post-mortems, to Nicola Long for being such a willing and observant beta-reader, and to my editor Danél Hanekom, for plucking me from the slush pile and adding value ever since!